HELLBOUND

CHESTER D. CAMPBELL

Also by Chester D. Campbell

Post Cold War Political Thriller Trilogy:

Overture to Disaster (3)
The Poksu Conspiracy (2)
Beware the Jabberwock (1)

Greg McKenzie Mysteries:

A Sporting Murder (5)
The Marathon Murders (4)
Deadly Illusions (3)
Designed to Kill (2)
Secret of the Scroll (1)

Sid Chance Mysteries:

The Good, The Bad and The Murderous (2)
The Surest Poison (1)

To all the good folks at City Road Chapel
United Methodist Church in Madison,
Tennessee who joined me on a memorable
trip to New Orleans twenty years ago.

Notes and Acknowledgments

Originally written around 1997, this story is the most realistic I have ever tackled. Realistic from the standpoint of the basic path of the bus trip it depicts. My wife and I went on the exact same junket a few years earlier. Where it departs from reality is the Mafia angle, the bus's engine problem, and the hurricane. Other than that, the journey follows our itinerary exactly, including places we stopped, sites we saw, and the mule-driven tour of the French Quarter some of us took.

The characters are all fictional, though a few of them may resemble real people in some respects. Most of the French Quarter driver's spiel is almost word-for-word as I recorded it with a small pocket recorder.

Thanks to members of the old Quill & Dagger Writers Guild for helpful suggestions with the manuscript. Much thanks to Jaden Terrell for a topnotch editing job. And thanks, as always, to my wife Sarah for her love and support.

1

Moving like a hurricane ready for landfall, slow, deliberate, destruction on his mind, Boots Minelli paused at the door. With that innate sense of the totally committed, he felt the payoff almost within his grasp. After years of chasing down false trails and blundering up blind alleys, he would soon see the terror in the traitor's eyes. The bastard who had nearly wrecked the Vicario "family" no longer had his days numbered. It was now only a matter of hours.

The thin metal pick looked like a toothpick in his beefy hands, and though he hadn't used the gadget in years, Boots wielded the thin metal pick with the ease of a locksmith. Pulling the heavy, wood-paneled door open, he squeezed through. Not that the doorway was any narrower than normal, but Boots had the size and demeanor of a snorting bull.

In his black outfit, he could have passed for an undertaker, which wasn't that far off the mark. He lingered in the slate-floored foyer, stared into the living room, noted the faint lemony odor of a cleaning spray. It led him to suspect the room's tidy, vacuumed appearance was the result of a housekeeper's recent visit. The only thing out of place was a folded piece of paper on the floor.

The effort of stooping to pick it up left him panting, mouth agape, like some dumb-ass hound he might have chased off to fetch a stick. Ridiculous, he thought. Maddening. But that was the way a lousy fate had treated him lately. A big man in his middle fifties with abundant black hair, he had a bloated face, a joyless twist to his thick, pursed lips, and a body that made him a prime candidate for by-pass surgery.

Boots unfolded the paper and tilted it toward the light from the window. A heading identified the sheet as the itinerary for Lovely Lane United Methodist Church's "LLSS New Orleans Tour."

Beneath that was a list of dates and times for the week, starting with Monday:

"7:30 a.m. Board Bus, Depart Lovely Lane.

"1:00 p.m. Lunch at Barnes Crossing, Tupelo, MS.

"2:00 p.m. On to Natchez, MS, to spend the night."

The gold Rolex on Boots' massive wrist showed not quite seven a.m. A little earlier, parked in his rental car a short distance up the quiet suburban street from the red brick ranch, he had watched the man who called himself Bryce Reynolds pull out of the driveway in a four-year-old charcoal gray Buick. If Reynolds was leaving on the church bus at 7:30, Boots had a detailed schedule of where the man could be intercepted along the way to or from New Orleans.

But Boots had worked too hard and too long to risk any slip-ups. He needed a positive ID. Shoving the paper into his pocket, he launched a quick search of the house. Three-bedrooms, two-and-a-half-baths. One of the bedrooms had been furnished as an office. He pulled on a pair of sterile gloves and began to probe about the desk with surgical precision. He found a few utility bills, brochures promoting investment newsletters, an ad for a music CD club. Mostly he spotted Post-It notes stuck everywhere. It resembled a mini-billboard jungle—reminders of bills to pay, events coming up, checklists of things to do. One note confirmed Reynolds' plans to be on the New Orleans bus tour. *He's in his seventies*, Boots thought, *tends to forget things if they aren't written down.*

Though certain Reynolds was not the man's real name, Boots found nothing around the desk that would hint at a concealed identity. Next he turned to the family room. He found strictly masculine furniture, heavy wooden pieces informally placed. But he had an odd feeling that something was missing. Then it hit him.

No pictures. Not a single photograph was displayed anywhere in the house, the mark of a man with a hidden past.

As he shifted his gaze about the wood-paneled room, Boots thought of the years of searching that had finally paid off. He finally had a current name and address for the man whose testimony at the big New York Mafia trial in the early nineties had decimated the Vicario stronghold.

Though there were no photographs, Boots noticed the walls had been decorated with paintings. They included a tranquil mountain village draped in snow, a melancholy lighthouse beside foaming breakers, a drab old grist mill amidst a fiery display of fall foliage. Boots had no taste for art, but he guessed these were valuable paintings, not knockoffs turned out in some assembly line operation. The traitor had money. He could afford the real thing.

Boots stared at the grist mill, but his thoughts strayed to the contact he had employed in Tennessee to dig into Reynolds' background. There was little to be found. The man kept to himself, made no close friendships. He had bought the house in Madison, an unincorporated suburb on the northeastern side of Metropolitan Nashville, in 1995. His only slip had been a mention that he came from Tulsa.

A check in Tulsa turned up records of a Bryce Reynolds who had gone bankrupt in 1992. He started drinking heavily, and his wife left him. He disappeared from the radar screens shortly afterward. Presently he would have been in his early sixties, but Boots' source said the Madison Reynolds was likely over seventy.

The bright colors of the leaves around the grist mill slowly dragged Boots' attention back to the painting. Then he had an idea. He walked over and pulled the frame away from the wall enough to peek in back. Nothing. He checked the lighthouse, in a smaller, vertical frame. This try rewarded him with the outline of a cutout panel.

The thump of excitement in his chest triggered a brief return of breathlessness. Boots took a moment to catch his breath then removed the painting from the wall. He pried the panel open with a pocket knife, revealing the combination lock of a wall safe. Probably an old one, he thought, put in when the house was built back in the sixties. A simple "box job." Safecracking was a skill he had learned from a fellow student during his happily brief sojourn at a New York facility for the education of the criminally inclined, otherwise known as the state prison at Attica.

He flattened a large ear against the safe and gingerly twisted the dial. In the silence of the room, he listened to the soft click as the tumblers landed in position. He had the door open quickly. Inside lay a stack of "C notes," crisp hundred-dollar-bills bound with rubber bands, probably a few thousand bucks' worth. The safe also contained a handgun, but what caught his eye was a photograph and a long, thin case. He checked the picture first.

Bingo! A man and a woman, with two smiling younger men. He immediately recognized Patrick Pagano, his wife, Ellen, and their sons, Paul and Phillip. He knew what was in the case before he had it open. A star-shaped medallion with the word VALOR beneath an eagle's outstretched wings, attached to a blue ribbon emblazoned with white stars. On the back was engraved "Sgt. Patrick O. Pagano, December 22, 1944, Bastogne, Belgium."

The Congressional Medal of Honor. A flag-waving patriot despite his problems with the government, Tony Vicario had proudly bragged about having a Medal of Honor winner on his payroll.

Boots mustered the first genuine smile he had allowed himself in ages. He had withheld details of Pagano's new identity from his boss until he could be certain he had the right man. Now he would tell Vicario he had accomplished the seemingly impossible.

2

THE CHURCH parking lot had not seen so much activity this early on a Monday morning since a visitor tossed a burning cigarette into a trash can, starting a mini-conflagration that turned a nearby fence into charcoal. In addition to cars pulling up to liberate hopping, skipping, squealing youngsters headed for the Lovely Lane Day Care Center, others dropped off an equally excited, though less demonstrative, group of folks at the other end of the time spectrum. They tugged and dragged stuffed travel bags over to a big red and white bus with Nova Tours painted on the sides, highlighted by a stylized shooting star logo.

The bus blocked one lane of the parking lot beside the impressive stone building, its diesel engine rumbling impatiently. Not half as impatient, though, as the tall, thin woman who lingered beside the open door. Her angular face, accented by wide green eyes that kept searching for someone, was topped by a shock of frilly gray hair that overhung her brow like tendrils of Spanish moss. Her glasses, encased in thin metal frames, had been tilted up and jammed into her hair. At sixty-nine, Matilda Ellis was a marvel of movement, a highly charged bundle of energy.

"If forty-three other people can get here by seven-thirty," she said in the deep voice that rang from the alto section of the choir on Sunday mornings, "you'd think Sadie Blevins could, too."

"Want me to go in and call her, Tillie?" asked a short, dumpy woman standing nearby. "Surely she didn't forget."

Tillie Ellis gave a deep sigh. "Don't bet on it. That woman would forget her name if it wasn't printed on her Social Security card. Go ahead and call, Polly. If she's still there, tell her we're about to send the sheriff after her."

The tardy passenger represented only a minor annoyance.

The real source of Tillie's frown lay on page five of the morning newspaper stuffed among her belongings on the front seat. A story that ran barely five paragraphs, the item chronicled a tropical storm that had just reached hurricane status in the West Indies. A retired travel agent, Tillie had listened with growing anxiety on numerous occasions to a colleague's harrowing tale of being trapped in Miami by Hurricane Andrew seven years ago. The possibility of a similar fate had plagued Tillie during hurricane seasons ever since, a hangover from a fear of storms acquired when she was still in pigtails. The prospect concerned her even more now, with all the time and effort she had invested in this trip.

She turned to the driver, a stocky black man with thinning salt-and-pepper hair, dressed to match his bus in white shirt, dark red pants and tie. "Have you ever been on a bus caught in a hurricane, Chick?"

Chick Townes leaned against the door and shook his head. "No, ma'am. What's more, I got no desire to."

"Well, let's pray it doesn't happen this time." She glanced over at the church. "It looks like we may have a little delay, though, waiting for Sadie Blevins. That any problem?"

"Not unless the weather really turns ugly on us," he said. "If we get away by eight o'clock, we ought to be in pretty good shape."

Most of the passengers were already in their seats, dressed in a variety of casual outfits, some topped off with sweaters or light jackets. That would change the farther south they went. A few of the men were out strolling around the parking lot. Tillie stepped down to the asphalt and encountered Polly Pitts waddling up like a small, plump duck.

"Sadie said she was just going out the door," Polly said. "Claimed she'd be here within fifteen minutes."

"Thanks." Tillie shrugged off a twinge of remorse. "I guess I shouldn't talk about her. I'll probably be worse than that when I'm eighty." *And I may feel like eighty a lot sooner if that hurricane doesn't stay down in the tropics where it belongs*, she mused.

A RETIREE from the DuPont plant across the Cumberland

River in Old Hickory, Fred Scott kept pace with his casually dressed companion as they strolled past the bus toward the street, where a changing traffic light brought a wail of screeching tires. He tried to think of something that might get Bryce Reynolds talking. "Looks like old Tillie's really keyed up this morning," he said. "Bet she spent half the night getting everything ready."

"Yeah," Bryce said. His face showed no trace of what he thought about it. "Putting this together must have been a monstrous job."

"You ever done one of these bus trips before?"

"No."

"Guess you were too busy making a living."

Neither his voice nor his expression changed as Bryce replied. "Guess so."

They walked along in silence, Fred adjusting his John Deere cap and puzzling over how to do a better job of pulling his new friend out of that hard shell he'd erected around himself. Fred knew he'd made a little progress, recalling Tillie's telephone conversation a few weeks back after he had suggested she call Bryce about this trip. Fred had listened in on an extension in the church office. After introducing herself, Tillie launched into a persuasive sales pitch.

"Fred Scott suggested I call you about our Lovely Lane Silver Shadows trip to New Orleans. It will be six days in October, a real fun-filled adventure. Are you familiar with our Silver Shadows group?"

"Senior citizens, isn't it?" Bryce asked.

Tillie had glanced at Fred and waved a hand. "I'd say we were more than just a senior citizens group. Anyway, I think most of us prefer to be known by the more genteel term mature adults."

"I don't think I've ever been with a group of mature adults," Bryce said, a hint of humor in his voice. "I'm not sure I would fit in."

"Of course you would. Fred has told me all about you."

Fred groaned. That "all" was actually quite limited. Bryce said little about himself.

Tillie charged on. "I think you'd find the group very convivial.

We have lots of single ladies signing up for the trip. Actually, most are widows. The males are just about all accompanying wives.”

“So I would be the token bachelor? I’m really a widower, you know. My wife died several years ago.”

“I’m sure you won’t be the only one,” she said.

In the end, she had talked him into signing up.

When Fred and Bryce reached the sidewalk that bordered the parking lot, they turned toward a black asphalt apron surrounding a drugstore that abutted the church property. A solitary mockingbird serenaded them from a nearby oak tree.

“I heard a new joke yesterday,” Fred said, glancing around. He caught a flash of the odd twist Bryce’s straight slash of a mouth showed with the telling of a funny story, one of the few bits of emotion he had coaxed out of the man.

“This another farmer tale?” Bryce asked, his wide brown eyes beginning to shine.

“I’m really just a farmer at heart, you know.” Fred lived on a small farm down in Neely’s Bend, a part of Madison formed by one of numerous serpentine twists the Cumberland River took while meandering through Nashville. The area was an anachronism, a small chunk of rural America plunked down in the midst of a heavily populated suburb of Metropolitan Nashville.

“Okay, let’s have it,” Bryce said.

“Seems this farmer called the vet about a problem with a cantankerous bull that kept breaking out of the pen, giving the heifers a hard time. The vet says, ‘I thought I sent you some pills to keep that bull from getting so excited.’ ‘You did,’ the farmer replied. ‘But I had to throw ‘em away.’ ‘Why on earth?’ asked the vet. The farmer said, ‘Because my wife found out what they were for and I was afraid she’d put ‘em in my coffee.’”

Bryce shook his head as he laughed. “Fred, you’ve got more stories than McDonald’s has hamburgers.”

THEY WERE halfway down the lot when something odd caught Bryce’s eye over near the drugstore. He stopped abruptly and stared at a tan car with the driver-side door open. A leg protruded from it. The rest of the man's body appeared to be leaning the other way.

"That guy looks like he's in trouble," Bryce said. He ran toward the car.

Fred jogged behind him.

As they approached the vehicle, Bryce saw an expensive-looking cowboy boot stuck out the door like a large leather exclamation point. The man appeared monstrous in size. He clutched one hand to his throat.

"Are you all right?" Bryce called out.

As he leaned into the car, a shock wave froze him into numbness. He stared at the flushed face of Boots Minelli, one of the most feared capos in the Vicario crime family.

3

O_N LEAVING Pagano/Reynolds' house, Boots had decided to go by the church and check on the bus. He remembered passing the rambling stone structure on the way in and knew he would have no trouble finding it. Afterward, he would contact his young sidekick, Dominick Locasio, and the three other "wise guys" who had accompanied him to Nashville. They would rendezvous at the car rental agency before heading south.

Elated at what he had found after all those years of fruitless searching, Boots drove with a semblance of a smile, a decided change from his normal dour expression during those difficult times. He had never remotely considered giving up, of course. He was the most loyal and devoted subordinate of the The Boss, Anthony Vicario, who had chosen Boots as a young stalwart to enforce one of Tony's main credos, "death to traitors." Let a turncoat get away and it would spread like an infectious disease.

Rush hour traffic was building as Boots pulled onto Gallatin Road, the main drag through this northern suburb. A mish-mash of fast food outlets, cloned service stations, small retailers, and a few chain stores crowded each other for exposure along the busy strip. He had seen enough of Nashville. He hated country music, and he was sick of hearing about the Tennessee Titans. Thank God he'd be leaving shortly. According to the itinerary in his pocket, the bus would travel down the Natchez Trace Parkway, with the group scheduled to spend the night at a Days Inn in Natchez.

That would be the place to take care of business, he thought. A call to his room would lure Reynolds out. They would whisk him off to some secluded spot where he would have the opportunity to sweat over his misdeeds, then Boots would ventilate the bastard's head with 9mm slugs. In his view, it was a simple business proposition, a permanent solution to an annoying problem. It made him quite a different breed, or so he reasoned, from such ogres as serial killer Jeffrey Dahmer or mass murderers like Charles Manson. Boots looked forward to making his report back to The Boss that Pagano had ceased to exist.

As he drove along, dodging the zany Nashville drivers, Boots saw a couple of boys jostling each other as they waited for a school bus and recalled his own life as a youngster in Brooklyn. Monstrous in size even then, he had liked nothing better than making things miserable for other young punks. Though not well-educated in a formal sense, he had the equivalent of an advanced degree in street smarts. He graduated from petty larceny to armed robbery, then joined the outfit as a "soldier" in a group involved in loan sharking. He loved to knock heads when some poor slob got behind in his payments.

In the 1980s he was made a capodecina, captain of his own crew involved in mob activities. He escaped the trials brought on by Pagano as he was on an overseas sojourn back in the old country, recovering from a shooting injury. He hid out for three years, then returned after the heat had subsided. Intensely loyal to Tony Vicario, he happily took on the mission of tracking down the traitor who had tried to destroy the family.

When he arrived at the church, Boots saw the bus in the parking lot with its engine running. Noting several men wandering about, he decided to see if he might be able to target the traitor, although Pagano had doubtlessly attempted to alter his appearance. Boots parked beside a twenty-four-hour drugstore next door, took out a small pair of binoculars and swept the area. Remembering Pagano as a man of average height, he focused in on one figure that appeared about the right size. The man walked beside a taller companion.

Taking a closer look, he realized the strolling figure appeared a bit slimmer than the Pagano he remembered. That was something that could easily have been changed. The white hair fit, but he recalled a balding spot in front caused by a receding hairline. While considering this disparity, he picked up on something. The man's hair had been combed forward at an angle.

So it would cover a bald spot?

As he studied the face framed like a bullseye in the circle of the lenses, he knew it resembled Pagano in many ways. Yet, in others, he wasn't so sure. He hadn't seen the man in several years.

A person could alter a lot of things about himself, he reflected, but it would be difficult to hide peculiar mannerisms. He concentrated on recalling all he could about Pagano. Then it came to him. Pagano had an oddball grin, a sort of half-smile that pulled his mouth to one side as though his face were warped.

As he watched the man talk, the quirk showed up almost on cue. That same peculiar twist of the lips he remembered. Now he was certain. He had tracked down Pat Pagano, the traitor. Excitedly, he reached over and tapped his fingers atop the Medal of Honor case that lay on the seat beside him. It would be his war trophy.

Like any hunter, Boots was eager for the kill. So eager, in fact, the passion it generated set off a totally unexpected reaction inside his overburdened body, something for which he was ill prepared. First came a return of that damnable pain in his chest. Then a growing numbness invaded his left arm. His jaw began to tingle. Something told him this was not just another irksome episode of angina.

Reaching for the cell phone on the seat beside him, he punched in the motel number and asked for Dom Locasio's room.

"Yeah?" Locasio answered in a laconic voice. He never bothered to say hello.

"Dom, this is Boots. I've found him." He spoke rapidly, his voice tinged with anxiety.

"Pagano?"

"Right. He's about to get on a red and white Nova Tours bus packed with senior citizens. It's at Lovely Lane United Methodist Church on Gallatin Road in Madison."

"Damn! Where are they headed?"

"New Orleans. I got a paper with times and all. They'll be on the Natchez Trace Parkway, spending the night at a Days Inn—"

His voice choked off as the searing pain suddenly intensified, almost like a knife jabbed into his chest.

"Where?" Locasio asked.

"Oh, God." Boots gasped, fighting to get his breath.

"What's wrong?"

"The heart...get an ambulance." Boots was sweating now. He reached a hand up to tug at his collar.

"Where are you?" The strain colored Locasio's voice.

"Drugstore...by the church parking lot."

"Lovely Lane Methodist? Hang on, Boots. I'll have somebody there pronto." Then the younger man apparently realized he was still missing a vital piece of information. "Wait. Where did you say they were spending the night?"

"Natchez." It was almost a whisper.

Boots dropped the phone. He needed air. If he could just open the door. Fresh, cool air. He reached over and pulled the door handle, then pushed against it with his foot. The exertion was too much. He fell back against the seat and fumbled with his collar. Sweat soaked his shirt.

Boots felt light-headed. Was this it? Was he cashing in his chips? His heart raced and the rushing blood pounded in his ears. He barely heard voices nearby.

"He must be having a heart attack," Fred said. He gazed over Bryce's shoulder.

Bryce's own heart had taken a jump in tempo as he stared at the burly figure sprawled across the car seat. He spotted the binoculars, the telephone.

They had found him.

"He's having trouble breathing. I know CPR." Fred pushed Bryce aside as he spoke, apparently believing his friend had been numbed by indecision. "Go call nine-one-one."

Save your executioner, Bryce thought? This man was clearly the enemy. Every bit as much as the Germans he had faced during the war. But did he really have any choice? If he refused to help, it would require a lot more explanation than he was prepared to give. And at the moment he was not sure just how badly his cover had been breached by the mob.

Displaying no emotion, Bryce nodded. "I'll alert them at the drugstore." He trotted across the parking lot. Before he reached the store's entrance, the shrill wail of a Metro Nashville Fire Department ambulance cut through the morning chill. Flashing lights appeared down the street. Moments later he waved the paramedics toward the tan car with the open door.

As the ambulance crew took over from Fred, Bryce heard Tillie Ellis' voice shout from the bus.

"Fred, come on. We're ready to leave."

Sweating from the exertion, Fred grasped his open jacket on either side and began to fan with it. His beak of a nose made him look like some kind of tall bird flapping its wings. "Let's go, Bryce. They'll take care of him now. Nothing else we can do."

Bryce pondered the enormity of what he had just seen, of what it boded for his future. The binoculars told him Boots had been watching him. Had Boots used the phone to call 911, or had he called someone else? He thought it unlikely the old capo would have come after him alone. But how much did the others know? He doubted Boots was even aware of the bus tour. Probably the big man had followed him from his home.

Bryce had been meticulous in covering his tracks. He did not use credit cards, never gave out his Social Security number. In fact, he had never applied for Social Security benefits. He kept only a small balance in the bank and withdrew funds from his foreign account in checks of odd amounts under five thousand dollars, sums calculated to arouse no suspicion. He never filled out those prying warranty questionnaires; he would not even mail in the cards. He had no passport and he never registered to vote. How could they have found him after all these years?

When they reached the bus, Tillie stood beside the door, watching them with the critical eye of a mother hen. She nodded toward the ambulance. "Tell me what that's all about after we get on the bus. Sadie is here and we're ready to roll."

Bryce felt a sudden urge to bolt and run. This might be his last chance. But, just as quickly, a strange sense of calm came over him, an odd feeling of dispassion. He held his ground. Was it sang-froid or resignation? He wasn't sure, but if they had located him after all the precautions he had taken, was it hopeless to keep running any longer?

The questions still tormented him as he stepped aboard the bus and moved down the aisle in search of his seat-mate, who would also be his roommate at motels along the way. Funny, he thought, he had been looking forward to this trip as something of a new beginning, an effort to put behind him all the sadness, the hurt, the self-recrimination, the depression that had dogged him for so long now. But just when he was like an old spy ready to come in out of the cold, a deadly specter had risen from the ashes of his past. Now he faced the prospect that his anticipated tour of liberation could turn into a deadly journey to hell.

4

THE RECTANGULAR window above the massive windshield, where the bus's destination would have been displayed on a Greyhound, bore the whimsical designation GOIN' PLACES.

Inside, the decor was warm and inviting, a soft gray with red trim, scalloped fabric above the windows like small red awnings. Fuzzy red covers topped the seat cushions. It appeared such a perfect setting for this leisure-minded group to begin its latest adventure that almost to a person, they would have scoffed at any suggestion it might come to some kind of tragic end.

The only one who would not have taken such a suggestion lightly stowed his brown canvas carryon bag on the overhead shelf and slid into his place on the rear bench seat.

"I was afraid Tillie might go off and leave you," said Troy Walden from his position by the window. A short, heavyset man with clipped gray hair that resembled bristles on a brush, he had a round, smiling face.

That might have been the best thing for me, Bryce thought. "Fred Scott and I got delayed by a little emergency."

At that moment the ambulance siren began to wail again and its flashing lights sped past in the nearby street.

Troy glanced through the window, then turned back to Bryce. "What happened?"

Bryce explained about the man with the apparent heart attack, leaving out any speculation of who the victim might have been. He was just finishing the story when Tillie's voice came over the PA speakers mounted above the seats.

"Before we get under way, Dr. Trent wants to say a few words. I warned him to keep it short. We're running a little late. For you non-Lovely Laners, Dr. Trent is our senior pastor."

Peter Trent leaned forward as though ready to lunge down the aisle, a necessary maneuver to accommodate his six-foot-six frame. He had played basketball before starting his seminary studies. He took the mike from Tillie with an amused grimace, as if accustomed to being the target of one of her lectures.

"You folks had better mind her on this junket or she'll have you across her knee," he said. "I just wanted to wish you a great trip. Tillie has done a fine job planning it. I'm sure you'll see and do a lot of interesting and exciting things. Just don't get too carried away down there in Sin City." The last comment was accompanied by a wide smile. Then his face turned serious. "Let's have a brief prayer, and then you'll be on your way."

Listening in the back, Bryce could only hope the trip did not get overly exciting. He was probably the only one in danger of literally getting carried away in New Orleans. It was a known Mafia stronghold. Had Boots died, he wondered? And even if he had, how much had he told his henchmen about Bryce Reynolds beforehand? Should he consider himself safe for the moment, or was it likely they would be coming after him sooner than later?

"Gracious Lord," Dr. Trent said into the microphone, "we pray your blessings on these, our brothers and sisters, as they head out on a journey of fun and fellowship. Keep them safe, help them to be your ambassadors of goodwill, and bring them back renewed in their faith and refreshed in their outlook on life. In Jesus' name we pray. Amen."

Bryce added his "amen" to those voiced around him. He could not have asked for more—safety, renewal, a fresh outlook on life. But he had an overwhelming gut feeling that fate was dealing from an entirely different deck.

As the bus rolled out of the parking lot, Tillie came back on the loudspeaker. "Listen up, people. I'm going to pass out your trip kits, then we'll go over what's inside them. I'll keep you updated on our whereabouts as we go along."

Her commanding presence reminded Bryce of an old first sergeant he had known back in the war. World War II, of course. All the fiftieth anniversary commemorations and recent movies had revived interest in that critical period of history among Americans of all ages. For him it had stirred half-century-old memories that had long been locked away. Now he wondered if he was headed for a new kind of combat. It made him wish he had brought along the small .44 caliber revolver he kept in the bedside table at home. Actually he had thought about bringing the gun, having once heard that New Orleans was a city with a high murder rate and one of the most corrupt police departments in the country. He didn't know if that were still the case. Anyway, it didn't seem quite right to pack a gun on a church-sponsored bus loaded with senior citizens. Instead, he had stuck a pepper spray device in his carryon. It looked like a plump ballpoint pen, complete with clip for attachment to your shirt pocket.

When Tillie reached the back row, she handed the last two red folders to Bryce. "Give one to Troy," she said. "We're happy to have you with us, Mr. Reynolds."

"Bryce," he said, working on a slight smile. Over the past several years, he had come to think of himself solely as Bryce Reynolds, training his mind to show no reaction when someone called "Pat" on the street.

"Very well, Bryce," Tillie said. "Fred Scott told me about that poor man over at the drugstore. He said you saw him first and ran over to check on him. I hope they got him to the hospital in time."

"Yeah," Bryce said. He couldn't bring himself to add *so do I.*

Tillie headed toward the front of the bus. Bryce thumbed through the folder, noting the cover printed with "Lovely Lane Silver Shadows Fall Tour" and the dates. Inside, the first item was a revised copy of the itinerary, giving a few more details than the original he had received in the mail. He felt in his shirt pocket for the other one, but it wasn't there. He had left home in a hurry but remembered folding it up and shoving it into his pocket. At least he thought he had. Or had he? It was annoying how you could forget little things like that in so short a time. He used to think he had a mind like a steel trap. Now it was more like a rusty spring. He was forever walking into the kitchen to get something, only to stand there puzzled, trying to remember what he had come for.

Next in the kit was a list of all those on the bus, complete with addresses and phone numbers. He noticed only about half of them had Madison addresses. Most of the others lived in adjacent communities. After that came a few descriptive sheets on the Parkway, on Natchez and New Orleans, then several pages of inspirational poems.

Tillie's voice again livened the speaker. "First, let me acknowledge a typographical error before some of you eagle eyes start calling me to task. On the last page of the itinerary, you'll notice the day we come home listed as 'Friday.' Obviously, that should say 'Saturday.'"

When she finished going through the kit, Tillie wound up her spiel with a small bit of housekeeping. "On a longer trip, where we would be spending a lot more time on the bus, I would suggest rotating seats after each stop. It would give everyone equal opportunity at sitting in front and back, as well as both sides. But we won't be on the bus all that long. You might want to swap around on your own, though. It would give you the chance to sit with some different people, make some new acquaintances."

Troy looked askance. "Better watch her. She's a manipulator. She might try to get you hooked up with some lonely old white-headed widow." He snickered. "Maybe you'd like that."

"I've been alone for too long now," Bryce said. "Another woman would probably find me too difficult to live with." It wasn't altogether true, but it was an excuse he had come to depend on. A reason for keeping his distance, for declining to get into any kind of relationship that would require revealing details about his background.

Troy's face suddenly took on a clown's painted look of sadness. "Fred told me how you'd lost your wife to cancer. Sometimes I wonder what's worse, seeing a healthy spouse get suddenly ill, struck down in the bat of an eye, or having to watch one slowly deteriorate, knowing there's not one sorry thing you can do to stop it."

"Is that the case with your wife?"

"Parkinson's Disease." He moved his fingers as he stared at them, as though seeing a woman's trembling hands.

As he thought about it, Bryce wondered if the fact that his wife, Ellen, did not linger might have been a blessing. Of course, he hadn't felt that way at the time. Watching her rapidly waste away had been agonizing. In the end she had become only a shrunken parody of the once-beautiful woman he had loved and lived with for so long. Her abundant blonde hair, which in recent years had taken on a silken, silvery sheen, was gone, a victim of the powerful chemicals that had tried but failed to halt the deadly cancer's spread.

When she died, he laid the full blame at his own doorstep. It was the culmination of a series of blunders, of fatally flawed decisions he had made. Blunders that had not only contributed to his wife's surrender to the disease but to the fiery deaths of his two grown sons as well.

Sitting there beside Troy, he had to admit the threat to his own life had never been greater than now. But was he only getting what he deserved? And what, if anything, could he do about it?

5

WHEN LOCASIO and his three companions arrived at the drustore parking lot, they found Boots' abandoned rental car but no sign of the tour bus beside the church. No doubt it was on the road to Natchez, Locasio concluded. Which was no cause for concern. He was confident they could catch up with the bus in Mississippi. The condition of his capo was something else. At a trim and virile twenty-nine, Locasio had difficulty relating to obesity and heart problems, but he knew Boots had been courting disaster for some time. The man had become so obsessed with finding Pagano that he had let everything else, including his health, go to hell.

As he slid behind the wheel, he saw Boots' cellular phone and binoculars, and the odd-looking case beside them. Familiar with his boss's habits, he reached beneath the seat and retrieved a 9mm Bernardelli semiautomatic, which he slipped into his pocket. Thank God it wasn't on Boots when the paramedics arrived, or it would have brought in the cops.

Locasio pulled a cigarette pack from his jacket, tapped one out, stuck it between his lips and lit it with a flick of his lighter. He drew the smoke into his lungs and relaxed. He'd had to curtail his smoking habit around Boots lately. Just a hint of cigarette smoke would propel Boots into paroxysms of coughing, triggering a return of that ungodly chest pain.

Using the telephone, Locasio called to find out where they had taken Boots, then punched in the hospital number. The report was not good. Mr. Samuel Minelli of New York City was listed in critical condition. The doctor was not available.

"I can't give out any other information," the nurse said. "But I would advise you to get his family down here right away."

Boots' wife was dead. There were some nephews, but Locasio was about as close to family as anybody. Locasio had been selling dope in high school when he first attracted Boots' attention. The boy had passed along word that he was looking for more interesting action than peddling dime bags to pock-faced, snotty-nosed teenagers. His parents had divorced when he was fifteen and neither showed any inclination to take on the task of trying to rehabilitate an incorrigible teenager. Boots pulled him off the streets and treated him almost like a son. Almost. But there was never any real parental bonding. It was more of a teacher-student relationship. Locasio drew praise when he did a slick job of passing counterfeit bills or fencing stolen goods.

Locasio was twenty when he underwent the ceremonial spilling of blood and swearing of allegiance to the mob. He had been a faithful soldier ever since. Now he knew what he had to do.

Locasio clicked off the phone and turned to the others. "Boots is in damned bad shape. Let's get back to the motel. I've got a call to make."

The morning fog, which seemed more of a misty haze, had begun a gradual retreat, opening the way for what would likely be a pleasant, sunny day in Nashville. As Locasio drove Boots' rented car along Briley Parkway past the Opryland Hotel complex and the sprawling Opry Mills Mall, he speculated the place probably drew its share of good-looking chicks in need of companionship. Regretfully, he put the thought aside. Much more weighty matters required his attention. With his captain fallen, Locasio felt he was the logical choice to take over as leader of the operation. There was no time to delay while the family sent in some more seasoned executioner from New York. Anyway, knocking off an old guy in his seventies couldn't be all that much of a problem.

Back at the motel, he placed his call and got the current consigliere on the line. He explained what had happened to Boots and that he knew where to find the traitor, Pat Pagano. Locasio related his story cryptically, aware there was a good chance the FBI was listening in.

"Hold on," said the consigliere. "I think you'd better talk to The Boss."

A few moments later, a voice came on he recognized instantly. It was the slow, measured but forceful tones of the old Don himself, Tony Vicario. "Your mentor has expressed great confidence in you," he said. "Can you do what is required?"

Locasio's chest swelled with pride. It was like being tapped by the sword of a sovereign. "Yes, sir. I can."

"Good. Leave someone there to look after our friend. Take the others and resolve the problem."

Locasio hung up the phone and turned to his colleagues, a look of satisfaction on his face. The baton had been passed. He was now in charge. Locasio's voice took on a commanding tone as he turned to his troops.

"The Boss has given our marching orders. Marco, you are to stay with Boots. You can keep the rental car. Give the word if there's any change in his condition. Joe and Ferrante will come with me." He gave them a diabolical grin. "We're going to pop old Pagano and send him to join his ancestors in hell."

6

THE FIRST HINT this might turn out to be something other than the typically smooth-sailing Silver Shadows outing came at mid-morning in the vicinity of the Tennessee-Alabama state line when the bus began to labor on hills. Up to that point it had been a page torn from a travel brochure, with the historic Natchez Trace unfolding before them like a serpentine ribbon of asphalt, played out beneath a backdrop of azure blue punctuated by a few fluffy white accent marks. Occasionally, Tillie pointed out significant spots along the scenic two-lane parkway, which wended its way southwest from Nashville following the trail first trod by animals, then by tribes such as the Choctaw and Chickasaw, finally by white settlers in the late eighteenth century.

"Most of the travel was one way back then, headed the opposite direction from us," Tillie said. "Some of you may have heard the story of how it was used. People floated their crops and products down the Mississippi to sell them at Natchez or New Orleans. Rather than try to fight the river current back upstream, they would dismantle their boats and sell the wood, then head north on the Trace by foot or by horseback."

"If this bus breaks down, we may have to do the same thing," Fred said from his seat a few rows back.

After the laughter subsided, Tillie leaned toward the driver, then spoke into the mike. "Chick assures me his bus will not break down. But if it should, we'll make Fred get out and push."

The prospect of Lovely Lane's chief usher nudging his shoulder against the rear of the bus appeared a real possibility when the vehicle began to have difficulty climbing the modest hills. Since the time had come for a pit stop anyway, Chick pulled off the parkway at a small wooded area with back-to-back rustic restrooms.

Bryce joined Fred at the rear of the bus where Chick had the engine compartment open, probing around.

"What's the problem?" Fred asked. "I was starting to worry that Tillie might really want me to get out and push."

Townes scratched his head thoughtfully. "We started losing power a few miles back. I'm not a diesel mechanic, but I know a little about these monsters."

He had left the engine idling and reached in to tug on the throttle cable. As the engine revved up, a burst of black smoke billowed from the exhaust pipe.

The driver looked around, a frown on his dusky face. "Not good."

"Too rich a mixture?" Fred cocked his head to one side.

"Would be in a gasoline engine, but not a diesel. Usually means low compression or a problem in the injection system."

"What can you do about it?" Bryce asked.

"Nothing till we get to Tupelo. I just hope there's not too many hills between here and there."

Tillie charged up, brows pinched toward her nose. "What's the trouble?"

Chick gave her the bad news.

"I wondered why you seemed to be slowing down so. Is this going to delay us much?"

Chick shook his head. "I hope not. I'll get it looked at while you folks are eating lunch. Maybe we can make up some time this afternoon."

Though clearly not pleased with the situation, Tillie took a deep breath and spoke with finality. "We need to be in Natchez by suppertime."

She devoutly hoped this was not an omen of worse things to come. When she had herded everyone back on board, she switched on the microphone. "We're having a little problem with the bus," she said. "Chick says it's losing power. Makes it tough getting up hills. He doesn't think there's any danger of a real breakdown, but he plans to get it checked out in Tupelo. That's where we'll be stopping for lunch."

Though she had tried to downplay the potential for further problems, she recalled that newspaper story about the hurricane and couldn't help wondering if this trip had somehow acquired a jinx that might dog them the rest of the way.

WHEN BRYCE explained the problem, Troy took the news with a disgruntled frown.

"That's annoying," he said.

"Chick's taking the bus to a garage in Tupelo. We'll have to wait and see what they say about it." It was more than just an annoyance to Bryce. His concern was the slowdown in their progress, which would give anyone in pursuit a better opportunity to catch up.

The peaceful view of cleared fields and still-green forests that spread out beyond the bus windows made the situation a bit more palatable for Troy, however. After gazing out the window dreamily, he turned to Bryce.

"Reminds me of when I was growing up. I'm an old farm boy. Raised on a fifty-acre plot in Sumner County. You ever live in the country?"

Before the trip, Bryce had considered how to handle questions about his background. He wasn't sure how his usual policy of vagueness would play in this crowd. Making the choice even more difficult was the fact he genuinely enjoyed Troy's friendship.

"Afraid not," Bryce said. "I was a city boy."

He didn't elaborate, but the place where he grew up was nothing at all like this. And the name he was born with, Pat Pagano, was equally foreign to the one he used now. The son of a brash, hustling, black-haired Italian father and a shy, compassionate, red-headed Irish mother, he was raised in the desert country of southeast Nevada. Vince Pagano, his father, worked on the giant Boulder Dam project in the early thirties. When the dam was completed, he moved his family to Las Vegas, where he landed a job as a dealer in a small casino. That remained home for Bryce until his fateful move to New York City.

He looked back at Troy. "Why did you decide to give up the rural lifestyle?"

"I still get a hankering sometimes for the peace and quiet, but I deserted the farm as soon as I got out of college. Didn't want to have anymore to do with smelly old cows and labor-intensive crops like tobacco. Got a job selling insurance and just kept at it till I retired."

"What kind of insurance?"

"Life and health. Course, in later years it got more sophisticated. I added a lot of initials after my name. You know, CLU, ChFC, called myself a Financial Services Consultant."

Bryce shifted in his seat. "What did you do then?"

"Still sold life and health insurance, but concentrated more on business people than common folks. Handled a lot of buy-sell agreements, retirement plans, investments, things like that."

"Stocks and bonds?"

"Yeah, some. I never got into that end of it too big, though. If a client wanted securities, I'd recommend something. Didn't like to sell anything I wouldn't buy myself."

Now that he was almost reconciled to the fact that his cover had been blown, Bryce found himself caught in the limbo of uncertainty over how far to go. Did he really need to continue all this shadowboxing with reality?

"I used to be involved in investment counseling myself," he said, letting his guard down.

"One of the big brokerage firms?"

"No, I worked for a relatively small company for several years, then handled investments for a corporation."

As they sat quietly watching the pastoral scene pass beyond the window, Bryce recalled the accidental meeting that put him in the brokerage business.

After the war, he earned a degree in accounting, then signed on with a Las Vegas firm that counted casinos among its clients, including one his father managed. During a pre-wedding party at his father's place one night, an accountant friend introduced him to the maid of honor-to-be. A petite, smiling girl named Ellen Davidson, she had long blonde hair and a face he could only describe as angelic. Overall, the effect was so stunning he felt he would melt right there in his shoes. She proved such a distraction that when he tried to set his empty wine glass on a small busing table, he missed and dropped it to the floor where it shattered.

"Sorry," he said, red-faced. "I'm not usually this clumsy."

She put one hand to her mouth and whispered, a twinkle in her large blue eyes. "Hopefully the manager didn't hear it."

"If he did, he'll make me clean it up."

"You're kidding. They wouldn't do that to a guest."

"Not most guests. But the manager happens to be my dad."

She flashed that heart-stopping smile again. "Of course. Mr. Pagano. He's a friend of my father's."

"Really? In that case, I'm going to be mad at him."

"Why?"

A waiter came by with a tray of wine glasses and Pat stopped him, turning to Ellen. "Red or white?"

"White," she said. "But why would you be mad at your father?"

He handed her the glass as he gazed into those stunning eyes. "He should have introduced me to you a long time ago."

He learned she worked as a secretary in her father's securities brokerage firm and was the same age as he. They were soon dating regularly, and the following year they married. When Mr. Davidson offered him a job as a stockbroker, he took it.

Troy brought him back to the present with a smile that gave Bryce a sinking feeling. A feeling that he might have said too much.

7

THE BLUE Cadillac sped down the sun-drenched highway. A short, wiry man with a sharp nose sat behind the wheel, a watchful look on his face. His real name was Joseph Capparella, but he had been known as Joe Blow since the day he had almost destroyed his high school chemistry lab during an unauthorized experiment with a few unstable compounds. Explosives fascinated him. Independence Day fireworks displays were always the high point of his year.

"We haven't seen any sign of that bus," Joe said, wary eyes scouting the road ahead.

Sprawled on the back seat, Locasio waved his hand dismissively. "It'll take a while to catch up. No problem, long as you don't get us busted for speeding."

"Hey," Joe said, "you told me—"

"He's jerking your leg, dumbass," said Ziggy Ferrante from the front passenger seat.

Joe gave him an icy look. Solidly built, Ferrante had an odd, high-pitched voice that did not seem to match his body, plus the blank stare of a boxer who had lingered too long in the ring. He had been a pretty decent fighter at one time but joined the mob after running afoul of the law for throwing a couple of high-profile fights.

"As long as this thing works, we're copacetic." Joe patted the small radar detector mounted on the dash.

The speed limit on the Trace was 45 m.p.h., but Joe kept the speedometer around sixty.

Ziggy turned to the rear seat passenger. "Exactly what did Boots tell you about this bus?"

Locasio lit another cigarette and took a long drag before replying. "It's a Nova Tours bus. Red and white. Should have Tennessee plates."

Joe was still troubled. "How you gonna know which geezer is Pagano?"

"We keep our eyes open. We check out everybody on the bus."

Ziggy looked skeptical. "Maybe we ask them for a list of everybody, huh? What if he ain't using his right name?"

Locasio flicked a long ash into the tray at his side. "I thought of that. He probably isn't. And Boots didn't give me his alias. I'll have to come up with a plan. But we'll get the bastard if we have to take out every guy on that bus, one at a time."

Joe considered that for a moment. With his talents, he could take them all out with a single blow. He saw the problem, though. Squeezing the steering wheel, he frowned. "Did Boots show you a picture of him?"

"No. Did he show you one?"

"Boots didn't tell me shit. You know how he gets sometimes."

"I know." Locasio stared at the glowing tip of the cigarette between his fingers. "He said he'd tell us everything when he got damned good and ready. I'm sure he wanted to put a bullet between Pagano's eyes before he told us."

Joe persisted. "Didn't he give you any hints?"

"Basically, I remember him saying Pagano was average size, a little hefty last time he saw him."

Ziggy scowled. "Great! That covers about half the population."

"One other thing. He has a scar on the calf of his right leg, from a shrapnel wound during the war."

"Maybe they'll have a swimming pool at the motel," Joe said. He started to smile.

"That don't make no sense, Joe," said Ziggy. "People don't go swimming in the middle of October."

"They do down here, man. This is the South. People act different from the way we do in New York."

Locasio shook his head. "You two are gonna drive me batty. Shut up and let me think this thing out."

Joe had his own ideas about the sort of things that could be done. When the Vietnam draft caught him just out of school, he had volunteered for an explosive ordinance disposal team. He thought he had landed in heaven. The Army taught him everything he had always wanted to know about explosive devices of every sort, from grenades to bombs to mines. His job was to dismantle them or explode them under controlled conditions. But in order to take them apart, he first had to learn how to put them together. That talent assured him of employment when he returned to New York after his Army hitch.

Joe had an uncle who was a long-time acquaintance of Boots. One of the first to welcome the young ex-GI back from the killing fields, Boots posed a proposition that only a fool would have refused. Joe was nobody's fool. He became the Vicario family's booby-trap expert.

"You know what's funny?" Joe said.

Locasio growled. "No. What's funny?"

"The Boss once had me do a job to get revenge against the guys who blew up Pagano's place and killed his boys."

"That was back in the eighties, wasn't it?" Ziggy asked.

"Yeah. As I recall, his twin sons were home for Christmas. Both of 'em went to expensive schools. Seems one was studying to be a doctor. The other was into some kind of space shit."

"Boots told me about it," Locasio said. "It was the Bonannos that put the hit on him. Boots said The Boss gave Pagano bodyguards for a while. Then the sorry ass turned stoolie. His day's coming real soon."

8

THE BUS continued down the Trace, encountering difficulty only on the hills. Troy picked up the conversation where Bryce had dropped it.

"Have you met Hamilton MacArthur? He's an old investment hand."

Bryce liked the idea of shifting the emphasis to MacArthur. "Fred introduced us out in the parking lot. I thought he headed an insurance company."

"He did. They brought him down here a few years back to be president. But before that, he was director of investments for one of the big life insurance companies in New Jersey. He's done pretty well for himself. Retired last year."

Bryce glanced up the aisle where MacArthur sat. "If looks mean anything, he sure gives the appearance of success."

He was about Bryce's height, but stockier. Deeply tanned, he had sun-bleached sandy hair and looked like a prosperous yachtsman in his blue blazer and white cravat.

Troy's mouth twisted into a sneer. "Yeah. But I think he's a lot of bombast. At least he had enough sense not to get involved in derivatives the way the guy did he replaced."

"Derivatives?"

"Like the ones that sank that big bank over in England a few years ago."

"The Barings Investment Bank."

"Yeah. That was it. Don't guess you ever got into that sort of thing."

"No," Bryce said. But he had been a careful student of speculation in the monetary system. In the seventies he had discovered the seemingly random shifts in currencies of various countries were really not so extraordinary when you considered the fundamental factors that determined a currency's worth.

Locating a bank in Switzerland where he could buy a money fund in U.S. dollars, he borrowed three times that amount in Swiss francs. Converting the proceeds into dollars, he bought more fund shares. The interest on the Swiss loan was only three percent, while the U.S. fund earned eighteen percent. When the dollar rose against the franc, he cashed in and earned a huge foreign exchange profit.

Troy looked back at Bryce. "I'd say MacArthur is pretty well-heeled. I'm sure he owns a big chunk of the company. His wife does okay, too."

"Why didn't she come with him?"

"She's a vice president of some sort with one of the big hospital outfits in Nashville. She's about sixteen years younger than he is. Fred said MacArthur was partly interested in this trip because his wife will be at a meeting in New Orleans while we're down there."

Bryce gave him a puzzled look. "Isn't this a bit of a slumming exercise for him? I'll bet it's been a while since he saw the inside of a Days Inn."

Troy laughed. "That's a sure bet."

"Maybe he just wants to get a look at how the other half lives."

"Actually, I think he came along at the urging of Emma Gross. She's the big woman with the off-center hairdo he's sitting with. Her husband is a retired Methodist preacher. He's currently serving as associate pastor of the church MacArthur goes to in Hendersonville. They're a couple of the non-Lovely Laners who were invited to help fill up the bus."

"You said Hendersonville?"

"Yeah."

The town of Hendersonville was a suburb just across the county line to the east of Madison. It was home to such country music legends as Johnny Cash and included a stretch of Old Hickory Lake shoreline studded with high-ticket mansions.

"I'm sure the passenger list shows MacArthur as living in Madison," Bryce said.

"It's wrong if it does."

"Then you'd better tell Tillie Ellis."

Troy gave him a wry grin. "You gotta be kidding. She'd have

me for lunch. Take a braver man than me to tell old Tillie she's wrong."

Bryce's laugh was less amusement than an expression of relief that he had successfully avoided further discussion of his background in the investment field.

BRYCE WAS reading the information on Natchez and New Orleans when Tillie's voice boomed over the speakers. "We're approaching the Tupelo Visitor Center turnoff. After we see a short movie about the Trace, you'll have a few minutes to look through the gift shop. We should be there no more than thirty minutes. Since we're running a little behind time, you'll need to get back on the bus promptly so we can leave for the Mall at Barnes Crossing. That's where we'll eat lunch. To keep down congestion, the driver's side will get off first, then the curb side."

Although the big vehicle had coughed and wheezed occasionally, like a metallic monster trying to catch a cold, Chick brought the bus to a smooth stop near the entrance to the Visitor Center, a small, modern-looking structure that also housed headquarters for the Natchez Trace Parkway, a project of the National Park Service.

After stepping down to the walkway, Bryce moved away from the bus, paused to stretch and loosen up stiff muscles. He was not accustomed to sitting for long periods on a bus seat. He felt like a spring toy that had been compressed into a small box. On looking around, he saw somber clouds nudging each other about the darkening sky. Then he caught himself scrutinizing the tree-lined area and realized that, unconsciously, he had begun to search for potential pursuers.

He admonished himself for such paranoid behavior. It seemed highly unlikely Boots' people would know where to find him, particularly not this soon. But he hadn't survived to this point by being imprudent, so he acknowledged there would be no harm in keeping an eye out for anything unusual.

What he saw a few minutes later caught him off guard, however, although it certainly qualified as out of the ordinary. As the curb-side passengers emerged from the bus, one of them attracted Bryce's eye immediately. He recalled having seen her earlier, though only in a brief profile view. Now he realized that if ever he had encountered the personification of growing old gracefully, this was it. Curls of golden brown wreathed her face, interlaced with strands that glistened silver beneath what little remained of the mid-day sun. She radiated a healthy glow with only a touch of makeup. Sparkling blue eyes, a short patrician nose and delicate lips shaped almost like a cupid's bow had been created in perfect harmony. She wore white slacks, a white blouse embroidered with two small cardinals and a lightweight red jacket. The LLSS badge clipped to her jacket identified her as Marge Hunter.

She had an understated elegance about her that almost caused him to miss the one blemish in the picture. As she started to walk past him, he noticed the shoelace of her right sneaker had come untied. Without thinking, he did something quite out of character. He stopped her with a raised hand and a broad smile, pointed at the shoe and spoke in as pleasant a voice as he could muster. "Let me tie that for you before you trip over it."

Glancing down, she shook her head. "Thanks, but don't bother. I'll get it."

He had already dropped to one knee. "No bother."

When he had finished, he started to get up but found his leg muscles reluctant to cooperate, something that had plagued him on occasion lately. "Mind giving me a hand? The old legs don't always perform like they were meant to."

As she took his hand and let him pull against her to regain his feet, her face took on an odd, uncertain look. "I'm sorry," she said, withdrawing her hand as soon as he released it. "You said it would be no bother."

A thin smile registered his embarrassment. "I sometimes exaggerate. I guess I should claim it was the result of an old football injury, but there's no use lying. Getting older has its drawbacks."

She looked thoughtful. "Older? Not getting old?"

That brought a grin. "I still have a long way to go yet."

"Marge," said an impatient female voice up ahead. "Are you coming?"

Marge Hunter glanced up the walkway, then turned to Bryce,

expressive blue eyes shining. "Thank you. That was very thoughtful. I hope you enjoy the journey."

Watching as she walked away, he wondered if she were referring to this trip or to that longer journey he had alluded to, the trek into old age? Then he glanced at his right hand, recalling the softness, the warmth he had felt as he'd held her hand. Had that been just a casual grip to steady a tottering stranger or a truly sensitive response? With an almost imperceptible shake of his head, he jammed both hands into the pockets of his jacket and started toward the Natchez Trace Visitor Center. Had it been so long since he'd experienced the warmth of a woman's touch that simply lending him a hand had the power to send him into flights of fancy?

9

LOCASIO GROUND out the cigarette and leaned back in the seat. A smile crossed his chiseled face as he thought about his new status. He hated what had happened to Boots, but he enjoyed having his own chauffeur and the luxury of a back seat to himself. Joe and Ferrante had been quiet for a few minutes, giving him a chance to study the problem he faced.

He badly needed a passenger list for that bus. Otherwise, it would be a hit and miss proposition to check out the men on board. There should be lots of opportunities to look them over. He knew buses had to make rest stops every so often, and he figured it was even more critical with a load of old people. He remembered how often they'd had to stop on the way to Nashville to let Boots take a leak.

If they only had a photo of Pagano, things would be so much easier. Boots said some idiot had trashed the guy's pictures in anger over his court testimony. Sounded like something Marco might do, Locasio thought.

He slipped the pack from his pocket and found only one cigarette left. "Joe," he called out. "Next time you see some place to stop, pull off. I'm out of smokes."

Joe frowned. "That'll cost us some time."

"Hell, man," Ferrante said, laughing, "you're some kind of Dale Earnhardt. You can catch the bastards."

Joe glanced around. "You come up with any ideas yet, Locasio?"

The young mobster rubbed his chin. "Yeah. When they stop for the night, we'll break into that bus and look for a passenger list. They've got to have one around there somewhere."

"What help will that be?" Ferrante asked. "You said Pagano wouldn't be using his real name."

"Right. But it will show us who we're dealing with. Give us a list of all the men, make it easier to check everybody out."

"Here's an exit with a service sign," Joe said, swinging the Cadillac off to the right.

BRYCE ENCOUNTERED Troy inside the Visitor Center, thumbing through a display of books on various national parks.

"I saw you met my ex-sister-in-law," said Troy.

"Who?"

"Marge Hunter. She was married to my brother, Keith. He died several years ago."

Feeling a slight letdown, which he would have denied even to himself, Bryce tried to remember the names on the passenger list. Now that Troy had brought up the subject of Marge Hunter, his curiosity was aroused. "Her current husband isn't on the trip, is he?"

"Hardly. He died last year."

"Sorry to hear that," Bryce said.

"From what I hear, it's the best thing ever happened to her."

Bryce raised a questioning eyebrow. "Would you care to elaborate on that?"

"The guy was a real horse's rear. I don't know the whole story. I guess she's too embarrassed to talk about it. At least with me. I got a smattering of it from Betty Lou Scott, who's closer to her than anybody. It's a shame. Margie is really a great gal."

"Let's go, fellas," Tillie said as she breezed past. "They're ready to show us a movie in the theater."

Troy rumpled his brow. "Better follow orders."

"We'll catch the flick, then you can tell me about Marge Hunter." Bryce turned with a shrug.

The movie described the Trace's origins and history through the early 1800s. The biggest year was 1810, when more than 10,000 boatmen and others traveled north toward Nashville. The largest southward migration came when General Andrew Jackson led his troops down to the Battle of New Orleans during the War of 1812. According to the narrator, the arrival of the steamboat *New Orleans* at Natchez that year signaled the beginning of the end for the Trace's popularity.

When the group filed out at the end of the movie, Bryce and Troy bought soft drinks and moved to the front of the building. The parking area appeared as shrouded as late afternoon, the sun now blotted out by churning clouds.

Bryce gazed up at the darkened sky. "Looks like we might get some rain. I didn't think that was in the forecast for today."

"Yeah. And I didn't think our bus was supposed to act up, either." A twinkle brightened Troy's eyes. "So you want to know about Margie Walden Hunter. She's a looker. You wouldn't think she was in her early seventies, would you?"

"Hardly."

"Yeah. She and Keith were married forty years. He was an unassuming, personable type, always wore a smile. One of those people who inspires trust just to look at him."

Bryce sipped on his drink. "Sounds like a nice guy."

"He was a natural at selling real estate. His one shortcoming was an inability to have children, something Marge had really wanted. Keith was sterile. Funny thing, though, about the time they finally decided to use other measures to have a baby, Marge suddenly changed her mind. She apparently got caught up in some kind of weird mid-life crisis." He shook his head and dropped the subject. "She and Keith lived in a big house on the river in Madison. They were pillars of the church...Lovely Lane, of course."

"What happened after he died?"

"She was at a complete loss. They had been constant companions. Often talked about traveling, but rarely found the time. They were looking forward to that after his retirement in another three years. He was only sixty-two when he died. It took her a good while to adjust to being without him."

"Where did she meet Hunter?"

Troy leaned back against the wall. "At a high school reunion. He was an old beau who had gone into the Navy as soon as he graduated. After he went to sea, they lost contact. They hadn't seen each other until he moved back to Nashville after retiring as a navy captain."

"He must have been pretty sharp to make captain."

"He seemed that way at first. In contrast to most of the other guys at the reunion, you know, bald, fat or stooped, Herb Hunter stood stiff as a ramrod. He had a thick head of black hair, hardly any gray in it. In high school, he was a smooth-talking, supremely confident character, took the lead role in school plays. You know the type. It had been a long time, but he seemed like the same old Herb to Marge."

Troy related how Captain Hunter had called Marge the next week and invited her out to dinner, to reminisce about old times. She was reluctant to go, but Betty Lou Scott convinced her this was exactly what she needed. A few years had passed since Keith's death, but she was still holding back. She needed to get on with her life. So she agreed.

Hunter was a jaunty host, according to Troy, oozing self-confidence, full of himself and stories about his travels and his service. Marge felt almost as though they had picked up right where they left off during the war. A few months later, she gave in to his persistence and agreed to marry him.

"The way Betty Lou told it, he was Prince Charming on their honeymoon trip to Hawaii," Troy said. "When they got back, Marge told her she couldn't have been happier. Then things apparently went to hell in a handbasket. Their first Sunday back at church, Fred did his usual thing and gave her a monstrous hug. She told Betty Lou that Herb stiffened like a board, fire in his eyes. As they moved down the aisle, he leaned toward her and snarled, just above a whisper, 'Who does that son-of-bitch think he is?'

"Well, Margie was mortified. She whispered back, 'Watch your language, Herb, you're in church.' To which he replies, 'You'd think we were in a whorehouse the way that bastard grappled at you!'"

Bryce frowned in disbelief. "He said that?"

"So help me, God. Least that's what Betty Lou said he did. She made me promise not to tell Fred, said it would wound him something fierce, might cause him to resign his job as head usher. I can't imagine walking into church on Sunday morning without Fred there to greet us."

Bryce knew what he meant. He had first met Fred on the walking track that circled above the gym floor in the Fellowship

Center at Lovely Lane Church. Fred's friendliness and persistence had finally prodded him into laying aside some of his reticence.

"What happened after that?" Bryce asked.

"Betty Lou wouldn't tell me anymore, except that when Fred greeted Marge the same way a week later, she had to pull her crazy husband away so he wouldn't deck old Scott right there in the narthex. They moved across town the next week. I didn't see her again until after Herb died last year."

10

DURING HIS quiet years in Madison, Bryce had lowered the barriers only once, allowing himself to get close to someone, and that had resulted in another shocking case of regret, triggering a return of the "blue funk." He had befriended a young woman at the mall where he walked daily. She invited him to Christmas dinner at her parents' home in a small town north of Nashville. When it started snowing hard on Christmas Eve, Bryce suggested she drive up the next morning with him, but she insisted on going after work to help her mother. She died in an accident not far from where her parents lived. Bryce blamed himself for not being more adamant that she ride with him. It had compounded his feeling of being a modern version of the Ancient Mariner wearing an albatross around his neck.

So when the passengers flocked off the bus at the Tupelo mall, he reverted to the loner image that had served him so well in the past. Lagging back while Troy joined a few of his friends, Bryce moved into the large food court and steered away from the milling crowd of Silver Shadows. He found a place that served sub sandwiches, ordered a half portion, which still looked monstrous, and chose a table on the periphery.

As he ate, he kept searching the tables until he finally found Marge seated with the Scotts and another woman he couldn't identify. He thought she was the one who had called to Marge after the shoe-tying episode. He felt a little silly gawking around like this.

In the solitude of his corner spot, Bryce let his mind churn over what had happened that morning at the church parking lot and what the incident might mean for his immediate future. Basically, he saw two possibilities. One, Boots had died or was incapacitated and had not communicated his findings to anyone else. In that case he was, at least temporarily, home free. Two, Boots had survived mentally intact or had already told others what he knew about Pagano/Reynolds. If that were the case, he could expect company at any time. What that might mean for the innocent bus passengers was a major concern. He would have to remain vigilant, wary of any strangers approaching the group. His only advantage was he had been around them long enough he felt he could spot a Mafia hood a block away.

After he had finished lunch, Bryce encountered Troy standing in line at an ice cream shop, waiting to order a cone of frozen yogurt.

"Want me to get you one?" Troy asked.

"No thanks," Bryce said.

"Where'd you go? I looked around and you'd disappeared."

"I went to the sub sandwich place. Almost got more than I could eat." Bryce patted his stomach.

"Know what you mean. Say, if you don't mind, Fred would like to swap seats with you on the next leg. We're both on the Trustees at church. He's chairman. He has a project he wants to discuss with me. You'd be sitting with his wife, Betty Lou."

Marge's friend, Bryce thought. "No problem," he said. But he wasn't so sure.

They headed out to the front of the mall and found Chick waiting beside his bus. Tillie Ellis had just begun to question him when they walked up.

"They found some bad injector nozzles," the driver said.

Tillie pulled her glasses down and stared. "I have no idea what that is. Did you get it fixed?"

"They did a rush job for me. Got new nozzles. The mechanic said it looked like they may have been purposely contaminated."

"What do you mean 'purposely'?" Troy asked.

"Sabotage." Chick had a grim look on his face.

"Who would have done that?" Bryce stared at him in disbelief. Though it sounded like the sort of thing that might be expected from the Vicario family, could that be possible? Had Boots known about this trip beforehand?

"The company fired a couple of mechanics a few days ago. Only thing I can figure is they might have done it to get even."

Tillie shook her head. "If that's the case, let's hope they didn't do anything else."

"I called the company and told them to keep another bus on standby in case we should need it," the driver said. "But this one seems to be running fine at the moment. Only problem I see now is the weather."

That was hardly the only problem Bryce saw. If Minelli's crew had already been out making mischief, he faced the challenge of blending in with his fellow passengers while avoiding anything that might single him out as the target for a Mafia hit squad.

11

A few minutes later, Bryce eased into an aisle seat near the front of the bus and said, "Hi, I'm Bryce Reynolds."

Betty Lou Scott had short gray hair and a plain, uncomplicated face. As she smiled, her crinkled brown eyes viewed him from behind oval-shaped, gold-rimmed glasses. "Fred has spoken of you many times."

Right now he was more interested in talking about anybody but himself. But he replied, "Favorably, I hope."

"Fred's one of those people who think you shouldn't say anything about a person unless you can say something good."

"I've noticed."

She leaned toward him, speaking in a conspiratorial voice. "I'll tell you a little secret, though. He'd dearly love to get you to church or Sunday School, but he won't push you because he's afraid it might turn you off."

Bryce shrugged. "Maybe after this trip's over I'll drop in some Sunday and surprise him." *If I'm still alive*, he added silently.

"That would make his day. Dr. Trent was kidding him last week about falling down on his recruiting job."

"Any vacant seats back there?" Tillie asked over the loudspeaker. After a chorus of "no's," she continued. "We must be all here then. For all of you who've been worried about the bus, it's fixed. At least for the present. We'll head on down toward Natchez, where we'll eat supper. Chick will give us a rest stop after a couple of hours. Polly Pitts has a big bag of cookies she's going to pass out when we get on the road."

"Which one is Polly?" Bryce asked.

"Short woman in the front seat on the left. Looks sort of like Humpty Dumpty. She raised four kids. Obviously she ate all the leftovers. I might have been that way with my three, but fortunately we had dogs to take care of the table scraps. You have children, Mr. Reynolds?"

"Please, just call me Bryce," he said. "No, I don't have children any longer. I'm afraid there's nobody left but me. I committed the unfortunate sin of outliving my wife and kids."

"I'm sorry to hear that. But I sometimes think a little solitude would be nice. Seems we spend half our time hauling grandchildren around, baby-sitting, going to ball games. I spend at least two days in the kitchen before a holiday."

Bryce turned to get a better look at her face. "And I'll bet you love every minute of it."

"I suppose so." Her expression was a cross between a smile and a grimace. "It's nice to be around a bunch of young folks now and then. Keeps you from feeling so old. On the other hand, I guess it can get pretty lonely when you're left by yourself."

"It was rough at first, but I stayed so busy I didn't have time to dwell on it...except at night."

But the nights had been more than enough. After he had slipped a sheaf of documents out of the consigliere's office and turned them over to the FBI, they took him into protective custody. During those lonely nights of virtual house arrest, he berated himself for the mess he had made of his life, for the curse he had put on his family. By the time the case went to trial, he had begun to accept that he could do nothing for his wife and sons except try to destroy the criminal conspiracy that had led to their deaths. His testimony was the prosecutors' key weapon against the mob. They guarded him like gold at Fort Knox, then gave him a new name and spirited him off to Portland, Oregon, where they proposed to give him a new start.

He had other ideas. He didn't trust the FBI any more than he trusted those they called the Cosa Nostra. He would rely on his own abilities. After a brief sojourn on the West Coast, he suddenly took his leave, resurfacing some months later in Nashville as Bryce Reynolds, a retired businessman from Tulsa. He had detoured to Oklahoma City, posing as a homeless old man, borrowing the Reynolds name from a fellow derelict who died of hypothermia not long after they met. The real Reynolds had no identification on him when he died and was buried nameless in a pauper's grave. Pat Pagano found a battered Social Security card among the meager possessions in the man's cardboard shack. Using the number, he learned a few basic details about the man, enough to construct a plausible story should he find one necessary. But, up to this point, he had managed to avoid any problems by living as a quiet, unobtrusive retiree who existed comfortably on the proceeds of his investments.

Betty Lou remained silent for a few minutes, gazing out at a peaceful view of a small valley darkened by clouds that jostled one another in a crowded sky. She appeared to wear the lines around her eyes proudly, like service stripes earned for tolerance, patience, and endurance.

When she turned back to Bryce, she had a look of uncertainty on her face. "I understand you were asking Troy about Marge Hunter."

"I was curious about her," he said. "Actually, it was after Troy volunteered that she was his former sister-in-law."

"Then he told you about her second marriage?"

"Yes. What he had learned from you, I believe. Which wasn't a lot. Sounded like a real sad situation, though. I once knew a man like that, had a major hang-up with jealousy."

"If you ask me," said Betty Lou, "it was pathological. He insisted they move to a another church, one he selected after checking out several different ones. She said it was a church where the people were cold and indifferent. There were several adult Sunday School classes, but nobody invited them to join one until they'd been there almost a year."

"That sounds kind of bizarre."

"That was just the start. He forbade her to associate with her former friends in Madison. Especially me, when he found out I was Fred's wife. Marge and I had been close friends since she and Keith were married."

"Was she physically abused?"

"Not that I'm aware of. But she's been pretty reluctant to talk about any of it."

Bryce rubbed his chin. "I remember some Army officers in the war who thought they were God, could do anything they pleased. I think it's one of the hazards of a military career. Why didn't she leave him?"

"That's the question people always ask, isn't it? But there's no easy answer. I think at first she was too shocked to believe what was happening. Her high school alumni association had written it up in their newspaper, called it a fairy tale romance."

"One that ended up a horror story," Bryce said, shaking his head.

Before Betty Lou could reply, a jagged flash of lightning struck in a nearby field, lighting up the interior of the bus as if it had been bracketed by a spotlight. A blast of thunder quickly followed, shaking the bus and rumbling off into the distance, triggering a chorus of "Oh's" from the passengers.

"That was close," Bryce said, gazing out the window.

Betty Lou blinked and composed herself. "Yes. I guess that wasn't too far from the shock Marge felt over the way Herb acted." Rain began to pelt the window beside her. "After the shock wore off, I think she went into denial. Except for one earlier period in her life, she was always the strong one. She'd stand up in a community meeting and tell the mayor exactly what she thought."

"Sounds like a gutsy lady."

"She was, before Herb Hunter came along. But after a while, she apparently came to accept that she'd made a horrific mistake in marrying him. Still, she endured it. She told me once her mother had lectured her on making a marriage work. There'd never been a divorce in the family. Whatever happened, she was too embarrassed to tell any of her old friends."

Bryce recalled Marge's reluctance to accept his well-intentioned assistance outside the bus and understood why.

"Did you talk to her during that period?" he asked.

"I called a few times. She'd say she couldn't talk but she would call me back. She never did. I got my feelings hurt and finally gave up. I wish I hadn't. It took a terrible toll on her self-esteem. After Herb died, it was a while before she could muster the courage to come back to Lovely Lane. Just about six months ago. She hasn't told me the whole story, but it's more than she's told anybody else."

Bryce gave her a curious look. "Why are you telling me?"

Her cheeks colored a bit, like a little girl caught doing something naughty. "I'll admit, I probably shouldn't. But I got the idea you might be...well, interested in her. It was my fault she dated that horrid man in the first place. Don't get me wrong. I'm not implying anything about you. As I said, Fred thinks the world of you. But I just thought you ought to know. She's finally gotten herself straightened out, rebuilt her self-confidence."

Betty Lou's face softened into a grandmotherly grin. "What she needs is plenty of good old TLC."

Bryce thought about that for a moment. He had to admit, he was definitely interested, but what were his real intentions? Did he have the right to even consider starting a relationship with Marge, or anyone else for that matter? After all, he was under a death sentence that could easily be carried out at any moment.

As that thought began to sink in, it touched off a spark of ire. Was he going to continue to let these cutthroats dictate his every move? He hadn't hesitated to step up and meet the threat during the war. After the Mafia trial, he had changed identities and adopted a subliminal existence for good practical reasons, an overwhelmingly clear and present danger. But there was a big difference between fear and prudence. If these guys were out to do him in, he did not intend to make their job easier.

What he felt most was anger and frustration. Right now he had no clear idea of the dimensions of the problem. All he knew for sure was that Boots had found him just before he boarded this bus. The next move was up to his pursuers.

12

STREAKS OF lightning flashed overhead and the dark clouds began to unburden themselves as the Cadillac cruised down the Trace south of Tupelo. Locasio's cell phone rang. He punched the talk button.

"Yeah?"

"Dom, it's Marco."

Locasio leaned forward in the seat and slipped a cigarette from the pack with his free hand. "How's Boots?"

"Not too good. They've got him hooked up to all kinds of tubes and monitors. He hasn't opened his eyes. He's in the Cardiac Care Unit. They'll only let me in to see him every few hours."

Locasio clicked his lighter and took a short puff. He knew only family members could visit patients in the CCU. "Who did you tell them you were?"

"A nephew traveling with him," Marco said.

"Good move." Marco wasn't the swiftest cat in the litter, Locasio thought, but he wasn't a total blockhead.

"They let me check Boots' clothes and I found something that should be a big help to you."

"What's that?" Locasio blew out a stream of smoke and moved the phone to hear Marco better.

"It says Lovely Lane United Methodist Church LLSS New Orleans Tour Itinerary. It has dates and times for where they're going to be."

"Did you find a passenger list?" Locasio asked.

"No. Just this itinerary."

"Damn, Marco. That's not much help. We know where they're headed, and we know they're staying at the Day's Inn in Natchez tonight. We can follow the bus on to New Orleans."

"Sorry, Locasio. That's all I found."

"Well, get the hell back in there and keep an eye on Boots."

Locasio had just switched off the phone when Joe Blow let out a loud whoop. Locasio gave him a surly look. "What the hell was that for?"

"We've caught 'em," Joe said. "That's the Nova Tours bus up ahead."

A grin spread over Locasio's face. "Just follow it and let's see what they do. Pagano, get ready. We're after your ass."

The rain had turned to a slow drizzle by the time Chick turned into the rest area north of Jackson. Bryce followed Betty Lou off the bus and found Marge and her seatmate huddled under a large red umbrella. Betty Lou tugged Bryce beneath a small, collapsible model as she made the introductions.

"Bryce Reynolds, this is my sister, Sarah Anne Yeager. She's from Chicago."

"Nice to meet you, Sarah Anne," Bryce said, smiling.

Sarah Anne was a little taller than her sister, and a bit thinner. She also had a more sophisticated look, which he took as the mark of a girl who had spent most of her life around the big city.

"Actually," Sarah Anne said, "I live on the north side of Chicago, in Evanston."

"And this is Marge Walden Hunter." Betty Lou emphasized the middle name. "I believe you two have already met."

"Very informally," Bryce said with a nod. "We read each other's badges."

"Mr. Reynolds tied my shoe for me this morning," Marge said with a look of distraction. "I'm sure you heard about it."

Betty Lou rumpled her brow. "Oh, yes. Clara Holly made a beeline to where I was standing. She couldn't wait to tell me."

Bryce cocked his head to one side. "Am I missing something here?"

"Small minds fixate on small details," Sarah Anne said.

Betty Lou threw up her hands. "You'd have to know Clara."

Marge looked at him, a trace of sparkle in her eyes. "I'm sure you'll meet her soon enough."

The building beyond them had restrooms on one side, drink dispensers and snack machines on the other and a small lobby in between. Betty Lou turned to Bryce. "I don't want to point, but see the terribly fat man and the skinny little woman going into the lobby?"

"Betty Lou," her sister said, frowning. "You shouldn't call him terribly fat."

"Who just said something about small minds? Anyway, I call it like I see it. Clara Holly is skinny and Horace is short and fat."

Sarah Anne smirked. "I'm sure you've noticed my sister doesn't mind expressing her opinions, Mr. Reynolds."

"Hey, I'm Bryce," he said. "Everybody keeps calling me 'Mister.' Makes me sound like some kind of dignitary. I'm just plain folks."

"Sorry about that, Bryce," said Marge in a contrite voice. "We certainly want you to feel at home. I've spent time in some places where the only shoulders around were cold ones. I guarantee you, Lovely Laners are the friendliest people you'll ever meet."

They walked on up to the building, where the women headed for the restroom. Bryce wandered into the cluttered lobby, which had the feel of a shopworn country store overrun by a horde of scavenging city dwellers. A large map of the state hung on one wall. Tourist brochures were displayed nearby, along with a variety of other information. He was looking over the map when a nasal voice spoke up beside him.

"How far do we have to go?"

He turned to see a rail-thin woman with straight hair the shade of dried corn shucks. She looked at him with wide gray eyes beneath a forehead that appeared permanently creased. He got a glimpse of the badge that identified her as Clara Holly.

Bryce gestured toward the map. "I'd have to check the scale to be sure, but I would guess in the range of fifty miles or so."

She moved closer to him, glanced at the map, then stared at his badge. "Reynolds. Used to be a company by that name that made aluminum."

"I believe they still do."

"Oh, that's right. They make that foil stuff you cook things in, don't they? You any kin to the aluminum Reynolds?"

"Don't I wish. If that were the case, I'd probably be rich."

"Are you from Dalewood?"

That was another Methodist church in a nearby section of Nashville. He had heard some Dalewood members were on the bus. "No. I don't live too far from Lovely Lane. I walk on the track. That's where I heard about this trip."

She stood quite close to him, her right hand gripping her left, her feet spread wide apart like someone staking claim to a spot of turf. She gave him a thoughtful frown. "You remind me of a banker I used to know. What did you do before you retired?"

Bryce narrowed his eyes. "Who said I had retired?"

"Most everybody on this bus has retired. That's what folks do at our age. Where'd you come from?"

He hated encounters like this. He didn't want to be rude, but with the possibility of stalkers lurking in wait for him, he had no desire to be quizzed about his past life. "I came from out West," he said. "I like lots of space. Maybe that's why I like to walk so much." He took a half-step backward to emphasize his point.

That seemed to shift her focus into chatterbox mode. "You must walk in the mornings," she said. "I come over afternoons. I keep telling Horace—that's my husband—I tell Horace all the time he ought to come with me. He needs it more than I do. Heavens to Betsy, that man has more excuses than a ninth grade dropout. He's got to have the car worked on or he needs to go by his brother's place to pick up something. Don't ask me what something is. Or he's got a cramp in his leg, or more likely a cramp in his head. I was telling my brother, John—he lives in Columbia..."

At this point, Bryce threw a switch in his brain that diverted his hearing mechanism, allowing her words to dribble out into space. He continued to focus his eyes on her and nodded now and then, but his thoughts wandered back to that "I came from out West" statement and the blunder he had made in leaving it.

A few years after developing his foreign currency gambit, Pat Pagano had a visit from a well-dressed attorney from New York who had heard of his success through Vince Pagano, a justifiably proud father. Pat had been investing relatively small amounts, but this fellow wanted him to put a quarter of a million dollars into the Swiss bank scheme. In a few short months, a currency shift took place and Pat presented Frank Salerno with a profit of $395,000—a 158 percent return, more than 300 percent on an annualized basis, since the money had been at work for less than six months.

Around the same age as Pat, Salerno cut a dapper figure. He was a handsome, smooth-talking lawyer whose gestures seemed designed to flash the large rings that adorned most of his manicured fingers. After tucking the check into the pocket of his tailored Italian jacket, Salerno smiled across the desk at Pat.

"I want you to come to work for the Alcamo Corporation," he said. "I'm chief counsel. We'll pay you double what you're currently making to handle our investments."

Pat stared in disbelief. "Come to New York?"

"Right. We will make all the arrangements. Find you a house, handle your move."

The offer had come so suddenly that Pat's head was swimming. "But I don't know anything about your company," he said, shaking his head.

"We're an international conglomerate, involved in such diverse fields as construction, transportation, and textiles." He didn't specify how they were involved in those fields.

Pat was intrigued. The money was fabulous, but even more exciting was the challenge, which would be hard to resist. And before the day was out, he had accepted.

Alcamo moved rapidly. In less than two weeks, the Pagano family had been relocated to a large home in a fashionable section of Long Island. But once in place, Pat quickly made a startling discovery. His new employer was really a front for one of the most influential Mafia families in New York, headed by an old Don named Tony Vicario. Although Alcamo sounded like a shortened version of some meaningful words, it was actually the name of the town in Sicily near where Vicario was born not long after the start of the Twentieth Century.

Fred jerked Bryce back to the present when he interrupted Clara's prattling. "Sorry, Clara," he said, "but Betty Lou is looking for Bryce here. She needs to ask him something."

Bryce directed a grim smile at Clara. "Nice meeting you."

Then he hurried off with Fred. When they got to the front door, he swiped a hand across his brow and exhaled noisily. "Phew! Thanks, pal. I believe she could have gone on until midnight."

Fred gave a big laugh and laid a hand on his shoulder. "You have now been officially initiated into the Lovely Lane Silver Shadows. Congratulations. Oh, that part about Betty Lou was true. She wanted me to tell you she'd like to visit a little while with her sister."

"Sarah Anne?"

"Right. Something to do with their ornery brother, I think. Anyway, Troy and I are still trying to iron out a problem with the church building. I hate to keep bouncing you around, but would you mind sitting with Marge Hunter till we get to Natchez?"

Troy had warned him that Tillie Ellis was a matchmaker. Bryce wondered if Betty Lou Scott might not be the culprit instead. Apparently she was satisfied that he posed no threat to her friend.

"Be happy to," he said.

Actually, he had mixed emotions. He felt a natural attraction for the woman, but what had happened a few hours ago drastically altered the landscape. Could he afford the distraction, and would he be putting her at risk?

THE RAIN had turned serious, pooling into small ponds along the sidewalk as they jogged out to the bus. Back inside, Bryce dropped into the seat on the left next to Marge.

She looked mildly amused. "Sorry you got stuck with me. They've had you playing musical chairs, haven't they?"

"My pleasure, really. Isn't this what Tillie told us to do, move around and make more acquaintances?"

"I noticed you just made one inside there."

Recalling the encounter with Clara, he grimaced. "Oh, boy. Did I."

"That must have been quite a conversation." There was a hint of mischief in her eyes.

"Actually, it wasn't much of a conversation at all. More of a monologue."

"I can imagine. She's really a good-hearted soul, though."

"That's nice to know."

Marge leaned down to get a tissue out of her bag, and Bryce watched every graceful move. He had to admit, for early seventies, she was quite a stunning woman.

"Troy told me about his brother," he said. He leaned back and folded his hands to hide his nervousness.

"Keith Walden was one of a kind." She spoke with a marked tenderness in her voice.

Bryce found that a neat way of leaving unsaid that her second husband couldn't hold a candle to him. She had class.

As the bus pulled out onto the interstate, the rain beat a steady patter against the window beside Marge while Bryce puzzled over the odd contrast in his feelings toward her. She radiated a warmth and concern that made him as comfortable as he had been with anyone in a long while, yet at the same time she stirred a sense of awkwardness in him. The realization triggered a momentary flashback to that night in the casino when he had dropped the glass on meeting Ellen Davidson.

Drawing in a deep breath to calm himself, Bryce turned to Marge. "Troy told me Keith had a real estate firm. Did you sell houses, too?"

"Oh, no. I just helped out in the office. I'm no salesperson."

"Neither am I," he said. Then, inexplicably, he proceeded again to break the vow of silence about his past. "When I worked in a brokerage firm, it was a bit of a handicap. The real salesmen were always on the phone to their clients, touting some great stock issue, or plugging a bond they thought was sure to go places. I mostly waited until a client called me, ready to invest his money. Then I would suggest what I saw as the best move. Fortunately, most of them made money."

"Sounds like you didn't need to be a great salesperson. Giving people what they came to you for was the main thing, wasn't it?"

"I suppose you're right. Success is usually measured by results."

She twisted the tissue in her hands, looking a bit forlorn. "I've had some experience with that, too...on the negative side."

No doubt she was referring to her life with Captain Herbert

Hunter, he thought. Seeing the pain in her face saddened him. He decided to shift the focus to something more pleasant. "I've really been looking forward to this trip. It's a long time since I was in New Orleans."

She spoke with a faraway look in her eyes. "The last time I was there was for a Sugar Bowl game. I don't remember what year it was. Once when the Vols were playing down there. Keith and I both graduated from the University of Tennessee."

"My last trip down, I did a sightseeing ride on the St. Charles trolley line. Saw a lot of interesting houses. I wondered if we might cover some of that area on the bus?"

"I think so. When we were over at church one day, Tillie discussed the itinerary in some detail with Betty Lou and me. Seems like she mentioned St. Charles Avenue. After the bus problem and now the rain, I just hope things take a turn for the better. I'd hate to think we might run into something like that Hurricane Nora that was in the news."

THE POSSIBILITY of a hurricane showing up was not what concerned Bryce, but something far more potentially threatening. He had an active imagination, and the longer he had to think about the possibilities, the more alarming they became. Sitting beside Marge, he wondered if his own latent troubles could not easily become a serious problem for her, as well as the rest of the tour group. What if somebody should try to take him out with a long-range rifle shot? Anyone standing near him would be at risk.

But was that a likely scenario? No, he decided. From all he had read and heard, Mafia executions were normally carried out at close range. Nobody at Alcamo had confided in him, but he had picked up some whispers that gave him a good idea of what went on. There had been some notable cases of mob leaders murdered face-to-face in restaurants and hotels, even barbershops. Still, there were other cases where someone they were after simply disappeared, like Jimmy Hoffa. Bryce did not think they would harm innocent people just to get at him. If that were true, his best defense would be to stay in a group, avoid getting in a position to be isolated.

13

THE INTERIOR of the bus was almost dark. Bryce gazed out the window where the oncoming traffic appeared as yellow spots of light flitting through the rain, like trails of fleeting fireflies.

Tillie's voice blared over the loudspeaker. "We're on the outskirts of Natchez. I just talked to Day's Inn on my cellular phone. They'll have a room list and keys ready when we get there. I'll go in and pick them up, then pass them out before you get off the bus. But since I've heard rumblings about people starving to death, Chick will let us out at Shoney's first."

Chick Townes eased the bus up to the restaurant. Among the first off were Marge and Bryce, who dashed just inside to wait for Betty Lou and her sister. The two women hurried in a few minutes later, Sarah Anne toting a large floral-printed fabric handbag.

Marge pointed to it. "I don't know if you ought to carry that thing down here, Sarah Anne. Remember, this is Mississippi. They might think you're a carpetbagger."

"Oh, I am," she said, working to moderate her Southern accent. "I'm one of those damn Yankees from Illinois."

"You are not," Betty Lou said. "You can take the girl out of the country, but you can't–"

"Madison doesn't strike me as particularly country," Bryce said.

Betty Lou shifted her eyes. "You know what I mean. Come on, let's go find a table for six. That'll leave room for Fred and Troy."

Marge looked around. "Maybe Bryce has someone else he'd rather sit with."

He wasn't sure if that was a subtle suggestion that he sit elsewhere or if she merely sought to keep from imposing on him. "You folks are about the only ones I've met. Well, that's not really true. I guess I could eat with Clara Holly, couldn't I?"

Betty Lou grabbed his arm. "Don't be silly. Come on."

The restaurant had few other customers and the Silver Shadows were given carte blanche to find tables anywhere in the dining room. Although the temperature had dropped outside, Shoney's enjoyed a warm, cozy feel. Several of the group piled their jackets on one table. Polly Pitts brought in her red "trip kit" but left the folder on the table with her jacket.

Bryce helped the waitress push two tables together, then sat between Fred and Troy. The three women took the other side. They looked over the menus, then ordered, most of them choosing to take the simple way out, opting for the salad bar. After they had settled down to eat, Betty Lou looked across at Bryce.

"Well, disregarding ailing buses and drenching rain, how have you liked the trip so far?"

"So far, so good. The conversation has been lively."

"Sarah Anne and I are the only ones you didn't get to sit with," Fred said. "Maybe we'll get a crack at you later."

Bryce grinned. "If I keep moving every time the bus stops, people will start calling me Reynolds the Restless."

Sarah Anne chuckled and gave a knowing nod. "That reminds me of something Fred threatened to do last time I was down here."

Her brother-in-law frowned. "What's that?"

"Remember when Betty Lou and I were watching that soap opera The Young and the Restless? You said you were going to write one called The Old and the Shiftless."

As they all laughed, Bryce fixed his gaze on three new customers who had just entered the restaurant. Dressed in dark suits, they looked like businessmen who had come in after work. Not an unexpected sight for an eating place on a main thoroughfare, but something about their manner left him wondering. As the waitress seated them at a table adjacent to the one piled with jackets, he realized what had caught his attention. The trio had an obvious swagger in the way they walked. A darkly handsome younger man, apparently the leader, arrogantly dismissed the hostess, then spoke to the waitress with a sneer and a broad wave of his arms.

He had seen more than his share of such characters around the Alcamo Corporation in New York. They were Mafia hoods, following old Tony Vicario's dress code. Since Vicario always contended that his people were just businessmen, he insisted they dress like businessmen.

Careful to avoid eye contact, Bryce stole surreptitious glances in their direction. There was something vaguely familiar about the younger one. Several years had passed, and he was ready to acknowledge a faulty memory, but he felt almost certain he had seen this man with Boots. The name escaped him, if he had ever known it.

The important question was how likely these men were to recognize him? He noticed all three kept shifting their glances from table to table.

He tried to keep up with the conversation among his companions while training a wary eye on the likely trio of Mafiosi. But when a peal of laughter erupted suddenly around him, he realized he had missed a chunk of the conversation. Sensing the glances of the apparent mobsters targeting him, he shrank into his chair.

Holding a cracker toward his mouth to partially obscure his face, he turned to Fred. "I missed that one. I was straining to read a sign across the way."

Fred continued to chuckle. "Troy was telling about a survey they were doing in the mall the other day. About senior citizens. When the lady asked what did he think about sex for seniors, he told her, 'Well, I think about it quite a bit. Don't do much about it, though.'"

Bryce joined in the laughter, though not nearly so heartily as he would have if that ominous trio had not been watching from across the room. Finally the men got up and headed for the cashier. As they walked out of the restaurant, Bryce tried to relax, but the tension remained.

They were gone. But he knew if they were who he thought they were, one way or the other, they would be back. And likely soon.

14

BRYCE WAS the last one back to the bus. As he sank into his seat beside Troy, he heard Tillie give her usual call for vacant seats. Assured that there were no missing persons, she opened her mouth to give Chick the signal to go when Polly Pitts jumped up and squeezed into the aisle. "I forgot my trip kit!"

Tillie frowned. "You what?"

"I took my trip kit in with me and left it on the table with my jacket. I didn't notice it when I picked up the jacket, so it must be still in the restaurant." She pushed toward the door. "I'll run get it and be right back."

Tillie signaled to Chick, who opened the door. After watching Polly stumble out, Tillie turned to the driver and shook her head.

Polly was back a few minutes later, disappointment showing on her chubby face. "It wasn't there," she said.

"Maybe somebody else picked it up accidentally," Tillie said. Then she got on the microphone. "Did anyone happen to pick up a red folder, one of the trip kits, from the table inside where the jackets were stacked?"

When she got only head shakes, she turned back to Polly. "The bus boy probably threw it away. I'll copy mine for you when we get to the motel."

Bryce had moved toward the front of the bus and was close enough to hear the conversation. As Chick drove toward the motel, Bryce reflected on what must have happened. Polly's trip kit he been picked up, not by an overzealous bus boy, but by New York enforcers. If so, they now had a passenger list and a detailed itinerary. His troubles were just beginning.

Tillie passed out keys to the pairs of roommates, following down the list alphabetically by the first name in the pair. Since Troy and Sarah Anne were the names alphabetized, Bryce found himself rooming next door to Marge. He offered to carry her bag to the room, but she declined, doggedly toting it through the rain.

"I noticed there was a restaurant up beside the office," Troy said. He poked his key into the lock. "Anybody like a cup of coffee or something?"

Marge shook her head. "Not me. I've seen enough of this rain for one day."

"Thanks, Troy," said Sarah Anne. "It's been a long drive. I think I'll just get a hot shower and rest on my laurels."

It was nine o'clock. Bryce had no interest in wandering around in the dark and the downpour with only Troy for company. "I presume we'll see you in the morning at the Continental Breakfast," he said. "Did I hear Tillie correctly that it was complimentary?"

"That's right." Sarah Anne waved her arm toward the front of the motel. "It will be up there across from the check-in desk. We'd better get there by eight. Tillie wants us to be all loaded and ready to go at nine."

Sarah Anne had the door open and Bryce waved as they disappeared inside. "Have a good night."

The room he shared with Troy was small but adequate, with one weary blue plastic-covered easy chair, two inviting beds and a TV that resembled a large vacant eye sitting forlornly on the long countertop.

Troy tossed his small carryon on the bed toward the back of the room, pressing his hand to test its firmness. "Guess these are about the same." He picked up the TV remote from the bedside table. "There's a playoff game tonight. Want to watch it?"

Bryce unzipped his bag. He wasn't much of a baseball fan. "Turn on whatever you'd like, Troy. I think I'll follow Sarah Anne's example, just get a shower and relax."

"I'll get mine in the morning." Troy dropped onto the side of the bed and started surfing the channels.

Pulling out his shaving kit, Bryce headed for the bathroom. The lavatory was in an open area, with the toilet and shower through a door to the left. He paused in front of the large mirror above the sink, compressed his lips and watched the creases ripple across his cheeks. Not exactly what you'd call a pretty face, he thought. Where had the time gone?

The hot water helped relax his muscles and eased the pain that nagged at his upper back after a day of sitting on the bus. The pain was a holdover from an old compression fracture he had suffered years ago. He had passed out with the flu and fallen in the bathroom. Too bad it hadn't been something more colorful that would be worthy of a conversation piece. Something Walter Mittyish like getting knocked down while apprehending a robber who had just held up a bank. He shook his head. The only exciting things he had done in recent years were ones he couldn't afford to talk about.

Reluctantly turning off the shower, he climbed out and toweled himself dry, pulled on a pair of blue-striped pajamas and padded back out into the bedroom. What he saw brought a big grin. Troy lay sprawled across the bed like a large rag doll. He snored softly while the sounds of an excited baseball crowd and the mindless chatter of the commentators poured from the TV. Bryce switched off the set and the bedside lamp and crawled into bed.

He laced his fingers behind his head and lay there wide awake. He was a night person. Always had been. He did some of his best investment analysis work at night. His normal bedtime was around one a.m. So he lay there and listened to Troy's snoring in the darkened room. Finally, the snoring subsided, and he could hear the faint humming of an air conditioner somewhere down the covered walkway. Almost drowning out the sound was the determined splatter of raindrops just beyond. Mumbling voices moved quickly past the door.

What if there were a knock on the door at three a.m.? How would he convince Troy that it shouldn't be opened? Confess who he really was? Explain that he was an innocent man being hunted by the mob?

Troy would likely believe his innocence about as readily as Matthew Kravitz, the FBI agent who had talked him into looking for incriminating evidence to nail the mob. Kravitz had courted him as a prosecution witness, but Bryce suspected the agent never really believed in his professed ignorance of the Vicario family's illegal operations. Actually, most of what he had learned about Mafia activities came from a newspaper writer to whom Kravitz had introduced him, a man from the *New York Times* who probably knew as much about the mobsters as the FBI, maybe more. Bryce was certain the introduction stemmed from a deal the agent had made to get information from the reporter. Bryce had agreed to an interview reluctantly, even though he knew the name Pagano was not one he would be using in the future.

The writer told him about the mob's involvement in labor racketeering, how they forced payoffs from businessmen to assure union workers would not delay shipments or cause trouble on the job. They were involved in skimming money from government contracts and union pension funds. He confirmed something else Bryce had suspected, judging by the people he had observed around the Alcamo Corporation. The Mafia's recruits came from tough, uneducated felons. The reporter had given graphic descriptions of how the soldiers were required to commit brutal crimes as their tickets to admission.

Even the Vicario leadership had been backward in their business practices. They remained highly leery of such innovations as the computer. Bryce used one in his investment work, but none of the bosses wanted to get near the machine. When he discovered the incriminating records in Frank Salerno's office, they were all hand-written.

As he thought about it now, he realized his best chance of coming out of this alive would be to outwit them. Although they were brutally tough, most of them were not the brightest of adversaries. He would have to stay cool, stay smart, play his game, not theirs.

When he heard a muffled thump, he lay still and strained to catch any further sound. There was none. He decided the noise had come from the room next door. Probably the result of a heavy suitcase dropping on the floor. The room was Marge's. Picturing her face in his mind, he thought about the new dimension her appearance had added to the equation. At this critical point in his life, did he really need a distraction like her?

If he were all that smart, he thought, wouldn't he act to

distance himself from Mrs. Walden Hunter right now? She had done nothing to encourage him, nothing that would cause him to think of her other than as just another passenger on the bus. He mused how women throughout history, like Samson's Delilah, Mark Antony's Cleopatra, Napoleon's Josephine, had always been the nemesis of driven men.

Driven men? Why had that notion popped into his mind? For most of his life he had been anything but driven. But there had been one exception. The winter of 1944-45. In Belgium—the Battle of the Bulge. More than half a century had passed, but it still lingered vividly in his memory.

DECEMBER 16, 1944. Nazi Gen. Gerd von Rundstedt's 5th and 6th Panzer Armies had launched a savage counterattack against the Allied forces that had been sweeping rapidly through France and Belgium. General Eisenhower's troops were stretched out along a 600-mile front when the Germans unexpectedly struck. They chose an 80-mile sector in the Ardennes forest of Belgium and Luxemburg, an area that had seen bitter fighting during World War I as well. The Panzers quickly overwhelmed the thinly-held American line.

Sgt. Pat Pagano's platoon was among the 101st Airborne Division troops rushed into Bastogne to shore up the forces that had been overrun and were retreating in disarray. He found himself facing bitterly cold weather. Fog and minimal visibility prevented any help from the air. Then the snow began to fall, making conditions even more unbearable.

Pat learned the Nazis had rapidly encircled Bastogne, and on December 22, a team of German officers appeared under a flag of truce to demand the division's surrender by its commander, Brig. Gen. Anthony McAuliffe. After the general gave his famous "Nuts!" reply, the enemy became even more determined. Pat's platoon held a perimeter area on the outskirts of the town. When the artillery that had pounded them all day suddenly let up, he knew something was about to happen. Something bad. The terrain was hilly and covered with trees, their branches bowed under the weight of the snow. Located on a small promontory, he had as good a view as possible of the area, though he could see only a limited distance in the snow. His platoon spread out to one side.

The enemy struck suddenly, overrunning and capturing the first squad. The second squad, in the center, was their weakest link. It was pushed back and headed for cover, though the Germans did not pursue. An errant shot, which may have been friendly fire, struck the platoon commander. He suffered a serious head wound. Pat ordered two members of his third squad to evacuate the officer. Staring into the snow, Pat saw the Germans approaching from two directions. One group moved stealthily along a rock wall, where they were silhouetted against the snow.

Pat was angry. His anger was directed at the people responsible for all this carnage and destruction in the first place, Adolph Hitler and his generals back in Berlin. But the enemy soldiers who carried out their orders were equally culpable. The small town of Bastogne was a shambles. He had seen far too many bright-eyed young men literally torn apart by exploding artillery shells.

This was decision time, and he knew what had to be done. From the numbers involved and the tactics used, the assault did not appear a determined one, designed to make a breakthrough. More likely this was a probing action, he thought, probing in search of a weak spot. And if one were reported, the troops would come pouring in like water through a crack in a dam. The lieutenant had called for backup, but Pat knew reinforcements would take time to arrive, and should the enemy penetrate any deeper, the whole division could be in peril.

He felt the anger smoldering inside, but an even stronger emotion was determination. A determination that he would be the victor, not the victim. The old dictum was "know thyself," and he was certain he was the best marksman in his outfit. Turning to the soldiers behind him, he whispered, "Stay down." He aimed his carbine and squeezed off a quick volley that dropped five Germans along the rock wall. Then he ordered his men to provide him with covering fire.

The adrenaline was flowing. A man on a mission now, his mission had become intensely personal. He was responsible for his men, for his unit. He had to take whatever action he could to blunt the threat.

Leaning forward in a crouch, he dashed across the snow-covered ground to the wall and dived behind it, his move at least partially masked by the staccato blast of friendly fire. Hidden by the wall, he saw the second group of Germans advancing beyond a line of trees. Resting his weapon on a chink in the wall, he trained his sights on the column moving forward. He downed five more men before the rest turned to flee.

Just as the first soldiers of a reserve platoon arrived with orders to hold the line, Pat dashed out ahead, calling on his men to follow. They quickly caught up with the retreating enemy soldiers, who had the captured squad in tow. Motioning his men to spread out, Pat fired his carbine and yelled "Halt!" in German. They wound up freeing the men and captured ten Germans. The final count: ten enemy killed, ten captured, one American squad freed.

Two days later, on Christmas Eve, the skies cleared and the beleaguered troops cheered as American transport planes began dropping supplies. The day after Christmas, General Patton's Third Army broke through the German lines and set the town of Bastogne free. The 101st Airborne's heroic stand had raised spirits back home as well as along the Allied front. For his part in the battle, Pat Pagano was presented the Medal of Honor by President Truman in a White House ceremony the following July.

Recalling that wintry day as he lay in the darkness of the motel room in Natchez, two thoughts stuck in his troubled mind. One had bugged him occasionally over the years. He never doubted that he had done the right thing on the battlefield, but the memory of killing all those soldiers was disconcerting. It lurked in the back of his mind, concealed there as a disturbing reminder of what he had once done, what he had once been. Might some day, some situation trigger a return of that deadly Pat Pagano?

The other thought dealt with his current problem. He could not help but compare his situation now to what he had faced back then. The conclusion was obvious. His present plight was every bit as critical as that day in 1944. There were two major differences, however, both of them negative. This time the weapons and the element of surprise lay in the hands of the enemy. If only he had brought along his gun instead of that pepper spray pen, which was next to useless against such firepower.

<h1 style="text-align:center">15</h1>

A LIGHT SLEEPER, Bryce went on instant alert at the shrill sound of the telephone. He looked over at the table, then across to Troy, now a shapeless lump that might have been a chunk of marble in the bed for all the movement the ringing noise had produced. Could it be the New York mobster, he wondered? Why would he call? To bait a trap?

The phone rang again. Troy still had not budged as Bryce lifted the receiver. "Hello."

"Troy...Bryce?"

He recognized Fred's deep voice and relaxed. "This is Bryce. What time is it?"

"Did I wake you up? It's about seven o'clock. I didn't know about you, but I know Troy sleeps like a log. He carries a little old travel alarm with him, but it's not loud enough to rouse a hibernating bear. Thought I'd better check and be sure you boys were awake."

"I am now. Glad you called, though. Looks like Troy might sleep till noon. See you at breakfast."

Troy had finally stirred. He turned over and squinted up through narrow slits as Bryce hung up the phone.

"You talking to somebody?"

"Your friend Fred Scott. It was a wake-up call. Time to rise and shine, Troy." He recalled the way his dad used to come in to awaken him and his brother in a sing-song voice. "Let's go, boys. Time to rise and shine. Three will get you five the sun'll shine all day." He was forever quoting odds on everything. Bryce wondered what kind of odds he might give on the chances of his son surviving this trip.

Troy lumbered out of bed just as his alarm began to beep on the bedside table. He reached over to silence the clock, then stood beside the bed for a moment, stretching tentatively and rubbing the back of his neck. "I'll get my shower," he said. He had begun to stir in earnest. "You can go ahead and shave if you want to."

Bryce shaved and dressed and switched on the TV. Using the remote, he tuned in the Weather Channel and saw a large map of the U.S. Snow and rain and clouds dotted the map, along with a few glowing balls of sun. Things looked basically normal. Snow in the Rockies, cold around the Great Lakes, rain in the East (it had moved out of Mississippi during the night) and warm temperatures in the South. Hurricane Nora in the Caribbean was picking up speed in the open sea and headed for Mexico's Yucatan peninsula. He had never been in a hurricane, but he had often thought it would be interesting to experience one. Some other time, though. And not in Mexico. He had been there, and though he found the country intriguing, Montezuma's Revenge was more than enough to deal with all by itself.

When Troy came out of the shower, he glanced at the TV. "Did you see a local forecast?"

"Sunny. High of seventy-five."

"You bring any walking shorts?"

"Yeah. I think I put in a pair."

Troy had a devilish grin. "Why don't we wear 'em and give the ladies a thrill?"

"You're something else," Bryce said. "I don't know that these old legs would thrill anybody."

"Believe me, it doesn't take much for most of these old gals."

Bryce changed from jeans into light blue shorts. Then they packed their bags, except for toothbrushes, and strolled across to the motel office. The sun was a pale red ball in the hazy sky. Warming rays radiating outward indicated the slight chill in the air would not be around for long. They met a few early risers straggling away from the breakfast area as they entered.

"Better get you one of those muffins before they're all gone," Polly said, her chubby face all smiles. She clung to a fat muffin wrapped in a napkin.

"I believe all that woman thinks about is food," Troy said.

The welcome aroma of fresh-brewed coffee greeted them, along with the pungently sweetish odor of cinnamon. A long table held muffins and donuts, an array of fresh fruit, a large coffee urn and pitchers of milk. As he followed Troy toward the display of food, Bryce glanced around the room. He spotted Fred and Betty Lou seated at a round table in one corner. Two other couples had joined them, including the Jack Spratt-in-reverse pair, Horace and Clara Holly. The small lobby would accommodate only a limited number of people, with barely enough seating room for two tables.

Holding a cup of steaming coffee and a paper plate bearing a large cinnamon-flavored muffin, Bryce strolled over to the corner table.

"Well, I see you got him up," said Fred, nodding toward Troy. Then he eyed their shorts. "You boys must be expecting summery weather."

Troy shrugged. "The TV said seventy-five."

Fred looked back at Bryce. "Ready for a little sight-seeing this morning?"

The itinerary called for a visit to three of the twenty-four antebellum houses on the Natchez Fall Pilgrimage Tour. Bryce had looked through the brochure at the magnificent array of colonnaded homes dating from 1798 to 1858. Being a non-Southerner, he was particularly fascinated by these colorful relics of the plantation era, a period of American history that had come to a tragic end after colliding head-on with a juggernaut known as the Civil War. But that was all in the past. Right now he had a war of his own to contend with, one that might break into the open at any moment.

"Sounds like an interesting tour," he said.

Fred swiped crumbs from his mouth with a napkin. "Should be. From what I hear, we won't likely be the only busload around."

Good, Bryce thought. The more the merrier. He should have no trouble getting lost in the crowd.

There was a low whistle behind them, followed by a testy voice. "I've seen better legs than that on a coffee table. You guys haven't devoured all the goodies, have you?"

Bryce turned to find Sarah Anne wearing a flippantly quizzical gaze, followed closely by a smiling Marge dressed in gray slacks and a pink-striped polo shirt covered by a lightweight yellow jacket. He was struck by the fact that the plainest attire seemed to take on a certain verve when she wore it.

"I think they just brought in some hot muffins," Bryce said.

"Morning, sis." Betty Lou gave a nonchalant wave of her hand. "Hi, Marge." She pushed her chair away from the table. "We're finished. You all can have these seats."

Marge attempted to give the chairs to Troy and Bryce, since they were there first, but they would have none of it. Chivalry lived. When the women were seated with their pastry and coffee in hand, Troy asked Sarah Anne about the status of her teaching job. After being a high school Spanish teacher, she had worked as an instructor at Northwestern University for the past few years.

"I'm still trying to get the kids to *habla Español*," she said with a shrug.

"I thought maybe you had retired."

"No. I still have a year or two left in me. I'm not as old as my sister, you know."

As they talked on, Bryce set his empty plate and cup on the table beside Marge, who was listening to the conversation across the way, where Clara verbally entertained the pair next to her. A couple with heavily lined faces, apparently in their eighties, they sat with the polite inattention of a captive audience.

The woman finally appeared to get her fill and broke in. "We'd better be getting back to our room. Nice to meet you, Clara. We certainly enjoyed the Continental Breakfast with you."

As they got to their feet, Clara looked up with large, sincere eyes. "You know what Continental Breakfast means, don't you?" she asked. "It means it's free."

With an incredulous frown, Marge glanced around at Bryce, who stood beside her.

He whispered in her ear. "You can't say this trip isn't educational. You learn something new every day."

With her audience filing out, Clara turned her attention across the table. "Sure glad to have you back with us, Marge."

"Actually, I've been back at Lovely Lane for several months now," Marge said.

"I know you have. But this is the first Silver Shadows trip

you've been on. Horace and I never miss one. Do we, Horace?" She turned to him.

Solemnly, he replied on cue. "We never miss one, Clara."

"Did that church you came from have a group like this?" Clara asked.

Marge had a slightly pained expression. "No, not like this."

"You know, I heard one of the ladies, she's a Baptist, I think, say that her church quit having trips after a couple got in a fight at a motel. The woman got a black eye and some bruises. He was one of those abusers, you know. She said—"

"We'd better get back and finish packing," Bryce said, cutting her off. He held out his arm, making a show of staring at his watch. "Don't want Tillie Ellis to get on our case this morning."

"That's for sure," Marge said. She jumped up and tugged at Sarah Anne's arm.

As they started past, Clara gave Bryce a perceptive look, as if she had just discovered gravity. "You must have been in the war, Mr. Reynolds," she said.

The comment stopped him as effectively as a brick wall. He stared down at her, frowning, with a puzzled expression. "Why do you say that?"

"That scar on your leg. My brother has one exactly like it, only his is a little higher up. He got hit with some shrapnel during an artillery barrage in Europe."

Bryce was so caught by surprise that his reply was barely audible. "So did I."

As they started walking away from the building, Sarah Anne glanced back at him. "Clara doesn't miss a thing, does she?"

"You're right about that," he murmured, still shaken by the observation.

He had begun to reflect on his answer and wonder if he might have made a serious gaffe. Hopefully not. But if he had thought about the scar earlier, he would have made some excuse to skip wearing the shorts. The mob obviously knew about the war wound, since the Alcamo company doctor had given him a physical.

"Bryce and I still need to pack our toothbrushes," Troy said. "You girls going back to the room?"

"I guess I could use a trip to the bathroom," Sarah Anne said. "We've already put our bags on the bus."

A few members of the group were out doing their morning walks, circling the motel. "I should be doing that," Bryce said. "I missed yesterday."

Troy looked thoughtful. "If I was home, I'd be getting my exercise lifting Virginia and tugging her around."

"How's she doing?" Marge asked. "I haven't been by to visit with her for a while."

"She'd be happy to see you. She's holding her own, I guess. Gradually getting a little bit more unsteady."

As they followed the driveway from the office around to the main building, they passed a separate structure on the left that appeared to house meeting rooms. The building was long and low-slung, with a parking area in front. When Bryce glanced over that way, what he saw had the same effect as someone raising a large red flag. It took a force of will to shift his eyes away, to keep from staring.

A late model, dark blue Cadillac sat in the parking area, facing outward, with two men in the front seat, one in the rear.

They were too far away for any positive identification, but Bryce was ready to quote some of his dad's sure-thing odds that the occupants were the same trio he had seen last night at the restaurant. He was more convinced than ever now. This was the Grim Reaper's advance team.

16

THAT SCAR on his leg suddenly felt as if etched in a glowing neon red. With a swift but smooth, and what he hoped appeared natural, move, he stepped around Troy and Sarah Anne, edging slightly ahead so they would be between him and the Caddy. He still had no idea if the deadly trio knew his identity, and he could only speculate as to whether they were aware of Pat Pagano's scar, but he would err on the side of caution. As soon as they reached their room, Bryce slipped the key into the lock, twisted it and pushed his way inside.

He turned to Troy. "You can go first."

As the bathroom door closed, he pushed the heavy drapery aside enough to peek through the window. He could see no one but a few Lovely Laners outside.

His bag lay open on the bed. Hastily, he pulled off the shorts and slipped on a pair of jeans. He was packing the shorts away when Troy stepped out of the bathroom.

"Hey. Why'd you do that?" Troy frowned at him.

Bryce grasped at the first thought that came to mind. "I found a tear in a seam. I was afraid it might rip open on the bus."

"Dang. Now I'll be the only one in shorts."

"Sorry," Bryce said. "You'll have to be the lady-thriller all by yourself."

When their bags were zipped, he followed Troy out to the sidewalk. "Want to see if the girls are ready?"

"Sure." Troy knocked on the door, and it opened immediately. "We're heading for the bus," he said. "Y'all ready?"

"Let's go, Sarah Anne," Marge called over her shoulder. Then she stepped out onto the walkway.

Bryce caught a peculiar expression on Marge's face as she glanced across at him, then turned away. Was the look one of wariness? Fleetingly, he wondered if his changing into blue jeans might have prompted her reaction? But he didn't have time to dwell on the possibilities. His thoughts turned to more pressing matters as they walked up the driveway toward the bus, which was parked in full view of the blue Cadillac.

Bryce stepped into the crowd around the cargo bays, which stood open like gaping mouths ready to devour the luggage. He shoved his bag inside. Then he followed Troy to the door of the bus, where a smiling Chick Townes helped the women up the steps.

"Morning, Tillie," Troy said. She stood beside the driver's seat, checking her notes.

She looked up with a quizzical glance. "Still have your room key?"

"We left it beside the TV," Bryce said. "Sure is a beautiful morning."

Tillie smiled. "Just what I ordered."

Troy turned and gestured upward with his thumb. "She has a special line to the man up there."

I could use one of those myself, Bryce thought as he looked out the windshield to where the blue car sat waiting.

As soon as everyone was aboard, Tillie gave their marching orders. "We'll be visiting three houses this morning. The first one is called Gloucester. It was built around 1803 and was once the home of Winthrop Sargent, the first governor of the Mississippi Territory. After that, we'll see Magnolia Hall, then the Banker's House. The tour will wind up around noon at the Carriage House Restaurant, adjacent to Stanton Hall. We'll eat lunch there, then head on to New Orleans."

Chick put the bus in gear, backed out of his parking spot and began to maneuver the long vehicle out toward the street. Seated on the opposite side from where the Cadillac was parked, Bryce could only wonder at what action its driver might have taken. He knew he would find out soon enough.

After a short drive from the motel, they came to the large red brick mansion called Gloucester. As the bus rolled into the parking area out front, the classic two-story, white-columned portico presented a striking picture in the morning sun. Wrought iron railings painted white flanked the front steps and porch and an identical balcony above. Just beyond the portico, the walls began to angle back to form the house's unique octagon shape. Those with cameras began taking aim the moment they stepped off the bus. A nattily-dressed man, one of the owners, awaited them at the top of the steps, accompanied by an attractive, hoop-skirted guide.

When he reached the porch, Bryce glanced back toward the parking area and spotted the blue Caddy, parked a discreet distance behind the bus. The three occupants had climbed out and begun to stroll toward the house.

Bryce joined the line of Silver Shadows trooping through the front door as Tillie checked them off. Inside, they were herded into the sitting room, where the blonde-haired young woman in the swirling blue silk skirt began to tell about the house and its period furnishings.

"This home is one of the finest and best preserved of the old Southern mansions," she said. "It was built in 1803 and was once part of a five-thousand-acre plantation."

She went on to describe nineteenth century silver objects from France, delicate tables and lamps from New Orleans, paintings from Europe and furniture handsomely carved by craftsmen from the early 1800s.

As the group moved around the room, Bryce found himself standing beside Marge and Sarah Anne. When the mellow-toned docent described one of the chairs, he leaned toward Marge and whispered. "Doesn't strike me as too comfortable. Looks like something a stiff-backed old maid aunt would sit in."

Her reply was quick and mirthless. "Or a stiff-backed old navy captain."

"Not my style, at any rate," Bryce said. "I'd prefer something you could lean back in and prop up your feet."

"That sounds like Keith Walden," she said with a nostalgic nod. "He was never much on formality."

Bryce grinned. "My kind of guy."

A few minutes later, the guide led them out into the hallway toward the dining room, located at the opposite end of the front section. She stopped along the way to comment on a variety of paintings and other art objects. While they listened, Bryce glanced back toward the sitting room and saw the wavy black hair and thick, squarish brows of the well-dressed young hood he had seen last night at the restaurant.

Suddenly, out of nowhere, the name popped full-blown into his mind: Dominick Locasio.

He was certain now. This was the young sidekick he had observed with Boots Minelli in New York. They had never met, but Frank Salerno had given him the name, along with the comment that "Dom" would likely turn out exactly like his mentor. Bryce translated that to mean "deadly."

The fact that he could recall a name from several years back when he sometimes had trouble remembering people he had met the week before puzzled him. Then he realized his mind had been working like a computer, the way a microprocessor manipulates information on a particular subject in the background while an entirely different set of data is being accessed on the screen. Undoubtedly his brain had been subconsciously at work, digging around in old memory banks ever since the discovery he had made last night at Shoney's.

Positive identification of the Mafia hood was a sobering accomplishment, and the prospect of what the man was doing here made Bryce even more ill at ease. Standing in a who-gives-a-damn slouch, Locasio spoke with broad hand-waving gestures to a small wisp of a woman with unruly white hair that she kept pushing to one side. She wore a Silver Shadows name badge.

He felt a sudden, overwhelming desire to eavesdrop on the conversation. Was Locasio inquiring about someone named Bryce Reynolds, or was he just digging in a blind hole?

Bryce turned to Marge. "Who is the little lady over there talking to the black-haired guy in the suit?"

She followed his gaze. "Oh, that's Pauline Sanders. You don't often see her talking like that, especially to strangers. She's more comfortable with children."

"She have a large family?"

"None at all. She never married. But she's been involved in the Children's Department at Sunday School ever since I can remember."

How could he approach Pauline Sanders and find out what

he needed to know without being unacceptably frank, Bryce wondered? "I presume she's retired. Where did she work?"

Marge shook her head. "She never worked. She had a sister a couple of years older, who worked as executive assistant to the head of one of the insurance companies. She passed away a few years ago. Pauline kept house and looked after their father until he died. She's a funny little thing. You may have noticed how she stands around the edge of a group of people. She doesn't talk much but she sure hears a lot. I think Tillie cultivates her to gather all the gossip."

An eavesdropper? As they followed the guide on into the dining room, Bryce tried to recall if Pauline might have been standing near him sometime, listening. He was certain he had seen her. What had she heard that she could tell Locasio?

Damn. He couldn't recall.

The guide droned on about place settings of old French silver and Sevres and Wedgwood porcelain and pre-Civil War artifacts, then the tour moved to the rear and across to the small brick outbuilding that housed the old kitchen. Bryce maneuvered to keep an eye on Locasio and his henchmen without attracting attention to himself. Other tourists joined the milling group and he shifted about to mask his presence by literally staying in the center of things.

A large gaggle of people had gathered outside the patched brick facade of the "winter kitchen," listening intently to a large black woman in a blue-checked dress with a short white apron. She and busied herself answering questions about how the slave women had prepared meals in the old days. But Bryce was more concerned about the scene a few yards away where Locasio had cornered Clara. She knew too much, and she was capable of telling the man much more than even he wanted to know. Bryce noted with some consolation, however, that she didn't appear to be pointing toward anyone, particularly himself.

Shortly, Tillie began herding everyone toward the bus. On the way, Bryce caught up with Clara and Horace Holly.

"You folks enjoy that?" he asked.

Horace waddled along like a lame duck. "Interesting," he said.

Clara shook her head. "They must have plenty of servants. Wouldn't you hate to have to clean that house? Specially after a bunch of strangers trooping dirt in all day long."

He saw just the opening he needed and jumped at it. "Speaking of strangers, who was that sharp-looking young guy in the fancy suit I saw you talking to?"

She frowned, deepening the wrinkles in her forehead. "You know, that was really strange. That young fella came all the way down here from New Jersey. He just called it 'Jersey.' I said 'that's a cow.' Anyway, he saw the Tennessee plates on our bus and wanted to know where we was from. I told him Madison, of course, and you know what he said? He said his father had a good friend lived in Madison, that he thought he went to Lovely Lane Methodist Church. Isn't that just too much?"

That was indeed too much for Bryce. If he had needed any further confirmation that the stranger was Locasio, that inventive little story supplied it. And those characters were no more from New Jersey than he was.

"Did he tell you the friend's name?" Bryce asked, trying not to sound too concerned.

"No, he couldn't remember the name. Said the man had only lived in Madison a few years. Wanted to know if that might fit any of the men on the bus." She paused a moment, lips pursed. "The only ones I could think of right off hand were you and Will Chandler and that MacArthur fellow."

That stung. Not just for the problems it might bring him but for what it might mean to the others. At the moment he had no idea how to deflect it.

Bryce forced a laugh. "I don't know anybody from New Jersey. I came from the other side of the country. Anyway, I'm not a Lovely Lane member. And neither is Hamilton MacArthur." He didn't bother to correct her, but, as he had learned, MacArthur was not really from Madison, either. Will Chandler was one of those Marge Hunter had told him about, though they were yet to meet.

Clara frowned. "He caught me sort of off guard. I guess I wasn't thinking too straight. He said it would be a nice coincidence if his father's friend was on this trip."

Bryce immediately thought of the scar on his leg and wondered if Locasio had mentioned anything about that, though he had difficulty imagining a context in which the subject might have come up. He had mixed feelings as he climbed aboard the bus. The good news was they obviously did not know what name he was using. The bad news was that Clara had placed him and the other two men in nomination for whatever deadly plans they proposed for Pat Pagano. And he was certain they would use any means at their disposal, including the use of whatever force was necessary, to find out which of the men was really Pat Pagano.

17

Durıng the remainder of the morning, the group toured two more mansions. First they swarmed over the Banker's House, an 1838 structure built in connection with the First Bank of Commerce. Then they stopped at stately Magnolia Hall, a classic example of Greek Revival architecture, last of the great mansions completed before the outbreak of the Civil War. Bryce spotted the Cadillac at a distance on one occasion but saw no more of the menacing trio.

Shortly before noon, Chick parked the bus in front of palatial Stanton Hall, a magnificent structure in gleaming white featuring massive columns and intricately fashioned decorative ironwork. The Silver Shadows streamed out for a leisurely stroll across the broad side lawn, past the twisting tentacles of massive rambling live oaks. Though obviously quite old, the trees appeared only slightly more gnarled than some of his fellow passengers, Bryce reflected. Bolstered by the reassurance of what he had learned from Clara, he took his time, pausing to read the explanatory signs along the way, no longer feeling the need to be on the alert for snipers. There was always the possibility they could decide to kill all three men, but he thought that unlikely now as they seemed intent on narrowing the field.

Bryce was the last to reach the flower-bedecked terrace that led to the Carriage House Restaurant. Tillie stood at the entrance to the dining room, where she had just dispatched the last foursome. She stood erect, head slightly bowed, in a look of guarded repose. Bryce was reminded of a basketball official during a time out, anticipating only a brief break in the action.

She turned as Bryce walked up. "Looks like you and me and Chick Townes are all that's left," she said. "He'll be here in a minute. Would you like to join us?"

Bryce smiled. "I couldn't pass up a chance to sit with the head lady and the main man."

She dipped her head and stared over her glasses, showing no sign of amusement. "If that's what you want to call us. Here comes Chick. Let's go find a table."

Bryce was forced to move with a lively step to keep up with her as she weaved in and out among the tables, gesturing to the costumed waitresses. She finally chose a spot to one side of her group, pausing to look them over with the proprietary gaze of a schoolmarm.

Bryce turned to greet Townes, extending a hand of welcome. "I'm Bryce Reynolds," he said.

"Nice to meet you, Mr. Reynolds." The driver turned to Tillie as he took his seat. "We're ready to head for bayou country soon as you give the word."

She waved a beckoning finger at the waitress. "After everybody finishes eating, we'll give them a few minutes to relax, then head toward the bus. How are we doing timewise?"

Chick glanced at his watch. "It'll be about dark when we get there. Depends a lot on the traffic around New Orleans."

After the waitress outlined the two entrees, all three of them opted for the chicken dish.

"We'll make Methodists out of you boys yet," Tillie said. "Us Methodists made chicken the main dish long before it became so fashionable."

After the waitress left, Bryce looked across at Chick. "You're doing a great job maneuvering that bus around. How did you come by the name Chick?"

His close-cropped black hair, sprinkled with gray, wreathed an oval-shaped face marked by lots of wrinkles at the corners of his eyes, a mark of frequent laughter. "Thanks. My real name is George Townes," he said with a grin. "Remember *Roots*? The character Chicken George, who was always involved in cockfights? Well, I was a young guy when that came out. Liked to bet on the ponies. I don't do that anymore," he hastened to say. "Anyway, some of the drivers where I was working started calling me Chicken George. It gradually got shortened to Chick."

"Did you ever meet Alex Haley?" Tillie asked.

"Yes, ma'am. I carried a busload up there when he had that place around Norris. I told him about the nickname. He got a bang out of it, said I looked just like he pictured the character."

Bryce searched the dining room for the table where Marge sat and got a sudden wake-up call. There, across the room, sat Locasio and his two accomplices. Bryce hadn't noticed when they came in, but they appeared intent on making themselves conspicuous now. He wondered if it was a conscious act of intimidation.

"Speaking of characters," Bryce said, nodding toward Locasio's table, "I saw those three fancy-suited dudes at Gloucester House this morning. They don't look like your typical tourists."

Tillie checked out the table with her glasses, then tilted them back up into her hair. "They said they were businessmen from New Jersey."

Bryce swallowed back his surprise. "You talked to them?"

"No. But Pauline Sanders did. She told me the good looking one cornered her."

"Really? What did he say?"

"He was looking for a friend of his father's, someone who goes to our church. Only problem was he didn't know the man's name."

The same story he had used on Clara, Bryce thought. "Was Pauline able to help him?"

Tillie shook her head. "He asked about any men on the bus who had only lived in Madison for a few years. Pauline told him she didn't know that much about everybody. Actually, I don't know that that's true, but her specialty is kids in Sunday School."

"Clara Holly told me he asked her the same thing."

"He did? Well, maybe Pauline was right."

"About what?"

"She thinks they're really detectives. Or maybe private investigators. I thought she had probably been watching too many mysteries on television, but I don't know..."

As the waitress set the plates of food on the table, Bryce gave Tillie a doubtful look. "I should think a policeman would identify himself up front. If he wanted to find out about somebody on the bus, the logical thing would be to approach the person in charge—you.”

Tillie paused before slicing into a crusty, golden chicken breast. “I guess you’re right. That would sound logical.”

Chick had listened in silence. Now he spoke with conviction. “I noticed those guys this morning. I don’t know where they come from or what they’re up to, but I know the type. I grew up in the projects. Fortunately, I was raised by a grandma who saw that I got out of there and made something of myself. But I know a bunch of toughs when I see ’em. They’re all the same. I don’t care if they’re dressed up or dressed down or if they’re black or white or something in between.”

Tillie frowned. “So what do you make of them?”

“I think you ought to pass the word around to be wary of ’em.”

“Not a bad idea,” Bryce said as he tackled his mass of chicken.

In fact, he mused, an excellent idea. That might deter any Silver Shadows from getting too cozy with Locasio, offering further hints about who might fit the criteria for the man they were after.

He had to admit that cold-shouldering the New Yorkers might go against the grain of some friendly Lovely Laners. Yet one innocent slip could have the effect of painting a big bullseye on his back.

After a few moments of thoughtful silence, Tillie pulled her glasses out of her hair and rested them on her nose. “Maybe I’ll just have a few words with Clara, tell her I’ve heard this young man has been approaching several of our group. Some are suspicious of what he’s up to. I think we can count on her to spread the word pretty effectively.”

When the tables began to clear and the bus passengers headed for the exit, the “businessmen” quickly joined them. As Bryce watched, he saw the trio separate, each of them mingling individually among the crowd. Then he realized they were checking the men’s badges. Were they looking for a particular name, he wondered, or perhaps checking out things like height and build? Undoubtedly they had a description of the way he had looked prior to the trial. And while he had done everything possible to change his appearance, height was one feature that defied alteration.

As Bryce joined Tillie and Chick heading for the exit, he saw the short man with the sharp nose turn on a path that would intercept them.

18

Bryce REACHED one hand casually toward his chest, deftly removed his name badge and slipped it into his shirt pocket. He avoided looking at the man as they passed near the doorway. What little satisfaction he felt was tempered by the knowledge that he was only delaying the inevitable. But he hoped the delay would be long enough for him to come up with some means to thwart whatever they planned for him. In the back of his mind, he knew he still held one trump card.

As they strolled across the broad lawn toward the bus, Bryce chatted casually with Tillie and Chick. At the same time, he kept an eye on the inquisitive trio, who wandered among a group that had veered off the path to view the front of Stanton Hall. Out at the street, he lingered around the door for a few minutes as the bantering passengers began boarding but saw nothing further of the men or their Cadillac.

When he started toward the back of the bus, Bryce spotted Troy in the aisle seat beside Marge and looked at him questioningly.

"We're pulling another little switcheroo," Troy said with a grin. "Betty Lou's sitting with Fred, and Sarah Anne's back in my seat. She's a good old gal. You'll enjoy getting to know her."

Bryce threw up his hands, glancing at Marge. "Like I said, this trip is certainly educational."

After Bryce had headed on toward the rear seat, Troy turned to Marge. "What do you think of him?"

She stared blankly. "Who?"

"Bryce Reynolds."

"Oh. I suppose he's all right. Seems like a decent sort." She rumpled her brow. "Why do you ask?"

"Just wondered," he said.

That brought a stern rejoinder. "Don't start on me like Betty Lou and Sarah Anne."

"Start on you?"

"They've been giving me all this stuff about Bryce Reynolds. Why don't I arrange to sit with him more? Why don't I get to know him better? If they wanted to fix me up with somebody, why didn't they make it that Hamilton MacArthur fellow? He's got money written all over him."

"You don't need money," Troy said. "Besides, MacArthur already has a wife."

"Really? Where is she?"

"Working. She's a lot younger than he is. Fred said she's running a company meeting in New Orleans this week. She's supposed to meet MacArthur when we get there tonight."

"Well, good for her. Anyway, Sarah Anne said Bryce would make a great catch. I told her I wasn't fishing, thanks. If she thought he was such a great catch, why didn't she throw out her line?"

Troy grinned. "What did she say?"

"What you would expect from Sarah Anne. Said she already had her eye on a professor at Northwestern."

Troy was silent for a moment. "He reminds me of Keith in a lot of ways."

Marge frowned. She'd had the same thought but didn't want to admit it. Her reply came out slowly, deliberately. "I have found that people aren't always what they seem at first blush."

"You're talking about Herbert Hunter, I suppose."

Her face tightened. "Why would you suppose that?"

He hesitated, a look of caution in his eyes.

Her voice sharpened. "Answer me, Troy Walden."

"Well, I...I knew what had happened at church. You know, the flap with Fred, when you all first came back. I just thought–"

"Did Betty Lou tell you something?"

He breathed a loud sigh of resignation. "Betty Lou just told me you'd not had a very happy marriage."

She looked exasperated. "Oh, God. I was afraid I might have done the wrong thing. I should never have told her. I'll bet it's all over the church by now." She felt sick at her stomach. She had only confided in Betty Lou after much agonizing, because they had been best friends for years. She had thought getting her problem out in the open might be cathartic. That little bit, anyway. Certainly not the whole story. Not the deep, dark secret she had managed to keep locked away for years.

"It isn't all over the church," Troy said. "She told me because I had been your brother-in-law. Forget Herbert Hunter. You were part of our family for forty years. I still think the world of you. All I want is for you to have the happiness you deserve."

"Who have you told?" she asked.

He swallowed hard. "Nobody."

"You're lying." She could see it in his eyes. Then she had a sudden premonition. "Bryce Reynolds. Did you tell Bryce Reynolds?"

He twisted his mouth. "Only that you'd had a rough time with Herb Hunter. That he was real jealous. I didn't give him any lurid details. Betty Lou didn't tell me anything like that."

She dropped her head down into her hand, slowly rubbing her forehead. She could not believe Troy had divulged such personal information to a virtual stranger. No lurid details? The whole marriage had been one long lurid detail. She hadn't told Betty Lou about the sexual part, but she had begun to wonder if the entire disgusting affair had not resulted from Herb Hunter's desire to get what he had been denied forty years earlier. And, of course, she had not dared even hint at the source of the hold he'd had over her, a mental hammerlock that left her completely subdued. Something so pervasive that, like an elephant freed from its chain, she had continued to feel almost a prisoner in her home for weeks after Herb's death.

He had known her secret.

Tears welled in her eyes and she turned her head away from Troy toward the window. The secret was not something trivial, something that might merely trigger embarrassment if it became known. It was horrendous. At times, just contemplating what she knew would literally make her ill, ready to retreat to the solace of her bedroom. She had been bedeviled over the years until she learned to lock the knowledge away deep inside her mind, like a deadly virus hidden from public scrutiny in some obscure government laboratory.

What had she done to deserve this, she reflected, her mood bordering on despair. Had it all stemmed from being so insensitive to the way Herb Hunter had been during that first year they met when she was a cheerleader at East Nashville High School?

Marge had grown up a few blocks down Gartland Avenue from the school's impressive facade, which had gained it a place on the National Register of Historic Places. The James family lived in a one-story frame bungalow. Her parents occupied one bedroom, while Marge slept with her grandmother. Her brother, Ed, several years her senior, claimed the third bedroom until he shocked everyone in 1937 by running off to take part in the Spanish Civil War. Unmanageable as a teenager, he made this his final act of rebellion. They heard nothing further of him except for a report that he had later joined the French Foreign Legion. It was confirmed by a classmate returning from World War II naval duty. He had encountered Ed James on his ship in the Mediterranean, dressed as a Legionnaire.

Quite the opposite of her brother, Marge caused her parents almost no problems as she grew into a striking blonde teenager. She never took boys seriously until the start of her junior year in high school. That's when Herbert Hunter literally barged into her life. As she sat on the lawn in front of the big brick building talking with a couple of girlfriends during lunch period one day, a tall, well-built boy with thick black hair almost ran over them trying to catch a football.

"Sorry, ladies," he said with an apologetic smile. He poked the ball beneath one arm, then froze, looking at Marge James with a curious semi-smile. "You're the cheerleader, aren't you?"

She nodded. "Sure am. Are you playing football this year?" Like everyone else in school, she knew who he was. She had seen him in plays and heard him MC various programs in the auditorium.

He laughed. "Hardly. I might knock one of these out." He bared his shiny white teeth. "Think what that might do to my thespian career."

Herb met her after school that afternoon and walked her home. He became a fixture in her life, and they were soon known as "steadies."

They went to movies and "sock hops" and did all the usual high school things. Herb also took her to every romantic spot he knew anything about and used all his formidable powers of persuasion to get her to make love with him. But it was fruitless. She had taken her mother's words to heart and made up her mind long ago. There would be no sex until marriage. Period. End of conversation.

During a football game that fall, a friend from church who had moved away showed up on the sidelines and chatted with her about old times. Herb grilled her afterward, demanding to know all about the boy. And though she didn't like his tone, she dismissed the incident in the excitement of winning a big victory over a traditional rival. There were other subtle hints of jealousy she should have heeded, but didn't. They would return to haunt her years later.

With World War II in full sway, Herb followed the news of naval battles constantly. A year ahead of Marge in school, he set out for the Great Lakes Naval Training Station early that summer with diploma in hand. Marge wrote him faithfully at first, though after he went to sea his replies became few and far between. The correspondence soon trickled to a halt. She heard nothing more of Herb until seeing him at that reunion a few years ago, where he had renewed his pursuit.

<h1 align="center">19</h1>

MARGE HAD sat with her head bowed, eyes shut as the past replayed in her mind like a TV documentary. Troy's voice finally broke into her thoughts, a voice as soft and gentle as a caress.

"I'm sorry if I've caused you any more hurt," he said. "It's the last thing I wanted to do. After that shoe-tying thing, I just mentioned to Bryce that you'd been married to my brother. When he asked about you, I thought he should know what you'd been through, so it would be easier for him to understand where you were coming from."

She opened her eyes and looked around. They felt moist from a hint of tears. "I know you meant well, Troy. But I'm not sure I'm ready for any new relationships. I don't think people realize what an experience like mine can do to a person. You tend to lose faith in your ability to judge people's character. What do I really know about Bryce Reynolds?"

Her initial impression of him had been favorable, though there had been two disturbing incidents. The first came during dinner at Shoney's in Natchez. Bryce claimed he had missed Troy's joke because he was concentrating on reading a sign across the restaurant. She sat facing him so she couldn't be sure what he had seen, but when she had a chance to look around, she found nothing that could have produced such a strange change in mood. His face had switched instantly from carefree to tense. He had covered it with a laugh when Fred re-told the story, but he had remained oddly detached during the rest of the meal.

The other strange mood shift had come that morning as they were walking back to their rooms from breakfast. She had no idea what triggered it, but Bryce had abruptly sobered and quickened his pace to move ahead of Sarah Anne and Troy. And then he came back out of the room changed from shorts to blue jeans.

Troy's reply broke into her thoughts. "Like Keith, he doesn't talk much about himself. He said he had been a stockbroker and an investment counselor for some corporation. Fred told me his wife died of cancer. I think he had some children."

Marge crossed one arm and rested a hand against her face. "He told Betty Lou he had outlived his family. But where did he come here from? Why Madison, if he has no family here?"

"I don't know. I'll ask if you'd like."

"Never mind. I was just trying to point out that aside from a few first impressions, we hardly know anything about the man. I also question whether he's so interested in me as you all seem to think."

"Why's that?"

"Well, he spoke to me at the first house we visited this morning. Since then I've hardly seen him around." She didn't mention that she had been left feeling a little disappointed. That made things a bit too confusing. "Anyway, I learned to my eternal regret that people aren't always what we think they are."

Troy raised a hand. "Okay. I got the message. I'll not bug you anymore. Promise."

Her features softened with a hint of a smile. "Don't take it personally, Troy. You, of all people, I can't fault. Remember, you were willing to be the father of the child I never had. And the way you've stood by Virginia through thick and thin, regardless of all the problems it's caused, ranks you right at the top of my list. I feel badly that I haven't been by to see her more often. I promise to do better after this trip."

"THERE ARE nine old geezers with Madison addresses on this list," Locasio said. He sat in the back seat of the Cadillac, a cigarette dangling from his mouth, as they cruised along in sight of the Nova Tours bus. "We've accounted for all of them except two that skinny old broad mentioned."

Locasio checked the notes jotted beside each name, such as "too tall" or "too fat." One, Will Chandler, was considered "possible," meeting the general profile he had heard Boots describe–"in his seventies, average height, on the heavy side." The others had not been identified.

"Which two?" asked Ziggy.

"Hamilton MacArthur and Bryce Reynolds. You guys try to pinpoint MacArthur next time they stop. I'll look for Reynolds."

Joe Blow glanced around. "Then what?"

"We gotta find out more about the possibles."

"How do we do that?"

"Don't push me, Joe. I'll let you know when I'm ready." Locasio glared at the list and cursed his luck. Why hadn't he asked Boots the vital question–what name was Pat Pagano using now? That would have made things so much simpler. And why hadn't Boots confided in him earlier about just who he was looking for? The answer to that one was obvious.

Over the years Locasio had learned to be wary of one troubling aspect about his mentor. Most of what Boots did, the threats, the head-knocking, even the executions, was accomplished without rancor. "Just business," he would say. But once in a great while something occurred that caused him to shift into an entirely different mode. On those occasions, "business" became intensely personal. He would stretch his own resources to the limit before calling for help. When Boots got on one of his missions, Locasio had learned to stay out of his way until invited in.

Boots had sought his help in some of the early legwork during the search for Pat Pagano. They had checked every known location where Pagano might have spent any time with relatives, friends or acquaintances. Thanks to a corrupted source inside the Justice Department, Boots had even managed to track down Pagano's move to Oregon under an assumed name, but the man they found there turned out to be an innocent guy who just happened to have the same name. End of trail. Pagano had covered his tracks well. Still, Boots never gave up. Whenever he came across a lead, he followed it with the tenacity of a bloodhound.

The new consigliere, Nick Caggiano, finally came up with the idea that led to the solution. He suggested looking into Pagano's trademark financial dealings with the foreign currency gambit. Going back over old documents, Boots found the name of the Swiss bank involved. Locasio accompanied him to Switzerland on a trip that proved productive in the end, though at the time things did not seem so promising. Despite Boots' efforts to put the fear of God in the old Swiss banker, he wouldn't budge. He could provide no information on accounts because everything was on computers, he insisted. Without the proper passwords, which only the account holder would know, nothing was available.

Back home, Boots had an idea. He had heard a nerd nephew brag about computers the boy had broken into. Boots financed an operation in which the nephew got help from some fellow hackers in Switzerland and finally cracked the bank's codes. They discovered funds had been moved from Pat Pagano's account into one in a new name, a name which Boots did not choose to share with Locasio. He did confide, however, that the address for the account was a mail service on the Isle of Man in the English Channel.

Boots had displayed typical ruthlessness in that case, killing the owner of the mail service and ransacking his business until he had located an address in Madison, Tennessee for the owner of the Swiss bank account.

Monday morning, Boots had left early for Madison after instructing everyone to remain in the motel room near the Nashville airport and await his call. Now Locasio wished he had insisted on knowing the details of what Boots planned to do, though he had to acknowledge pursuing that path would have brought nothing but a string of curses and the admonition to keep his mouth shut and mind his own damned business.

"What if we don't manage to figure out which guy is Pagano?" Ziggy Ferrante asked.

Locasio's heavy brows nearly met as he frowned. "I've been thinking about that. Hopefully, we'll manage. If not, we may need Joe to do his thing."

The driver cocked his head. "I didn't bring nothing with me."

"Then you need to contact some of our friends in New Orleans when we get there."

20

AT THE REAR of the bus, Bryce busily fended off questions posed by Sarah Anne. First she wanted to know what had happened to his name badge. He told her the clasp was sprung. He'd have to work on the gadget. She didn't hesitate to dig into his background or to explain, rather enthusiastically, why Marge would be the ideal person with whom to share the rest of his life.

Bryce had become quite adept at glossing over things when people became too inquisitive. He described a middle class background during the depression that could have fit half the people his age, then said he left Oklahoma to get away from too many painful memories.

"I lost my wife to cancer and my sons were killed in an accident. I wanted to make a new start somewhere else," he said. "I had attended a meeting at the Opryland Hotel and decided this would be a good place to call home."

"That's a nice area where you live," Sarah Anne said. "Did I hear Troy say you'd been a stockbroker, or something like that?"

"Something like that." He grinned and parried her question with one of his own. "What did Stan do for a living?"

She liked to talk and quickly seized the opportunity. "He was a home builder. It was quite a coincidence that Marge married a Realtor and I married a home builder. Stan worked the high end of the market where the profits were greater. It turned out nice for me. He built us a really fine home. Of course, I don't need all that space now. But my older daughter has two girls. They often and stay with grandma. Did you hear why Marge has no kids? Was some kind of problem with Keith, as I understand it. Something that made him sterile."

"Troy told me."

"She was disappointed, but I never heard her complain.

There was some talk once about going another route to have a child, but she decided against it. You won't find a kinder, gentler, more understanding soul than Marge Hunter."

He was glad she had gotten off him, but talking about Marge was a subject that left him equally uncomfortable. He felt attracted to her, yet he was hesitant to follow his instincts. Not with Locasio and his two muscle men trailing around like a trilogy of bad dreams. He had convinced himself that his blundering ways were responsible for taking the lives of too many people dear to him. Could he dare risk another?

21

WE'LL BE STOPPING at a rest area shortly," Tillie announced. "Let's try to hold it to about twenty minutes. That'll give you time to go to the restroom, get a Coke or whatever. We'll stop for dinner on the outskirts of New Orleans, then go on to the hotel." Apparently as an afterthought, she added, "By the way, Hamilton MacArthur has discovered another typo in our trip kit. His address is listed as Madison when it should be Hendersonville."

Clara frowned as she digested that bit of news. Had she known earlier, she wouldn't have mentioned MacArthur's name to that man from New Jersey. He asked about those who lived in Madison. On the other hand, had she known the fellow might be some sort of confidence man, she wouldn't ha`ve told him anything at all. What was this world coming to, she fretted? Things had gotten so bad you could hardly trust anybody anymore. What a far cry from the days when she had grown up as the daughter of a Nashville policeman.

TROY TURNED to Marge. "Since he is my roommate, would you have any objections if I invited Bryce to sit with us at dinner?"

She gave a slight shake of her head. "Of course not. I don't dislike the man. I just don't want you or your co-conspirators trying to push us onto each other."

"No problem. That's fine with me." He was through playing Cupid. That wasn't his game anyway. But they would make a handsome pair, he reflected. Both in obvious good health. They could enjoy the kind of active life he and Virginia had hoped for in retirement, until Parkinson's Disease had reared its ugly head.

Then he thought of something that instantly troubled him on several counts. It was something that might give Marge a more favorable insight into Bryce, but a subject he knew he shouldn't discuss. He tried rationalizing. In years past, Marge had served on the Administrative Board, the Trustees, just about every committee in the church. He wouldn't be confiding in a total stranger or someone new to the membership.

He had committed worse breeches of ecclesiastical etiquette, he decided.

"I guess you know I'm chairman of the Finance Committee at church," he said.

She looked at him curiously. "No. But it's nice to know our funds are in reliable hands."

He winced. If that were true, would he be doing this?

"Something real interesting happened a few Sundays ago," he said. No use stopping now. "Dr. Trent cornered me after church and said we needed to talk. Seems he had received a cashier's check for seven thousand dollars from a non-member. The donor wanted to remain anonymous. He had heard we needed theatrical lighting and a good sound system for the Fellowship Center stage. But he'd also heard we couldn't afford to put it in the budget. Dr. Trent thought I should know the details."

"Why would a non-member do that?"

"Said he appreciated what Lovely Lane was doing for the community. Things like making the track available to outsiders. Putting on musical shows and other programs in the Fellowship Center. He had attended the Dinner Theatre during the summer. Thought it was great."

"I haven't seen anything about this in the newsletter."

"It won't be announced until we get the equipment."

Marge looked pleased. "It's refreshing to hear that some people still want to do good things without seeking any glory."

"Yeah, it is. And I'm not supposed to reveal the name, of course, but I thought maybe you should know."

She frowned. "Why on earth should I?"

Troy lowered his voice. "Don't repeat it. I haven't told anybody else. It was Bryce Reynolds."

RATHER THAN make her feel more favorably inclined toward Bryce, the news of his unusual gift to the church caused Marge to view him with more uncertainty than ever. Why would someone with no obvious ties to Lovely Lane contribute such a large sum? Very few members gave that much over the course of a year. Marge was familiar with the street Bryce lived on. The neighborhood was nice but not luxurious. She speculated that either he had more money than he knew what to do with or he was seeking to absolve himself of some past sin.

AFTER CHICK let them off the bus at the rest area, Bryce caught a glimpse of the blue Cadillac parked nearby and knew his pursuers were heating up the trail. Before he had a chance to dwell too deeply on that prospect, however, he encountered Fred heading into the men's room.

Bryce knew that at seventy-four, Fred was obviously well acquainted with all the problems of aging, but the man seemed to have an unquenchable thirst for finding the humorous in life's many foibles. He attacked old age the way many people approached things over which they had no control—he made a joke of it.

"Looks like we'll have to stand in line," Fred said, checking the overflow crowd. "Reminds me of the woman who sent her little boy into the men's room."

Bryce twisted his mouth into a grin. "What happened?"

"He was gone for a while, then he came out with his pants all wet. When she asked him what went wrong, he said, 'Two old men were in front of me. One couldn't start, one couldn't stop, and I couldn't wait.'"

Bryce snickered. "I know the feeling. I've got a decongestant pill that slows you down until you've been there so long you get embarrassed."

"My problem's not a pill. It's just plain old rusty plumbing."

OUT IN THE open lobby with the inevitable map of the state and racks of brochures on nearby motels and attractions, Marge stood talking with Betty Lou and Sarah Anne.

"Did you hear what Clara's telling?" asked Betty Lou.

Her sister arched a well-drawn eyebrow. "What now?"

"Remember those three fancy-dressed men we saw on the tour and at the restaurant? She thinks they're con men from New

Jersey, down here to fleece a bunch of us gullible Southern seniors."

Marge frowned. "I saw the young, good-looking one talking to Pauline Sanders at Gloucester House this morning."

"Really?" Betty Lou's eyes widened. "You don't reckon, maybe...?"

Sarah Anne gave a skeptical shake of her head. "I doubt it. But who knows? Pauline would surely give the appearance of a likely prospect." She looked around. "You girls need to visit the ladies room?"

"I do," said Betty Lou.

Marge said she would wait for them.

As she stood opposite the entrance, she saw Bryce and Fred stroll in and head for a display of brochures. They began to pick through them, apparently not looking for anything in particular. When she became aware that someone had walked up beside her, she looked around and was shocked to meet the dark, probing eyes of the neatly-attired young man she had seen talking with Pauline that morning.

"Hi!" he said, glancing at her badge. "Ms. Hunter, I'm looking for a guy in your group named Bryce Reynolds. If he's around, I'd appreciate your pointing him out to me."

Though he sounded friendly enough, there was something disturbing about his eyes, a quality that left her feeling cold. Could Clara Holly be right about these men, she worried? She decided to face the problem head-on. "What did you want with Mr. Reynolds?" she asked.

He looked taken aback by the question but recovered quickly. "I thought he might be a friend of my father's." He gazed about the room. "Is he in here?"

How would Bryce have known his father, she wondered? Still, she didn't see how that could relate to any kind of scam. "He's the shorter of the two men over there looking through the brochures."

"Thank you, lady," he said. Then he strode across toward where Bryce and Fred were standing.

"CAN YOU believe they've got gambling casinos in Biloxi?"

Fred asked as he looked through a brochure. "When I was in the Air National Guard, back in the dark ages, we used to have summer field training at Gulfport. Bunked at Keesler Field. Biloxi wasn't much of a town back then."

"Pardon me, sir," said a sharp-edged voice.

Bryce turned to stare into the cool, unfeeling eyes of Dom Locasio. He tried to hide the shock but was not sure how well he succeeded. "Yes?" he said, brow furrowed.

"I'm trying to locate one of your people who knew my father, Nick Dominico, back in New Jersey. Ever heard of him?"

Bryce forced a grin and gave his best impression of Southernese. "Afraid not, young fella. Can't think of anybody I know from New Jersey."

"Somebody on our bus?" Fred asked with a curious frown.

Locasio eyed them coolly. "All I recall is he's a member of Lovely Lane Church in Madison."

Fred gave him an indulgent look as he rubbed his chin speculatively. "What's his name? I could probably tell you exactly where to find him. I know just about everybody at Lovely Lane."

Bryce spoke with a chuckle. "I think Fred's been there since they built the place."

"Not quite, but almost. I've been there some sixty years."

Locasio nodded. "Sorry, I don't know the name. Thanks anyway."

HAMILTON MACARTHUR was not a large man, only a man with a large ego. Those years in a corporate seat of power had left him with an inflated view of himself. He had become accustomed to making decisions involving millions of dollars, thousands of policyholders and hundreds of employees. And though he realized the days of underlings kowtowing to his every whim were gone, he still expected to be treated like the formidable personage he felt himself to be.

So far on this trip, he had not been disappointed. Matilda Ellis, who had done work for his company in years past, spoke quite flatteringly while introducing him to other passengers. Those he had talked with appeared duly impressed. His attire was a considerable cut above the crowd, which, of course, was what he had expected. When he encountered Troy Walden beside the drink and snack machines at the rest area, he was quick to imply his importance.

"Fred Scott tells me you were president of the Nashville Association of Life Underwriters at one time. The company I headed always swung its weight behind the agents' projects."

"As I recall, your company helped sponsor the Sales Congress when I was president," Walden said, smiling. "That's been several years back, though. I'm retired now."

"I stepped down last year myself. How do you like retirement?"

"No complaints. My company has a good retirement program. I imagine you did quite well."

MacArthur sipped on his Coke. "Our executives enjoy a quite liberal retirement plan. Of course, my stock in the company provides the backbone of my portfolio."

"Too bad your company doesn't take as good a care of its agents," Walden said. The smile had disappeared. "A friend of mine retired from there last year and got screwed out of his renewals."

MacArthur's eyes flashed. "Your friend must have neglected his clients. We have a point system. We take away points if you give poor service. It affects overall compensation, including retirement."

Walden shoved his hands in his pockets. "I understand you used to be in the investment end of the business. Are you still involved in that area?"

MacArthur rubbed the cold can against his cheek. With the temperature climbing, it felt good. And he was happy to get off the subject of retirement. He knew what Troy Walden was thinking. The company sometimes saw fit to take away points when an agent neared retirement. And those executives protected by a liberal retirement program were the ones who made the decisions.

"I'm only involved in investments for my own account," he said. "The past year I've enjoyed trading in commodities."

"You buy and sell futures?" Walden asked.

"Futures contracts and options."

"I've always heard commodities was a place where you could lose your shirt."

MacArthur gave him a smug smile. "If you don't know what you're doing. It is also a place where you can make a fortune, especially when prices are exceptionally volatile. Remember back when wheat prices hit a record high? I bought five May wheat contracts just as the price started to rise. With the leverage available through low margins, I only paid about twelve thousand dollars. A month later, the price had gone up a dollar-thirty a bushel. I closed out my position with a profit of over twenty thousand dollars."

Walden looked impressed. "If a fellow could do that every month or so, he'd be in hog heaven."

MacArthur took another swig of his Coke. "I've been trading lately in futures options. That limits your risk. And you can buy an option with very little cash."

During his tenure with the insurance company, he wasn't allowed to deal with anything but safe, low-risk investments like government bonds and blue ribbon stocks. Now that he was dealing with his own money, he could do as he pleased. Nevertheless, he was not a big risk-taker. He would invest only a small pool of surplus cash in the futures market. Where commodities were concerned, he was strictly a recreational investor. He played that market only for the thrill of the chase.

"I used to trade options on stocks," Walden said. "Is it any different with futures?"

"An option is an option. You need to watch your delta and use the gamma when it's favorable."

MacArthur slowly became aware of a solidly built man in a dark blue suit standing nearby, looking at him with an oddly blank stare. Finding the look a bit disconcerting, he turned to the man and asked, "Something I can do for you?"

The stranger fumbled in his pocket, produced a dollar bill, stepped forward and spoke in an unexpectedly high-pitched voice. "You got change for a dollar? I want to get a drink out of the machine."

Frowning, MacArthur fished a handful of coins from his pocket, selected four quarters and made the exchange. He promptly dismissed the intruder, turning back to Walden as the man headed for the machines.

"You should talk to my roommate," Walden said. "He was involved in investments before he retired. He made a fascinating play with interest rates and currencies."

"Really? How interesting."

As the man in the blue suit scurried past, clutching his drink can like a pack rat headed for his lair, MacArthur narrowed his eyes. "Wasn't that the strangest looking character? He could have gotten change out of the machine."

"I think he was one of those three odd ducks we saw at lunch in Natchez, dressed like they were headed for a funeral."

MacArthur pursed his lips. "Come to think of it, I believe you're right."

<h1 style="text-align:center">22</h1>

Back on the highway, Joe Blow pointed the Cadillac toward New Orleans and jammed the accelerator as though he were vying for an inside lane at Talladega. Beside him, Ziggy quickly recounted how he had put the make on Hamilton MacArthur.

"He's got to be our man," Ziggy said with certainty.

Locasio flicked his lighter and took a long drag on his cigarette. "What makes you so damn sure?"

"All that investment talk. About commodities and something called futures and options. It was way over my head. A lot of shit about deltas and gammas, whatever the hell they are. Sounded like Greek to me."

"Ziggy's right, Dom," Joe said. "Remember, Boots told us Pagano was a big earner for the family."

"I know." Locasio twitched his jaw. "Trouble is, when I talked to that Bryce Reynolds, I got a gut feeling he knew who I was."

"You ever meet Pagano?"

"No."

"Then how the hell would he know you?"

"I don't know, dammit. It just seemed like this guy did. Maybe he saw me with Boots back in my younger days. I'd say Reynolds and MacArthur are both possibles."

Ziggy stared at him and smoldered. The dour, stocky mobster had been born stubborn and hadn't changed in forty years. He wasn't happy with Dom's domineering. Sure, he knew Dom was being groomed for a leading role, while he and the others had been relegated to the status of bit players, but that didn't make him any more eager to be bossed around by some kid still wet behind the ears.

"I say it's MacArthur," he said. "What you gonna do about it?"

"I'll call Marco in Nashville, see what he can dig up."

Ziggy shrugged. "Better tell him to dig fast. What if Pagano gets scared and decides to blow?"

"We'll be watching. Anyway, I don't think he will. Remember this little jewel?" Locasio reached into his coat and pulled out the medal attached to the blue ribbon. "The old man's got balls." Then a devilish grin twisted his face. "And I plan to cut the suckers off and hang 'em over the rearview mirror."

THE SKY glowed brightly above a translucent net of wispy clouds that waited to catch the dropping sun. As Chick exited I-12 north of the Lake Pontchartrain Causeway, Tillie grabbed the microphone for an update.

"We will be stopping for supper in a few minutes at a restaurant near Lake Pontchartrain. I'm sorry you're going to miss what I'm sure will be a gorgeous sunset, but it'll be gone by the time we get back on the road. The causeway runs twenty-four miles across the lake and would've given you a grand view. But we'll have other opportunities.

"About New Orleans, a word of advice. It's no different than any big city that caters to tourists. In fact, it's not nearly as bad as some places in Europe, like Rome, for example. Fred and Betty Lou Scott can tell you about that. They were with me on a European tour a few years back. In Rome, the pickpockets are terrible. Bag snatchers will ride along the street on motor scooters, reaching out to grab handbags right off your shoulders. Thank God there won't be anything like that in New Orleans, but I just wanted to caution you to be careful. Ladies, watch your bags. Hang onto them tightly when you're in a crowd. And guys, look after those bulging billfolds. It's better to take out some of your cash and put it in a front pocket."

Fred spoke up. "I carry mine in a pouch that hooks onto my belt. Slips down inside the waistband of my trousers."

"Great idea," said Tillie.

The restaurant sat just north of the choppy, brackish lake. The big red and white bus pulled up at the entrance nearly at dusk and the Silver Shadows streamed off, the women dutifully clutching their bags. For some, the effort would be too difficult. To reach the dining area, they had to negotiate a trap baited with an endless array of souvenirs and overpriced bric-a-brac. Tillie found it necessary to coax several laggards into the waiting line for tables, including Polly, whose crinkled eyes gazed on a small doll in a green satin hoop skirt.

"You can shop after you eat," Tillie said.

MacArthur advised her that he would be in after using his cell phone to call his wife, giving her their expected arrival time at the hotel. Thinking about it, Tillie realized MacArthur was likely the only other passenger with a cell phone. Most of the seniors hadn't yet acquired one, and those who had seemed happy to be away from the annoyance of the perverse ringing machines.

WITH TOKEN reluctance, Bryce accepted Troy's invitation to join him and the same foursome that had dined together the previous evening. They were ushered to a round table near a wall that displayed an array of ancient, rusted farm implements, including a scythe with a wicked-looking blade below a curved wooden handle.

"You haven't lived till you've attacked a wheat field with one of those gadgets," said Troy, pointing at the scythe.

Betty Lou narrowed her eyes. "Don't tell me you really used one of those things."

"Well, maybe not in earnest. But I watched my grandpa use one many a time." He turned toward Bryce. "You ever encounter one of those?"

Bryce cocked an eyebrow. "Not except in the hands of the Grim Reaper."

"Hey, man," Troy said, feigning a frown. "Don't use that word in front of old people."

Sarah Anne turned up her nose. "Speak for yourself, Troy."

Betty Lou spoke up. "What did you think of Tillie's warning about pickpockets and bag-snatchers?"

"I wouldn't worry a whole lot about it," said Bryce. "Just use a little elemental common sense."

Troy leaned forward and said in a hushed voice, "I'm not sure how much of that you'll find in this crowd."

"Don't sell us short, Troy," Marge said, finally breaking

her silence. She sat facing the opposite corner of the table from Bryce.

Bryce gave her a salute. "Thanks for taking up for the common folks, Marge."

"Wouldn't be so bad if we were just plain common folks," Troy said, rumpling his brow, grinning. "But we're common old folks."

"What got you on this old people bashing kick, Troy?" Sarah Anne asked. "You make it sound like there's something wrong with being over sixty-five. Heck, we seniors are a great bunch. We're not the ones who commit all the crimes and cause all the violence and mess up the environment. You don't find seniors getting AIDS."

Troy propped his elbows on the table and stared at her. "What are you talking about, woman? We've got more aids than anybody. KitchenAids, Rolaids, hearing aids, Bandaids..."

That broke them up. When the waitress appeared in the midst of the laughter, she folded her arms and said, "How about letting me in on the joke?"

"You're too young," Fred said, still chuckling.

While the others were giving their drink orders, Bryce took a careful look around the dining room. Locasio and his two pals were nowhere to be seen. Was that a good sign? He wasn't sure. If the mobster had caught that startled look back at the rest area lobby, he might have concluded Bryce was his man. Would they be waiting for him at the hotel? Maybe the time had come to play that hole card he had been holding back.

He decided for the moment he should simply remain wary. He might as well enjoy whatever respite he got from this deadly game of tag they were playing.

As he turned back toward the table with an abrupt twist of his head, his gaze locked onto Marge's. He got the impression she had been staring at him. When he started to smile, she ducked her head toward the menu. Her cheeks took on a pinkish tinge, like a girl who'd been caught peeking at a forbidden book.

Betty Lou put the focus back onto his pursuers after the waitress brought their drinks and took their orders.

"When we stopped at the rest area this afternoon, I saw one

of those men from New Jersey that Clara was telling us about," she said. "I didn't hear anybody say if they'd tried to pull some kind of scam."

Troy looked skeptical. "One of the older guys approached Hamilton MacArthur while we were talking near the soft drink machines. He just wanted change to get a Coke or something. That doesn't sound very devious to me."

Not as devious as Locasio had been, Bryce thought. But had that approach been something more than just a desire for a Coke? There was no way to know.

Fred stirred his coffee deliberately. "The young guy came up to Bryce and asked if he'd ever heard of his father, somebody from New Jersey."

"Nick Dominico, or something like that." Bryce gave a wave of dismissal. It had been an obvious lie. "Never heard of the guy."

Marge nodded. "He asked me if I could point you out, Bryce. Mentioned something about his father then."

"Sounds intriguing," said Sarah Anne with a conspiratorial grin. "You should have told him you were his dad's best friend, Bryce. Maybe he died and left some money to a long lost acquaintance."

Bryce was not at all pleased to learn that Locasio had asked about him. He might as well put his badge back on. But he masked his concern with a laugh. "I guess I should go look him up, tell him I just remembered his father was an old buddy from the war. We were in the Battle of the Bulge together."

Marge's eyes snapped open wide. "You were in that?"

"The Battle of the Bulge? Yeah. Bastogne."

"My brother Keith was there," Troy said. "He was a sergeant in Division Headquarters of the 101st Airborne. Said it was really bad. One of his jobs was to process recommendations for medals. He said he never saw so many Purple Hearts."

Bryce's face sobered as he remembered. "Yeah. A lot of fine young guys didn't make it out of there. Some of them were good friends of mine."

"Keith never talked about it much," Marge said. "He told me a few things that happened, but it was obviously painful to recall."

Bryce looked across at her. "I know how he felt."

INSTEAD OF a sunset view, they got a moonlit crossing of Lake Pontchartrain, the big enclosed tidal bay that connected to the Gulf of Mexico through Lake Borgne. As they drove along I-10 toward downtown New Orleans, Troy, who had returned to his seat at the back, told Bryce about his chat with MacArthur.

"I still think the guy's full of bull," Troy said, "but it sounds like he's done well in the markets. If you can believe him."

"Which markets?"

"Commodity futures and options. Said he made over twenty thousand on one wheat trade. You ought to talk to him. You can probably relate to it better than me. I was too much of a novice to get into stuff like that."

"Sounds intriguing," Bryce said. He hadn't traded futures but he was familiar with the financial commodities market.

"Virginia and I have enough stocks and bonds, plus my insurance renewals, to afford a comfortable retirement," Troy said. He leaned back in the seat and locked his fingers behind his head. "But the investment I still like best is land. Waldens have always been close to the land."

Bryce gave him a bittersweet look. "My only tangible assets are my house and my car. There's nobody to leave anything to when I die."

He had thought about drawing up a will to dispose of the Swiss treasure trove he had amassed trading on his own account. He might give it to churches or charities, but he would have to hire a lawyer who would likely start digging into his background. He hadn't been willing to risk that. But without a will, his tidy fortune would probably wind up in some wily Swiss banker's pockets.

Troy looked thoughtful. "That's my problem, too. Since Virginia and I had no kids, and neither did Keith and Marge, looks like I'm the end of the Walden line. I still own half of the old family farm in Sumner County. It's now just outside the Gallatin city limits and getting more valuable every year. Marge owns the other half. I offered to buy her share after Keith died, but she wanted to keep it for sentimental reasons. Turned out to be a great investment."

"You and Sarah Anne both mentioned something about Marge changing her mind on having children. Were they thinking about adoption?"

Troy squirmed uncomfortably. "No. They had decided against that. It was something a lot more...well, personal." He paused and rubbed his chin. "It's also ancient history now, I guess. Was back in the sixties. Keith came up with the idea of using donor sperm. Marge's only objection was to having some stranger's baby. So Keith approached me on being the donor. That way the genes would be kept in the family. After talking it over, Virginia and I agreed to it. But just before it was to happen, they went on a trip. When they got back, Marge was a wreck. I don't know what happened. She would never tell anybody. But she said she couldn't have the baby. That was it."

Bryce stared at Troy, recalling what Betty Lou had said about a strange mid-life crisis. "She didn't offer any hint?"

"None. She had a terrible case of depression. It got so bad Keith wanted her to go to a psychiatrist. I thought he would have to commit her somewhere, but she finally pulled out of it. She's had her ups and downs since then, like all of us, but far as I know she's never experienced anything like that again."

"Where did they go on their trip?"

"West Virginia."

Not exactly a shocking place to visit, Bryce thought. He wondered what could have happened to her. From the sound of it, the trauma must have been even worse than her experience with Capt. Herbert Hunter.

23

THE HOTEL WAS a small one on Canal Street in the shadow of the expressway, just north of the main downtown area. Despite the relatively early hour for New Orleans, the wide sidewalk that ran in front of the hotel appeared deserted. Across the broad thoroughfare, the neon script of a drugstore sign glowed brightly in the humid night air. Chick parked his bus at the corner of the hotel building, and the Silver Shadows streamed off. Most of them hovered around the cargo bays as the luggage was being unloaded.

The small lobby contained a few green plants and a handful of vintage chairs across from the front desk. A restaurant was located opposite the entrance to the parking garage. One of the well-worn chairs was occupied by an attractive, auburn-haired woman who jumped up as MacArthur came through the door. She gave him a big hug and a kiss. He introduced her to Tillie, just as the tour director came around dispensing room keys.

"Mrs. Ellis, I'd like you to meet my wife, Andrea." His face glowed. "She's already got our key. I think I mentioned she was foregoing the Marriott to spend the night with us."

With us? Tillie thought. "Nice meeting you, Mrs. MacArthur. Your husband told me you were down here for a business meeting."

"Yes, this saves me from having to appear entertaining while some of my colleagues tarry too long at the bar." Her cultured voice bore an air of authority and her look was classic successful businesswoman, from the stylish hairdo to the pale green suit and matching high heel pumps. She clutched her husband's arm in what appeared a proprietorial grasp as they headed for the elevator.

AFTER GETTING his key, Troy found Betty Lou, Sarah Anne

and Marge waiting in a corner of the lobby. "Where's Fred?" he asked.

"He and Bryce are looking for one of our bags," Betty Lou said. "What room are you in?"

"Four-twenty."

"Sarah Anne and Marge are next door to you again. Fred and I are down the hall."

Troy set down his suitcase and looked around, spotting the restaurant. "Anybody want to come down for ice cream or pie and coffee after you get settled in?"

"Didn't you get enough to eat at dinner?" Sarah Anne asked.

"I didn't order dessert over there. Anyway, at home we usually have our ice cream during the ten o'clock news."

Marge glanced at her watch. "You won't have long to wait. It's nearly nine-thirty."

Fred and Bryce showed up with the missing bag moments later. Marge and Sarah Anne decided to call it a night, while Fred agreed to meet the two men in the restaurant.

"I'd better come with him," Betty Lou said, "to make sure he doesn't overdo this dessert business."

IN A CRAMPED second-floor room, Ziggy sat in a blue vinyl upholstered chair by the noisy air conditioner. Joe Blow perched on one bed in something akin to a lotus position while Locasio sat on the side of the other bed, the telephone receiver clutched in his hand.

"Anything you guys want to ask Marco?"

"I just want to know what shape Boots is in," said Joe.

"Ask him to find out about MacArthur's wife," Ziggy said, a scowl on his face. "I still think that rusty-haired broad was a hooker."

Locasio shook his head. They had been watching from just inside the restaurant when the tour group arrived. "You took too many nine-counts, Ferrante. He wouldn't have introduced a hooker to the old woman that runs the show."

With his credit card on the table, he punched in a long series of numbers and finally got Marco Rizzi at the motel in Nashville. Marco was tough as leather, with a demeanor about as smooth as the underside of a cow's hide. He was a large, muscular man who would have looked at home in a wrestling ring. Unfortunately, he wasn't the brightest bulb on the tree, which was the main reason Locasio had left him behind with Boots.

"How is Boots?" Locasio asked without bothering to identify himself.

"Not good. The docs say the next thirty-six hours is crucial. If he gets through that, he might make it. You guys find Pagano?"

"Has he been awake enough to ask him about Pagano's new name?"

"No. He ain't opened his eyes. You still don't know who Pagano is?"

"We got him narrowed down to three people. That's the main reason for my call. We need you to get us some facts about them."

He explained in painstaking detail what he knew about Will Chandler, Bryce Reynolds and Hamilton MacArthur, then outlined what he wanted Marco to do.

"I'll call tomorrow night to see what you've found. Remember, you got to be careful so nobody gets wind of what you're about."

"Sure, Dom. No problem."

Locasio wished he could believe that. He also wished he had some other contact in Nashville he could rely on. But he didn't. So his choice was Marco or nothing.

HAMILTON AND Andrea MacArthur occupied a room in one corner of the second floor. She had used her clout with the travel agency people to book it. There was a king-size bed, a round table with two chairs, an oversize counter (compared with the other rooms) with large drawers on each end and a TV set that looked like twenty-five inches or more. The room was the closest thing the small hotel had to a suite.

Andrea poured two glasses of wine from a bottle of imported Riesling that sat on the table.

"Come on, Mac," she said. "You can unpack later. Sit down and relax. Tell me about the big adventure."

He sat down, lifted his glass, cocked his head and pursed his lips. "It has been interesting."

"Is that spelled B-O-R-I-N-G?"

"The bus-riding part certainly was. I'm happy we don't have to travel with the masses on a regular basis. This morning I picked up a copy of *USA Today* to try and keep the world in focus. Wouldn't you know, they did not have one single word on that big fraud trial in Nashville."

"You poor dear. I don't know why you get so wrapped up in those cases."

"Simple. They fascinate me. I find the criminal mind most interesting. I'm intrigued by the methods people use to separate others from their hard-earned cash."

Her green eyes twinkled. "And you'd love to try some of them yourself, wouldn't you?"

"Come on, Andrea. You know I wouldn't touch any kind of deal that wasn't strictly legal, no laws broken."

"Emphasis on the strictly. You wouldn't mind if a few laws got bent."

He sipped at the wine with an emerging grin. "All right. As long as they don't crumble."

"How about your fellow-travelers? What are they like? Lots of good ol' Southern boys and girls?"

"Plenty of those. But, surprisingly, I found an oddly eclectic mix among them. One little old lady had been Nashville's first female judge. She had opinions on just about everything. Another was a retired science teacher who had built her own telescope."

"She must have wanted a new perspective on the world."

MacArthur grinned. "Right. I think she's ready to take over where Carl Sagan left off. Of course, there were others like the thin-as-a-fence-post woman who sat beside me at lunch. When she learned I was from New Jersey, she proceeded to tell me reams more than I ever wanted to know about that celebrated Southern delicacy grits."

"Sounds like you've been making out with the little old ladies," Andrea said. "I'd better check with Emma Gross to be sure you've been behaving yourself."

"Oh, I met several of the men, too. The inevitable insurance agent, a rather snippety fellow, and a retired DuPont worker who is obviously Lovely Lane Church's chief booster. There's one I'm curious about, though. I understand he's a former investment advisor. Maybe I'll run into him tomorrow." He shifted in the chair and gazed across at his wife. "And how about you, love? How was your day?"

There was a devilish look in her eyes. "I'm more interested in my nights, dear. Finish your wine and let's get ready for bed." She stood and began to slip off her clothes.

MacArthur gulped the last of the Riesling and followed. They had exchanged some harsh words when Andrea adamantly refused to drop her career after his retirement, but he knew the key to holding onto her was his prowess in bed. That was one reason he worked constantly at keeping his body in shape. She was his link to the Fountain of Youth.

MacArthur's first wife had divorced him because of a roving eye. Actually, a lot more than his eye had been roving. A private investigator she hired had caught him at a motel in Dallas with a well-endowed Cowboys' cheerleader. Now he was several years older and more cognizant that his life was a wasting asset.

He and Andrea had been married about five years. They met while working in the United Way campaign. Hamilton chaired the Allocations Committee and Andrea headed a group charged with studying and approving budgets for several of the key charitable agencies. Hamilton was so impressed that he took her out to dinner to discuss her ideas. The relationship blossomed quickly into something much deeper.

Andrea was touched to learn that his commitment to charity did not involve merely attending meetings during business hours and making contributions from company funds. Quite privately, he gave his own money to help people who "fell through the cracks" and could not get help from other sources.

The holder of a law degree as well as a CPA designation, Andrea had a sharp mind and a driving ambition. Her specialty was cost containment. She headed the hospital corporation's efforts to cut expenses and increase income. Andrea was also a divorcee. She had moved to Nashville from Pennsylvania with her first husband, but the marriage fell apart when he couldn't cope with a wife who was much more highly paid and held a position of more importance than his. This, of course, was not a factor with MacArthur. Although he had come from a Midwest family of modest means, he had done extremely well and never looked back.

THE SMALL front section of the restaurant was all that remained open. A thin waitress with ebony skin and a Jamaican accent brought strawberry-covered cheesecake for Betty Lou and Bryce, chess pie for Fred and a large chocolate sundae for Troy. There was a round of coffee for everyone. Black, no sugar.

Troy looked around as he dug into the mound of ice cream. "What has Tillie got planned for us in the morning?"

Betty Lou pulled out her schedule and looked at Wednesday. "A bus tour of the city in the morning. Then we go to the French Quarter for free time in the afternoon. We have dinner at Le Dauphin–that's got to be a French restaurant–then go to Preservation Hall for a jazz concert. Sounds like a busy day."

"We'd better rest up tonight then," Fred said.

Troy grimaced. "Rest up from what? You've been sitting on your can all day."

Bryce had checked out the place for Mafia minions and, finding none, turned his attention to the television set mounted on the wall near their table. "Take a look at the tube over there," he said. "Must be a hurricane bulletin coming."

As they lapsed into silence, the Hurricane Alert logo was replaced by a long-faced announcer at an anchor desk. A slowly twisting white radar image covered half of the screen. The sound was just loud enough for them to hear the newsman's voice.

"The National Hurricane Center in Miami issued a hurricane watch tonight for the Brownsville area along the Texas coast. Hurricane Nora smashed homes and businesses and downed power lines as it unmercifully pounded Mexico's Yucatan Peninsula today." The video image changed to scenes of destruction, roofs torn from buildings, trees uprooted or bowed like weary old men in the driving wind and rain. "Winds have diminished to just over a hundred miles an hour, reducing Nora to a Category Two hurricane, but they are expected to gain in strength as the storm moves back over the warm waters of the Gulf of Mexico. Weather forecasters also reported her track across the Mexican peninsula had slowed the northwestward movement to twelve miles per hour. If the storm continues on its present path, Nora should strike land again between Tampico and Brownsville. There appears to be no present threat to the Louisiana coast."

"Thank God for that," said Fred, turning back to what was left of his pie.

"He said if the storm continues on its present path," Betty Lou reminded him. "What if it doesn't?"

Bryce lifted his napkin and brushed a morsel of cheesecake from his lip. "In that case, I'd say things could get pretty exciting around here."

24

A CONTINGENT OF ten Lovely Lane Silver Shadows basked in the glory of a brilliant October morning as they strolled the broad sidewalk along bustling Canal Street. The sun glowed from a vast, seamless canopy of blue, moderating the hint of chill in the air and touching off a chorus of smiles. The day appeared fashioned by a generous Providence especially for sightseers. After a rocky start, their prayers had apparently been heeded.

Bryce would have preferred a more lively pace, but he held himself in check and strolled along with Marge and Sarah Anne. He thought he had spotted one of Locasio's accomplices just as they were leaving the hotel lobby, but he could detect no one following en route to the lunch (or, in this case, breakfast) counter at a five-and-dime store a few blocks down Canal toward the Mississippi River. The smell of bacon and eggs greeted him as he perched on a high stool at the counter, something he had not experienced in many a year. He felt a perverse charm in the idea, however, as he tried to imagine MacArthur and his suave wife seated there.

Aside from other obvious tourists, the counter, arranged in semicircular islands, appeared to be inhabited mainly by regulars. In addition to several likely workers headed for New Orleans' canyons of commerce, there were a few who looked rumpled enough to have slept on park benches. One disheveled old woman with dirty gray hair shuffled toward a stool, stopped, tottered back and forth like a windup toy as her weight shifted from one unsteady foot to the other. She pulled a coin purse from her pocket, painstakingly opened it and peeked inside. Though appearing somewhat uncertain about what she had seen, she carefully closed the purse, returned it to her pocket and climbed onto the stool.

Fred, who was seated beside Bryce, motioned to the waitress. When she came over, he leaned forward and spoke in a hushed voice. "Tell that little old lady her breakfast has been paid for by an anonymous friend. Give her whatever she wants, then bring the bill to me."

A large black woman with long hair tied up in a red-and-white-checkered bow, the waitress wrinkled her broad brow. "We call her Millie the Moocher. Sometimes she has enough to pay; sometimes she don't."

"This time she does," Fred said with a grin. "Don't let her know it was me. I don't want any thanks."

Bryce smiled. "That was a nice gesture, Fred. I should have thought of it." He realized his preoccupation with the Mafia stalkers had caused him to miss a lot of little things lately. He didn't intend to let down his guard, but he would try to get at least a whiff of the roses as he passed by.

"Fred does that a lot," Troy said. He was seated just beyond Bryce.

"Aw, that's no big deal." Fred sounded a bit embarrassed. "Really, it was kind of selfish. I get a big bang out of stuff like that."

The chatter slackened off as they ate, then Betty Lou spoke up beside Fred. "You boys better get a hustle on. Tillie'll have you drawn and quartered if you're not on that bus ready to roll by nine."

They paid their checks–Millie the Moocher's was only $3.50, not much by mooching standards, Bryce thought–and headed back up Canal Street to the hotel. He was pleased when he failed to spot either Locasio or the other two mobsters among those milling about the lobby.

PROMPTLY AT nine o'clock, Tillie checked for empty seats. Finding none, she introduced their guide for the morning tour. She was a small woman with short reddish-blonde hair, dressed in a candy-striped blouse and white skirt. Yvonne Deschamps, in her mid-thirties, had married a member of an old New Orleans Creole family.

Taking the microphone from Tillie as Chick pulled out into

the traffic on Canal Street, she greeted them with a cheery, "Good morning!" To which the Silver Shadows replied with an equally fervent, and more drawn out, "Good mornnnning!"

"I like that," she said, her round face wreathed in a smile. "New Orleans is an exuberant city and you appear to be in just the right mood for it. We're going to take you down to the Mississippi Riverfront, through the French Quarter, out to one of our unusual above-ground cemeteries, then to colorful City Park. But first, a little history. New Orleans was founded in 1718 by a Frenchman named Jean Baptiste Le Moyne, Sieur de Bienville. It was under French rule until 1762, when the Spanish took over. They turned it back to the French just before it was acquired by the United States in 1803 as part of the Louisiana Purchase."

She described how Canal Street started out as just what the name implied, a canal. Pointing to various sights along the way, she detailed improvements made around the waterfront as part of the 1984 Louisiana World Exposition. Then they headed into the colorful French Quarter with its unique balconies and French/Spanish-influenced architecture, past Jackson Square and the French Market, down to the northeastern edge at Esplanade Avenue.

"Those narrow streets look as bad as downtown Nashville," Troy said as they passed signs bearing names like Toulouse, St. Peter, St. Ann and Dumaine.

"And I'll bet parking is just as hard to come by," Bryce said.

Troy chuckled. "I'm glad Chick is driving this thing, not me."

And as Chick turned into Esplanade, Yvonne Deschamps directed their attention to the old U. S. Mint, which had been turned into a museum. Farther along she began to point out samples of French Quarter architecture.

"That long, narrow house over there is called a 'shotgun,'" she said. "It has four rooms, one behind the other. You could fire a shotgun through the front door and kill a chicken in the back yard."

Bryce laughed and turned to Troy. "Can't you just picture that." He enjoyed the thought of guns being used in some other context than by shady-looking New Yorkers.

The guide also cited examples of the Creole cottage and the swaybacked structure called a "camelback." They departed the French Quarter at Rampart Street and headed for their first stop, St. Louis Cemetery #3.

AS THEY STROLLED through the rows of solid masonry tombs, both plain and ornate, Yvonne Deschamps explained that because of the marshy ground, and the fact New Orleans has the misfortune to dwell six feet below sea level, the people had adopted mausoleum burials. Otherwise, the coffins would be engulfed by water as soon as they were lowered into the ground. The four-tiered vaults, primarily rectangular boxes about eight-by-ten, dotted the cemetery like rows of sugar cubes lined up on a table. Most were owned by families or organizations, she said. And though some were grandiose in size and architecture, most suffered scars of mold like dark slashes across their sides.

Yvonne Deschamps pointed out an engraved list of people buried in one of the vaults and noted there were several more names than apparent spaces in the tomb. She explained that a year after burial, the remains were placed in a box at the bottom of the vault, making way for a new occupant on top. As Bryce read the inscription on one elaborate end plate, he heard his name called and looked around to find a smiling MacArthur approaching. The retired insurance executive stuck out his hand in greeting.

"You're one of the few I haven't had the opportunity to meet yet."

Bryce gave his hand a firm shake. "Nice to meet you, Mr. MacArthur. Troy Walden told me about you."

"He was also my source of information on you," MacArthur said. "I understand you were an investment advisor. I held a similar position with an insurance company in New Jersey."

Bryce folded his arms. "I'm sure your company was much larger than the one I worked for. It was an interesting job, though. Troy told me you had been trading futures and options."

"Yes, in recent years. And for my own account. I could not deal in anything so risky with an insurance company. Were you involved in commodities?"

"No, but I was a close student of currencies and interest rates around the world."

"Walden mentioned that."

"I had devised a method of borrowing money in low-rate foreign currencies, then investing the cash in high-yield U.S. funds." He explained how the system worked.

"Fascinating." MacArthur's blue eyes gleamed. Then he paused a moment, rubbing his chin thoughtfully. "I vaguely remember reading about a fellow who did something like that once. Was some years ago."

Bryce felt a pang of apprehension. There had been a mention of his system in a *New York Times* article about him during the Mafia trial. Had he blown it again?

MacArthur quickly dropped the subject and turned to some of his own exploits. Bryce realized the retired executive was unlikely to make the link and cause him any problems.

But as they turned to follow the Silver Shadows group to another section of burial crypts, something caught Bryce's eye that proved much more disconcerting. He glimpsed a figure just around the corner of the tomb where he and MacArthur had been standing, a swarthy-looking man in a tan single-breasted jacket and an open-collared yellow and brown sport shirt. Not a ready-for-business attired character like the New Yorkers, but unmistakably Italian. The hair was black and brushed front to back, the brows full and straight, the mouth angled downward and the eyes an icy dark brown.

Was the man just another tourist, Bryce wondered, or somebody who had been sent to eavesdrop on their conversation? Or was this just a case of cultivating paranoia? Whatever, he would remember that face.

THEY STOPPED next in City Park, the 1,500-acre swath of green at the north end of Esplanade. Yvonne Deschamps pointed out the Dueling Oaks, where many an affair of honor had been settled in an earlier time. Other large, gnarled live oaks had been dubbed with identities of various people, including one named after band leader and march composer John Phillip Souza.

Chick parked the big bus beside a building that provided a

place to shop for food and drink and New Orleans bric-a-brac. While most of the passengers headed first for the restrooms, Bryce bought a cone of frozen yogurt and browsed around the gift shop, occasionally glancing about in search of suspicious faces. Instead, he encountered a trio of familiar countenances belonging to Yeager, Scott, and Hunter.

"Would any of you ladies like an ice cream cone?" he asked. "Or frozen yogurt? I'll be glad to get it for you."

Only Marge appeared interested but quickly declined his offer. "I'll get it myself, thanks," she said. She turned and headed for the line at the ice cream counter.

"Marge is pushing this independence thing a bit, don't you think?" Sarah Anne said, frowning.

Bryce finished off his yogurt. "After what she went through with Captain Hunter, it isn't surprising."

Sarah Anne stared at him, then at her sister. "Captain Hunter? Is there something here I should know about?"

Betty Lou shrugged. "He's talking about that incident at church when Herb Hunter took offense at Fred's hugging Marge. Troy told Bryce about it. I hardly think that has anything to do with the way she is now."

Bryce realized he had spoken too hastily. Obviously, Betty Lou had not confided in her sister about the extent of Marge's problems with her late husband. Hoping to affect a rescue, he donned an innocent face and asked, "What did you think of St. Louis Cemetery Number Three, Sarah Anne?"

She gave her sister a disgruntled look, then turned back to Bryce. "It was unusual, to say the least."

"I liked the way they stacked the dearly departed four deep," he said. "Saves space, saves money. Makes a lot of sense. I don't see why they couldn't do the same thing under the ground in Nashville."

"We're too tradition-bound for that," said Betty Lou.

"Good point," Bryce said. "I would also bet some people would be uneasy at being put on the bottom. A little too close to Hell for comfort."

Sarah Anne squinched her nose. "I think some of your roommate's weird sense of humor has rubbed off on you, Bryce.

You don't really hold the concept of Hell as a fiery furnace deep in the earth's bowels, do you?"

"Geologists say there's a red hot molten core down there. It fits, doesn't it?"

"I think people make their own Hell here on earth," she said. "The wrongs we do come back to haunt us."

How well he knew. Bryce thought of the way his own life had resembled a patchwork quilt of black and white squares. The good seemed more than offset by the bad. His stupid mistakes had rung up a terrible price. The grief they had caused was his own personal Hell. His face sobered.

"I'd have to agree with you there."

MARGE LOVED the flavor of peppermint. She grew the plant in her backyard and used the crushed leaves in iced tea. She kept peppermint candies in her living room, stored in a beautiful container of Waterford crystal Keith had given her once for her birthday. Peppermint was cool and soothing and not too sweet, with a dash of tartness, much more interesting than blander tastes. The flavor was a lot like the way she preferred to manage her life, calm and collected but with a dash of adventure to keep things fascinating.

As she walked toward her friends, nibbling on a cone of peppermint ice cream, she saw Bryce chatting with Betty Lou and Sarah Anne beside a display of T-shirts and baseball caps. Mostly, she noted, he just listened. He was a good listener, she reflected. She had always felt a sense of admiration for people like that. Too many she knew kept their tongues wagging so much they missed half of what others said.

She gave Betty Lou a teasing glance. "I'm surprised to see you without a bagful of goodies. I didn't think you could spend this long in a gift shop without buying something."

Betty Lou grinned. "We've been talking about deep subjects. But that reminds me, I really do need to put in some shopping time. Got to get a few things for the grand-kids, you know. You want to hit the shops this afternoon?"

Marge licked at the cone. "I don't have anybody to buy for. I'll go looking though. Want to try the French Market after lunch?"

"The French Market is more like a flea market," said Sarah Anne. "I'd prefer to browse through a little more upscale merchandise. Why don't we try the Riverwalk? I hear they have all kinds of shops there, plain and fancy. It's near the French Quarter."

"I went there on my last trip down here," Bryce said. "Stayed at the Hilton. You can go into the Riverwalk right out of the hotel." He recalled the long, mall-like collection of shops and eating places that were strung out at different levels alongside the river.

Marge accepted the idea with obvious reservations. "Okay. But I don't want to spend all afternoon traipsing through a bunch of shops. I'd like to see some sights as well."

"Why don't you take a carriage tour of the French Quarter?" Bryce said. "Some friends did that and really enjoyed it. I hear the drivers are full of New Orleans tidbits."

"Sounds like a great idea to me," said Sarah Anne.

Betty Lou turned to Bryce. "You'll join us, of course? I'm sure Fred and Troy will come along. From what I saw, the carriages hold six."

He frowned. "I'd just crowd you."

"Don't be silly. Like Marge says, we came down here to see the sights, didn't we?"

He hesitated a moment. "You've got that right. I sure didn't sign up for this tour just to ride a bus and eat. A little adventure should make things more interesting."

Unfortunately, he thought, he might be in for somewhat more adventure than he had bargained for. And though he had not seen anything today of the Mafia trio, that suspicious Italian lurking beside the mausoleum could easily have been a Louisiana soul brother. He knew for a certainty Locasio and company would be back. And next time, perhaps, with a vengeance. Should he play his ace in the hole now, he wondered? Considering the confrontation with Locasio at the rest stop yesterday, followed by the encounter in the cemetery this morning, he had no trouble convincing himself that the prudent thing would be to make his move as soon as possible. He would need to be on the alert for a little privacy and a telephone.

25

SUMMERTIME SNEAKED back onto the streets of New Orleans while they were eating lunch. By the time they boarded the bright red carriage in front of Jackson Square, Troy had pulled a large white handkerchief from his jeans pocket and was swiping the sweat off his neck. Betty Lou, seated between Troy and Fred, fanned herself with a brochure she had picked up at City Park. And in the seat across from them, Bryce adjusted his aviator shades as he sat wedged between Marge and Sarah Anne. The lanky driver, who had identified himself as Jason and looked to be about twenty, obligingly put up a collapsible black top to shield the glaring sun from their faces.

The carriage was pulled by a big brown mule with a white face and legs. As the long-eared animal clopped away from the curb on Decatur Street, Jason turned with a broad grin. A genial, confident young man, he wore a wide-brimmed, flat-topped straw hat that made him look like he'd just come off the plantation.

"Our mule's name is Ernie and he comes from Columbia, Tennessee. You folks know where that is, I guess."

"Just south of us," Fred said. "Used to be known as Mule Town. They still have a big celebration every year called Mule Day."

"Well, old Ernie is anxious to show you New Orleans," Jason said, pronouncing it *Nu-awlins*. He had a distinctive accent. Pointing to a building in the next block on the left, he began his patented spiel.

"Eighteen-ninety-one to 1974 they brewed Jax Beer over there. Not anymore. We import it now. They sold 'em the recipe, but they didn't sell 'em the river. It's no longer safe to drink."

"Sold the recipe for what?" Betty Lou asked.

"The beer."

"Jax Beer," said Fred.

"They brew it in Texas now," Jason said. "You can still buy it here, but it ain't very popular."

"Oh." Betty Lou pursed her lips.

"Yeah," Jason said in his fast-paced, sing-song voice, "the building got renovated for the World's Fair back in 1984. It's like a little shopping mall."

As Ernie plodded along, heavy shoes clopping a noisy rhythm on the pavement, Jason observed that the French Quarter was famous for its unique cuisine. Turning onto St. Louis Street, he identified one restaurant as the place where they originated the "po-boy," another was named Napoleon House.

He identified a succession of restaurants and bars, honky-tonks and jazz clubs. After awhile, Bryce could contain his curiosity no longer. "Are you Cajun?" he asked.

Jason chuckled. "I thought you'd never ask. Let you in on a little secret. I'm really a drama student from Cleveland. Had to take off a semester to raise some cash. I've been practicing a Cajun accent. How did I do?"

"I'm no expert," Bryce said. "But you had me convinced."

Sarah Anne's eyes widened. "If you're an actor, I'm sure you know New Orleans has a fine literary background. Sherwood Anderson lived here. Tennessee Williams, of course. Faulkner did some work here, too. And Frances Parkinson Keyes."

"Her home is just down Chartres Street here," said Jason. "It's called Beauregard-Keyes House. Was once the home of Confederate General Pierre Beauregard."

"What about my favorite, Anne Rice?" Troy asked. "Doesn't she live here somewhere?"

Jason looked around. "She lives in an antebellum house in the Garden District. That's across the other side of Canal Street."

"I think we'll be going by there tomorrow," Marge said.

"Anne Rice?" Sarah Anne gave Troy an incredulous look. "Don't tell me you go for all that vampire stuff?"

He smirked. "You mean you don't believe in vampires?"

"I prefer realistic themes," she said.

"Like Robert Ludlum," Fred interjected.

Sarah Anne knitted her brows. "Ludlum is realistic?"

Fred tugged at his cap. "It could happen."

Considering believability, Bryce wondered what they would think if they knew his real identity. And the interesting little fact that he was being hunted by a team of Mafia hit men. And then, as Jason steered his plodding mule around a tight corner, Bryce got a brief glance back at the carriage following them. All along he had been vaguely aware of its presence. At one point, when they stopped for a traffic light, Jason had bantered a few words with the other driver, a large black man wearing a brown derby. But what instantly flashed a red alert was what he saw in the passenger seat.

A lone "tourist" stared back at him, the same black-haired, heavy-browed, icy brown-eyed face he had seen around the corner of the burial vault at St. Louis Cemetery #3.

Bryce had long ago disabused himself of the concept of coincidence. This was a deliberate act. In the first place, he doubted a carriage driver would take a solo passenger unless he were paid well or frightened out of his wits. Clearly, Bryce was being followed. Whether the man was another New Yorker or a member of the local "family" did not matter. They were getting too close. He was convinced now that he had no choice but to make that phone call at the earliest opportunity. The time had definitely come to play his hidden ace.

"BETTY LOU'S in hog heaven," Fred observed as the men slowly strolled among the crowd. The women were in and out of every little shop along the Riverwalk concourse.

Troy laughed. "If they gave advanced degrees in shopping, she'd no doubt have her Ph.D."

At intervals along the complex, a set of stairs moved the shoppers up to another level. Bryce took advantage of each opportunity to look back at the crowd surging behind them, searching for familiar faces among the wave of tourists that swept forward like a relentless human tide. But he failed to spot any of the New Yorkers or the stranger he had seen in the French Quarter carriage. That, he knew, did not mean they were not around. Worse yet, if they had made contact with the local Mafia, there could be others following him that he might never recognize.

When they came to the food area, Troy suggested a refreshment break. Bryce and Marge opted for coffee, while the others chose something cold.

Betty Lou looked across at Marge and shook her head. "You'd drink coffee on the hottest day of the summer, wouldn't you, girl? That'd burn me up."

"A good cup of coffee relaxes you on a hot day," Bryce said with a shrug.

"That's what I've tried to tell her." Marge spread her hands. "She thinks ice tea's the only thing you can drink when the weather's warm."

Betty Lou fanned herself with a napkin. "That's what sensible people do. Sometimes I wonder about you, Marge."

"Better watch your words," Marge said. "Now you're insulting Bryce, too."

He chuckled. "I don't insult easily. I'm usually guilty as charged."

Noting a pay telephone on the wall nearby, he glanced at his watch. The afternoon was already getting late. "While you folks are finishing," he said, "I think I'll make a quick phone call. I have a friend I promised to get in touch with while I'm here. I only have his office number, though, so I need to call before closing time."

Bryce hurried over to the telephone, pulling a yellowed snippet of paper from his billfold. He had memorized the number years ago but didn't fully trust his memory at this late date.

As he punched in the digits, he felt a twinge of uneasiness. Would there be anyone to answer the phone in New York at this hour? What if the number had been changed? Then he heard the ringing sound and began to relax.

"Burger," a gruff voice answered.

"Matthew Kravitz, please," Bryce said. The FBI agent had given him the phone number back at the time he entered the witness protection program. He was to call the number for help in case of an emergency. He couldn't imagine any worse scenario than what he faced with Locasio Locasio and friends. But he was confident Agent Kravitz would know how to take care of the situation. Obviously there would be plenty of FBI agents in New Orleans.

"Kravitz?" said the man. "He retired over a year ago. This is Agent Burger. Anything I can do for you?"

Bryce put a hand to his forehead. He had never even considered things like retirement. Why hadn't he thought of that? "I certainly hope so. My name is Pat Pagano. I helped Kravitz in a case against the Vicario–"

"I know all about Pagano. What's your racket, buddy?"

"Racket? What do you mean, racket?"

"Pagano's body washed up on the Oregon coast west of Portland six months ago. He had been playing dinner host to a bunch of hungry sharks. Probably did something stupid that tipped off the mob to where he was hiding."

Bryce was shocked into a momentary silence. "That can't be," he said when he got his voice back. "I am Pat Pagano. They changed my name to William Holder when I was sent to Portland."

"Well, William Holder's friends identified the body as his. They said he apparently fell out of a boat. More likely he was pushed."

This was crazy, Bryce thought with a sudden feeling of helplessness. Obviously they had the wrong William Holder. He recalled having seen another one listed in the Portland phone book. He had even gotten some of the man's mail once by mistake. How could the FBI have been so easily fooled?

Then the obvious question hit him. "Didn't you check his fingerprints?"

"Ha!" Burger's voice was sharp, mirthless. "The sharks didn't leave fingers, much less prints. But there's no doubt it was Holder, meaning Pagano. I don't know what your game is, buddy. Maybe you think you can scam some money out of us. Well, think again."

With that, the line suddenly went dead. As dead as Bryce Reynolds' ace in the hole.

26

SLOWLY, HE replaced the phone, his head swimming. He remembered the first time he met Kravitz, not long after his sons' funeral. Pat Pagano was invited to lunch at a plush private club by an investment banker he had known casually. The bodyguard Tony Vicario had provided since the bombing that killed his sons was not allowed to accompany him into the club, leaving Pat alone when he met the banker in the expensively appointed dining room that overlooked the concrete and steel canyons of Manhattan. He discovered his host was not alone, however. Seated beside him at the table was a man who appeared to be in his late fifties, conservative blue suit, probing gray eyes.

The banker gave a typically ingratiating smile as he rose to greet Pat. "Sorry I won't be able to stay, but I have another meeting that's a must to attend. At any rate, the real reason for inviting you, Mr. Pagano, was to have you meet Mr. Kravitz." He nodded toward the other man, who appeared slightly shorter and considerably more stocky as he stood. "I have instructed the waiter to get whatever you gentlemen want. The bill is taken care of. Have a nice lunch."

And with that, the banker disappeared into an adjacent room.

"Nice to meet you, Pagano," said Kravitz with a look that held no trace of pleasure. He thrust out his hand and shook Pat's. "Have a seat. I don't know about you, but I'm not accustomed to this kind of treatment for lunch. I plan to make the most of it."

Kravitz signaled the waiter as they took their seats. He ordered the prime rib au jus. "According to this, it's the house specialty," he said.

Not all that hungry, Pat ordered a club sandwich. When the waiter had left, he looked across at Kravitz. "Should I know you?"

There was an intensity about the man that gave the

impression he preferred action to idle conversation. His gray eyes betrayed no emotion as he spoke. "I think not, but here are my credentials."

He handed across a small folder that contained his photo on an ID card and a badge that was engraved with "Federal Bureau of Investigation." It showed Matthew Kravitz, Special Agent.

Pat frowned. "Does this have something to do with the bombing?"

"It has everything to do with the bombing, and with your job in the Vicario family. I'm part of a task force targeted on old Tony and his mob. I presume you know why you were hit."

Pat did not like the man's implications. "I have no idea who did it or why. And I do not work for the Vicario family, as you call it. I am employed as an investment advisor for the Alcamo Corporation."

Kravitz tapped his fingers on the table. "Yeah, I know what you do. We have no evidence that you're involved in mob activities, but you're in a good place to know what's going on. As for the bombing, it was a rival family's way of sending a signal. They are damned unhappy with Uncle Tony's move into their territory in Vegas. They picked you for several reasons. One, you aren't Sicilian. You're not a 'made' member of the Cosa Nostra. But you come from Vegas, and they know you're a key money-maker for the mob."

Kravitz' abrasive manner was enough to turn Pat against him, but he was also aggravating the wound that had caused Pat so much grief. He had pointedly cited the involvement that left Pat with bloody hands where the deaths of his sons were concerned.

"How do you know all that?" Pat said. His voice dripped with skepticism.

"Simple, Pagano. I belong to an organized crime unit that has been digging into Tony Vicario for years. We listen to his phone calls. We read his mail. Oh, he's sharp all right. He doesn't give us enough to hang him, but we have a pretty good picture of what's going on."

"Well, I don't. And for all I know, Mr. Vicario is a legitimate businessman."

Kravitz gave a twisted laugh. "And I suppose you've never heard that he is a Mafia don, or that your immediate boss, Frank Salerno, is his consigliere?"

"I can read. I know what they say in the newspapers." Resenting a reminder of how he had allowed himself to be lured into an impossible situation, Pat matched the agent's scoffing tone. "I don't put a lot of stock in what those reporters write. They revel in painting everybody with horns. If they wanted to get on her case, they could make the late Mother Teresa sound like Ma Barker."

Kravitz grunted. "Well, nobody's going to confuse Tony Vicario with Mother Teresa, I promise you. But obviously you don't know what a precarious position you're in."

"What do you mean?"

"Whoever had that contract on you didn't complete his mission. Next time you won't be so lucky. They'll get both you and your wife."

Pat recalled what Vicario had said. "I've been told I'm not in any more danger."

"Oh? Then why did they give you a bodyguard? Or maybe you thought those guys were Boy Scouts working on a merit badge?"

Pat knew the agent was being deliberately goading, and it was getting to him. "They were assigned just to make certain there would be no more problems. I shouldn't think they would be around for long."

"You shouldn't think. There's a neat turn of phrase. Well, let me give you something to think about, Mr. Advisor. Tony Vicario is looking out for you right now, because that suits his purposes. But if the situation should change, and you suddenly became a liability, he would eliminate you in the bat of an eye."

Pat had already told his wife, Ellen, that he speculated as much. But he was not encouraged by having his suspicions confirmed by another source, particularly an FBI agent. "Why are you telling me all this?"

"Because we can help you, and you can help us."

"How?"

"Cooperate and we'll get you in the witness protection

program. Provide you a new identity, move you to a new location, help set you up in a new business."

"What kind of cooperation?"

"These people have their own peculiar kind of morality. Since you've been made a target, they may feel a bit closer kinship with you. If you're not lying about being so ignorant, some of them may open up a bit. Not Tony Vicario, for sure, but maybe someone like Salerno. Keep your eyes and ears open. Do a little probing of your own. Find some incriminating material, testify in court and we'll take care of you."

The prospect was quite intriguing. But would it be worth the risk, for Ellen's sake? He felt those cold gray eyes fixed on him as he pondered the thought. And in the end he decided too much risk was involved, plus he wasn't ready to trust his and Ellen's fate to this stranger. "I very much doubt I would ever have the opportunity to find what you're looking for," he said.

Agent Kravitz handed him a card with his name and phone number. "You may be surprised. If you do, give me a call."

THE OTHERS were just moving through a doorway onto a balcony overlooking the Mississippi river when Bryce walked up, still in a state of shock from the phone call. Up to this point, he had managed to dampen much of the impact of his pursuit by the Mafia hit squad by assuming that Kravitz and company were standing in the wings. Now he knew better. There would be no white knights in blue FBI jackets, no automatic weapons at the ready, no rescuers of any sort. He was strictly on his own.

Gut check time. For the moment, he could see no alternative but to go on as though nothing had changed. But obviously everything had. He was vulnerable and virtually defenseless. As one of three men Locasio had in his sights, he figured trying to run would do little good. Anyway, he had no intention of running.

As he followed the others through the doorway, he realized there was a good deal of comfort to be had in just mingling with friends, something he had been deprived of for so long now. He hoped he was not creating a potential hazard for them.

A stiff breeze that seemed one part fish oil and two parts petroleum residue met them on the balcony. The wind tugged at the ladies' hair and rumpled Bryce's own gray mane, forcing a squint that erased whatever consternation might have remained on his face. No matter, all eyes were fixed on the vast panorama of choppy water that spread out before them. Large tows with multiple rows of barges floated along, moving at such a leisurely pace they seemed to be drifting with the current. At this point, the broad Mississippi looked like a lake. A sea-going freighter moved past, gliding slowly upstream. Cranes that resembled the folded arms of a giant praying mantis sprouted from its deck.

"Wonder where that ship came from?" Troy asked of no one in particular.

Fred glanced up at the darkening sky to the west. "I don't know, but it looks like he may be headed for some bad weather. Check out those clouds."

Marge frowned. "I hope it doesn't rain on us. We've got another full day of sightseeing tomorrow, and the dinner cruise tomorrow night."

Standing beside her at the railing, Bryce tried to muster a hopeful look, as much for his own benefit as for hers. "Maybe we'll be lucky," he said. But as Hurricane Nora came to mind, he began to wonder if these clouds might be a foretaste of something really nasty. The way his luck had been running, that was a distinct possibility.

Gazing out at the waterfront, however, proved cathartic. The scene was a study in slow motion, a generous slice of tranquility. Movements appeared almost dreamlike. He found his mind wandering beyond the narrow confines of the present.

The view appeared to have done the same for Marge.

"When I was a teenager," she said, a dreamy look in her eyes, "there was a paddle-wheel boat called the *Idlewild* that used to come up the Cumberland River to Nashville every year or so. Our high school always had an outing on it one afternoon during its stay. We'd ride up and down the river for a couple of hours, acting as excited as if it was the *Queen Sarah*."

Bryce thought back to his own boyhood in Las Vegas. "They didn't have big boats where I grew up," he said. "We had a railroad, though. I was always fascinated by trains. When I'd hear that lonesome whistle blowing, especially in the dead of night, I'd conjure up all sorts of images of exotic places where it might be headed."

"I don't guess I was that imaginative."

He laughed. "If anything, I was overly imaginative. Thought of places like London and Paris and Rome. Places you could hardly get to by train. When I did make it over there during the war, though, I found things a lot different than I had imagined. Of course, I saw more countryside than big cities. Saw a lot of devastation, too."

"Have you been back since then?"

"Several times. On business. I got to see some of the more colorful areas of Europe, too, like the Rhine River and the mountains of Switzerland." He didn't mention the business that took him to places like Zurich, where he arranged or checked on secret numbered bank accounts.

"I've always wanted to go to Europe. Keith talked about going back to see some of the places he'd been during the war, but there never seemed to be enough time. He kept saying wait until I retire." She turned back toward the river, a look of sadness on her face. "Of course, he never made it."

"That's too bad."

"Look," she said, pointing.

Bryce followed her gaze toward the sky and saw where the clouds had formed what appeared to be an elevated horizon, a dark, undulating mass that resembled mountains, set off by the reddish glow of the soon-to-be-setting sun.

"It looks like fire on the mountains," she said. The hush of awe tempered her voice.

And as the sun gradually sank lower, the flames appeared to spread across the sky.

"That's quite a spectacle." Bryce looked around. "Did you ever see mountains on fire?"

"No, thank God. I love the mountains, the Smokies especially. Keith and I used to have a small place outside Gatlinburg, on the edge of the Great Smoky Mountains National Park. It sometimes looked like fire this time of year, when the sun hit all that beautiful foliage. The colors were magnificent."

Ellen had also been a lover of mountains, Bryce recalled. She had shown an almost childlike exuberance on one trip to Switzerland, when they had taken a chair lift and tram up the side of 7,000-foot Mt. Pilatus, near Lucerne.

"I went to see the Smokies last fall," he said. "Unfortunately, I picked the wrong time. I just missed the peak of the colors."

"You ought to plan to go next week. You'd probably hit it just right this time."

Plan to go, he thought? That implied a future, something of which he had serious doubts at the moment. "I haven't had too much luck with plans lately."

Marge looked back at him with a sympathetic smile. "I read recently where somebody said every time humans make plans, God laughs."

"I'm glad to hear he still has a sense of humor. Maybe there's a chance for me yet."

"You have a problem with the man upstairs?" That was not what she had meant to say, but probably came out, she thought, as a subconscious reaction to Troy's revelation about the big check Bryce had given Dr. Trent. The implication wasn't fair and she regretted it the moment the words came out, particularly after seeing the pain in his eyes.

"I rather think it's the other way around," he said. He turned to look out at a small boat that appeared totally insignificant in the vastness of the river. "I'm the problem, not him."

When Fred suddenly called from the doorway, Bryce realized they had been left standing alone on the balcony.

"Hey, you two. Betty Lou says we'd better get started back toward the restaurant. Don't want to be late for supper."

They had told Tillie Ellis they were going shopping and would meet the others in the French Quarter at Le Dauphin.

Marge headed for the door. "Tillie wouldn't be very happy if we're late," she said.

Bryce nodded as he followed her into the mall. This little interlude with Marge had made him forget for a short time that distressing phone call to New York. But he knew the whole landscape was changed now. What would the next siting of the blue Cadillac or its occupants bring?

27

"IT APPEARS that Mexico will escape another assault from Hurricane Nora, which blasted the Yucatan Peninsula late yesterday." The network news anchor spoke in dramatic tones as Locasio watched the TV in his hotel room. "The National Hurricane Center reports the storm has begun a turn to the north, away from the Mexican coastline. It is currently located two hundred and eighty miles southeast of Brownsville, Texas. Forecasters are unsure where it will head next, but they have issued hurricane watches for the Texas coast from Corpus Christi to Port Arthur. Nora has strengthened in the past few hours, with sustained winds near the eye now hitting one hundred and twenty miles per hour, placing it in Category Three on the Saffir-Simpson Scale. It has also picked up speed to fifteen miles per hour. The Weather Service reports that Nora has become a very large and dangerous storm, with hurricane-force winds reaching out nearly a hundred and fifty miles from the eye."

Locasio turned down the sound, lit the cigarette clamped between his thick lips and dialed the Nashville motel where Marco was staying. He had sent Joe Blow and Ferrante on with Johnny "The Barber" Barbarino, their New Orleans Mafia cousin, to keep an eye on the Lovely Lane Silver Shadows.

"Marco, how is Boots doing?" Locasio asked when his Tennessee connection answered.

"I just left the hospital, Dom. They don't think he's gonna survive the night."

"Damn! All the more reason to get that bastard Pagano. What did you find out for me today?"

"Not a whole lot, I'm afraid. I did like you said, told them I was a private investigator. That MacArthur guy has quite a layout. Right on the water, swimming pool, tennis court, the works. Throws dough around like it was going out of style."

"What did the neighbors say?" Locasio asked.

"He came down here a few years ago. Early nineties. Supposed to be from Jersey. He said he had retired as an insurance company bigwig. His wife is with a hospital company here. She's a lot younger than he is."

"The feds could have set him up with an insurance company," Locasio said thoughtfully. "What about Bryce Reynolds?"

"Lives in a nice house, but nothing to brag about. Neighbor says he's a retired businessman from somewhere out west. Oklahoma, I believe. Doesn't talk a lot. Just a quiet, friendly guy. You want to hear about Chandler?"

"Let's have it."

"He's a retired mail carrier. Lived in Madison off and on most of his life. He's been—"

"Never mind. He's obviously not our man." Locasio grunted dismally. "You're right, Marco. You're not much damn help. Still sounds like it could be either MacArthur or Reynolds. Call me the minute anything happens with Boots. If I'm not here, beep me."

He hung up the phone and cursed his luck. Actually, he hadn't expected much more than he got, but he had dared hope for a little better handle on which one was more likely the traitor. Now he would have to try and come up with another way to pin the tail on the donkey. Maybe they would spot something tonight that would point a finger in the right direction.

IN NASHVILLE, Marco Rizzi had just turned away from the phone when he remembered something. He had intended to chide Dom over the error the young man had made in passing along the information on Hamilton MacArthur. Marco had found the big home on the lake in Hendersonville, not Madison as Dom had told him. He picked up the newspaper laying on the bed and pulled out the sports section. Whether the guy came from Madison or Hendersonville didn't matter, of course. He had just intended to rib Dom about his miscue.

The only important thing now was Boots, whose life was

hanging by a thread. Marco had been with him since before Boots was made a capo. He would continue to check on him throughout the night.

<h1 style="text-align:center">28</h1>

CHICK HAD just parked along Decatur Street when Bryce and his friends arrived at the restaurant. The rest of the Silver Shadows were aboard the bus, except for MacArthur, who, Tillie had explained, was to pick up his wife and meet them at Le Dauphin. The lights glowed merrily along the busy street as everyone piled out of the bus.

Le Dauphin appeared undistinguished from the outside, as with most of the eateries and shops along the fringes of the French Quarter. Inside they found a narrow, high-ceilinged room with old French prints on the walls, along with a smattering of oval-shaped portraits Sarah Anne said bore the look of royalty.

Fred got them a table for six. As they took their seats, a black-tied waiter fluttered about the ladies like a hummingbird sampling petunia blossoms.

"Would you care for wine?" he asked. An indulgent smile covered his face.

"The dinner's paid for," Troy said. "But I'm sure wine's extra."

"I'll buy the wine," Bryce said. "If it's permitted on this tour."

"Methodists preach temperance, not abstinence," Fred said. "Wine's a good biblical drink, okay if used in moderation."

Bryce turned to the waiter. "Do you have a good Chablis?"

"Oh, yes. Very good," he said. He had a slight accent.

Betty Lou declined, but the others agreed to join Bryce in an apéritif. As the waiter was leaving, MacArthur and his wife strolled up and stopped beside the table. Mrs. MacArthur looked coquettish, and younger than her fifty-four years, in an embroidered white tunic and navy blue trousers.

"I would like you to meet Fred Scott, dear," MacArthur said. "He's the fellow who showed such great hospitality when I arrived at the church. This is my wife Andrea. She finished her meeting today and will be heading back to Nashville in the morning."

Fred, Troy and Bryce promptly rose from their chairs. Fred introduced the rest of the table.

Andrea MacArthur smiled at Bryce. "You're the investment expert Ham told me about."

"I lay no claims to being an expert at anything," Bryce said. "But I have been rather lucky at it."

"Don't be so modest. He was really impressed, and for him to be impressed, you have to be good."

Fred looked across apologetically. "I wish we had more room at the table. I'd invite you to join us."

"No problem," said MacArthur. "We promised to sit with Emma Gross and Mrs. Ellis. Incidentally, I've had some good reports about the food at Le Dauphin."

"I wonder where they got that name, Dauphin?" Betty Lou asked, rumpling her forehead.

"It was a title given to the eldest son of the King of France," MacArthur said. "Went out of vogue shortly after this area became part of America with the Louisiana Purchase."

Betty Lou's eyes widened. "That's interesting."

"It is also the name of a French province, isn't it?" Sarah Anne leaned forward on the table.

MacArthur turned to her. "Yes. With an 'e' on the end. That was actually the origin of the title. It is a region in the southeastern section of France, including part of the Alps. Grenoble is the major city."

Andrea MacArthur shook her head. "Don't get him started. He's an incurable buff when it comes to geography and history."

After they had moved on, the men resumed their seats. Betty Lou said, "Seems like a pretty bright guy, doesn't he?"

"Bright?" Fred frowned. "Young people are bright, Betty Lou. Old folks are supposed to be wise."

"What's the difference?"

"Bright means you know lots of trivia and can give snappy answers on quiz shows. To be wise, you got to know how to apply knowledge in useful ways."

Troy gave a slight sneer. "Based on that criteria, I would have to agree with Betty Lou. Hamilton MacArthur seems like a pretty bright guy."

The waiter turned out to be correct. The wine was good, and they enjoyed a zesty crawfish entrée. After dinner, the group filed out of Le Dauphin and began a leisurely stroll up St. Peter Street toward Preservation Hall. The warm night air felt heavily laced with humidity. A parade of noisy tourists crowded the sidewalks, most dressed casually, many in shorts, seemingly intent on rivaling the decibel level emanating from a succession of night spots.

Bryce watched them with an especially attentive eye, feeling a bit like a fox turned loose in a field of hounds. But where were the hunters?

A growing line meandered down the street from the doorway marked by a modest overhead sign that read "Preservation Hall." Tillie moved among them, passing out tickets, and soon they began to drift toward the entrance.

Whoops and shouts from a group of revelers just up the street brought a momentary pause in the line as Bryce handed his ticket to the wiry, white-haired man at the open doorway. The ticket-taker craned his head. "Buncha drunks. Cops ain't never around when you need 'em."

"You have much trouble around here?" Bryce asked.

"Not much." Then he bared a row of uneven teeth. "I keep a peacemaker handy just in case."

Bryce wondered what the "peacemaker" might be but dismissed the thought as he stepped inside a corridor that ran to the back of the building. Wooden benches, like old church pews, were parked against the wall on the right. A short distance back, a large doorway on the left led into an open area not a lot larger than his den. Toward the front of the building, a couple of steps went down to what passed for a stage. Three rows of seats flanked the narrow strip, putting the patrons almost at the feet of the performers, who perched on well-worn wooden chairs.

As people scrambled for the seats, Betty Lou, Sarah Anne and Marge slipped into the last three on the back row. The men took their places standing behind them, Bryce winding up in back of Marge. As he looked around, he couldn't help but grin at the idea of this being called Preservation Hall. The term conjured up visions of places like Carnegie in New York and Constitution in Washington. On a smaller and more modest scale there was Faneuil Hall in Boston, but even that was much more lavish and commodious compared to this tiny place. Dirty window panes opened to the street, where curious, would-be patrons on the sidewalk occasionally peeked in. There was no air-conditioning. The only thing to stir the warm October night was a floor fan in the corner behind the piano.

The area behind Bryce soon became packed with a murmuring, shifting crowd of standees. They filled the air with a variety of odors ranging from garlic to tobacco to a perfumed mixture almost as noxious as the others. Suddenly the room was cast into darkness, leaving only the musicians visible in the pale yellow glow of incandescent bulbs.

The laid back performers numbered five blacks and two whites who played piano, banjo, bass, clarinet, trumpet, trombone, and drums. The banjo and clarinet players were white-haired veterans who looked old enough to have performed back in the heyday of New Orleans jazz. And what they performed now was Dixieland at its best. A lover of most kinds of music, but particularly jazz, Bryce found the toe-tapping rhythm nearly enough to make him forget the threat that was ever-present, possibly lurking in the darkness behind him.

Nearly, but not totally.

That fact came to light after a rousing rendition of *St. Louis Blues*, with each musician taking his turn at an improvisational romp. Somebody, undoubtedly by accident, jabbed an elbow in his back while applauding vigorously. Bryce snapped his head around and heard an apologetic, "Sorry."

The incident jarred him back to the reality of the moment. He began to strain his eyes, searching the barely visible faces around him. Seeing nothing familiar, he decided to step out into the lighted hallway and take a look around.

A smattering of people, either foot-weary or somewhat indifferent to the lure of jazz, had come out to sit on the benches. One who likely met both criteria was Polly Pitts, the dumpy little woman who had shared her chocolate chip cookies on the bus.

She looked across at Bryce with a pained smile as he came through the doorway.

"You get tired, too?" she asked, stretching her legs. "My feet are killing me."

"Gets to you if you aren't used to standing," he said. Then he strolled leisurely up the hallway toward the front entrance.

The white-headed ticket taker leaned in the doorway, chatting with a couple on the sidewalk who waited patiently for admission to the next show. As Bryce looked past them into the street, he caught a glimpse of something that sent a low-level electric charge coursing through his body, a sensation that tingled up his neck. Three familiar figures in business suits stood on the sidewalk across the street.

Now he knew where the hunters were.

He stared across at Dom Locasio and his two sidekicks. Only the man from the cemetery and the carriage ride was missing. Had they finally figured out that he was Pat Pagano? Bryce wondered. If so they would have only one thing on their minds. Revenge. He was their target. And he no longer had the luxury of calling on the FBI for backup.

That thought rankled him. How could the Bureau so readily have assumed that he was the William Holder whose body had washed ashore in Oregon? And then the most plausible explanation hit him. Kravitz was gone. The agents in the office now probably considered Pat Pagano just another mobster who had ratted on his pals. They would not be unhappy at the prospect that he was gone. Good riddance. The shark-eating incident had likely generated enough notice that someone in the Bureau saw the name and made the connection, then did only a cursory investigation, prepared to accept what appeared to be obvious. One less name on the witness list to worry about, if, indeed, they ever really worried about such people.

He saw the trio start slowly across the street. For a moment they were hidden behind a passing van, then they appeared in the glow of the street lamps, apparently heading directly toward the Preservation Hall entrance. Their looks were somber. Their eyes seemed to stare straight at him.

The enemy was on the march. Cut from the same cloth as

those responsible for the death of his sons, these men intended the same fate for him.

His emotions had been on a roller coaster ride since Monday morning when he came face-to-face with Boots Minelli. Down, then up, then down again as the threat appeared to wax and wane and his feelings cycled from frustration to relief to anxiety to anger.

He had felt this same way half a century ago in that snow-covered field in Belgium. And now, as then, a cold dispassion took over. He faced a relentless, determined enemy with one obvious goal—his destruction. There was only one way to deal with the problem, the same way he had reacted on that icy December day outside Bastogne.

Only this time he was trapped without a weapon.

As he glanced about in a sudden frenzy, something caught his eye. A small table sat next to the wall behind the ticket-taker's empty station, a pile of ticket stubs on top. But what snared his attention was a drawer left partway open. A small revolver lay plainly visible. *I keep a peacemaker handy just in case.* The man's voice echoed through his mind.

Bryce recognized the black rubber grip and blued barrel of a Charter Arms .44 Special Bulldog Pug, identical to the gun he kept at home. The pistol had a two-and-a-half-inch barrel and weighed a mere twenty-five ounces. Loaded with five 200-grain rounds of .44 Special cartridges, the Pug was accurate as far away as fifteen yards, but built for close self-defense.

Once his mind had committed, his actions became reflexive. He slipped over to the ticket-taker's seat, reached into the drawer and pulled out the gun. A quick flip of the cylinder showed a full five rounds chambered. Locasio and his cohorts were now no more than fifteen or twenty feet away. They were strung out like the German soldiers he had faced that fateful day in Belgium, only much closer. Picking off beer cans atop a fence could not be easier.

He began to raise the gun.

29

BRYCE'S HAND stopped as he heard someone call his name.

Turning his head, he saw Marge a few feet behind him, leaning against the wall.

The spell had been broken. A wave of cold fear swept over him. Not fear of the mobsters—he had been ready to face them down—but fear of himself, of what he had almost done. He remembered that nagging dread that had troubled him early on, a fear that some day, under some dire circumstance, he might revert to the same coldly calculating killing machine he had been during the war. But regardless of the similarity between then and now, he knew this was different. Had he pulled that trigger, he would have become the same kind of savage animal as the Mafia trio. A ruthless killer without conscience. The idea sickened him.

And as the voices of tourists out on the sidewalk reached his ears, his pain deepened with the thought of innocents he might have killed accidentally. As if to punctuate that possibility, a group of laughing, chattering teenagers abruptly passed by, obscuring the mobsters.

The Bulldog Pug suddenly felt like a lead weight in his hand. Grasping the barrel, he shoved the gun toward the startled ticket-taker, who had also turned on hearing Marge's voice.

"Your peacemaker was lying out in the open over there," Bryce said. His voice sounded strange. "You'd better hide the damned thing before somebody uses it on you."

A dark frown on his face, the man grabbed the gun and shoved it into a back pocket. He started to reply, but Bryce turned away at a gasping sound and found Marge bent forward, hands grasping her stomach. A distressed look distorted her face, which appeared pallid and damp with perspiration.

Bryce ran back to her. "What's wrong? Are you ill?"

"I...I feel like...it's my stomach. Those crawfish must not have agreed with me."

Bryce helped her over to a bench and sat down beside her. "Do you want me to call a taxi and take you back to the hotel?"

She shook her head. "No. No, I'll be all right."

He pulled out a handkerchief and brushed her forehead, then handed it to her.

"Thanks." The color was beginning to return to her face, the color of embarrassment.

Betty Lou came out of the darkened hall and hurried over. "What happened? I wondered why you got up and left."

"She felt sick at her stomach," Bryce said. "It may have been the crawfish. She's looking a little better now. Getting some color back in her face."

"Chick should have the bus out front in a few minutes," Betty Lou said. "We'll help you out there."

Marge handed back the handkerchief and murmured in a soft voice. "Thank you, Bryce." Then she turned to Betty Lou. "Really, I'll be okay. Just let me sit here and rest a few minutes."

AS MARGE let her eyes flutter and close, Betty Lou watched her old friend with a growing sense of apprehension. She did not think the problem was anything Marge had eaten. They often joked about her "cast iron" stomach. She could eat the spiciest Mexican dishes with no difficulty. Betty Lou could recall other times when Marge had suffered similar attacks, though not in recent years. She couldn't be a hundred percent sure, of course, but Betty Lou was convinced the incidents had something to do with that fateful journey Marge and Keith had taken to West Virginia in 1965. The trip from which she had returned a basket case.

MARGE SAT with eyes closed, her thoughts racing back to the real cause of her queasiness, which had started in the darkness of the music hall when she heard a rustling sound behind her. Looking around, she saw Bryce head toward the hallway entrance. Although she had enjoyed the music, the heat and the closeness of all the bodies in that small enclosure had become stifling. She slipped out of her seat to join him in the hallway.

Curious, she paused and watched as Bryce stopped near the front entrance, apparently gazing at something out in the street. Then a sudden shock jolted her as she saw him look around, reach into a table drawer, pull out a pistol and turn back toward the street. What was he doing? Surely he wasn't about to shoot someone, she thought. But why else would he be standing there brandishing a gun? The uncertainty triggered a flood of horrible memories from that dreadful summer more than thirty years ago. The summer when she and Keith had driven up to visit friends in West Virginia. She cried out Bryce's name as the images poured back into her mind like a tidal wave, overwhelming her, touching off a churning within her stomach that brought on the nausea similar episodes had caused so many times in the past.

She recalled a more recent day a few years back when Herb had confronted her with a shocking revelation, triggered by her statement that she was leaving him. True to her mother's wishes, she would not file for divorce, but she had put up with all of the jealousy and abuse she could take. Then Herb had stunned her with his knowledge of the secret she had so closely guarded all those years.

"You are not going anywhere, lady," he said in that icy, commanding tone that had undoubtedly made his Navy subordinates cringe. "Unless you want the world to know about your brother."

Marge gasped. "What...about my brother?" He could not possibly know, she thought. It stretched belief. After all, she had found out only by being in the right place at the right time.

A diabolical grin broke out across his face. "I wasn't positive about it until now. That look tells it all."

"I don't know what you're talking about," she said.

"Oh, I think you do. And more important, I know who he is, and where he is."

Then he began to detail the complex web that had brought the puzzle together for him. Back during World War II, Herb

Hunter had been a seaman on the same ship in the Mediterranean as her brother Ed James' classmate, the one who reported encountering him in the white kepi of a French Foreign Legionnaire. Marge had told Herb earlier about her brother's involvement in the Spanish Civil War and the report of his enlistment in the Legion. Herb was quite intrigued to discover Ed on board his ship.

"I found him exercising on deck one day and told him who I was," Herb said, "that I had been dating his sister. He growled at me like a mongrel dog and grunted, 'I am no longer Edward James and I have no sister.' I wasn't sure what to make of that, but then he held out his right arm and pointed to a red tattoo. It said Freedom, and below that seven-dash-seven-dash-three-seven. Then he gave a bitter grin and said, 'That's the day I left Nashville. July seventh, nineteen hundred and thirty-seven. I will never go back.'"

At that moment Marge's faint hopes caved in. She knew what was coming. The tattoo was one of the ways she had identified her brother back in 1965, a time that qualified without doubt as the most traumatic period of her life.

Early that year the newspapers were full of stories about the bloody mutilation slaying of a family of seven in rural West Virginia. Vivid accounts of the crime horrified readers across the nation. A drifter had stopped by their farm looking for work. Neighbors said the family took him in and treated him as one of their own. But two weeks later, when another farmer came by looking for a tractor attachment, he discovered a grisly scene. The man and his wife lay dead in their bed, shot with the farmer's own gun, then literally butchered with a large carving knife. Their two boys and three girls had been shot and bludgeoned, their skulls shattered by blows from a pick handle. Evidently the slayings had occurred during the night. The drifter was missing.

The police put out a statewide alert and soon found the suspect hitchhiking westward some fifty miles away. He had spatters of blood on his clothing, which he claimed came from a cut finger. The cut, however, turned out to be only superficial. Tests later showed the blood was not his type but matched that of some of the victims.

Hailed in the press as one of the nation's worst mass murderers, the man was identified as Grantland Hemingway. They found a New York driver's license and a recently-acquired Social Security card in his billfold. His fingerprints were sent to the FBI, but no match was found in their files. This meant two things. He had no criminal record and had not served in the military.

The news media quickly jumped on the story and learned Hemingway had worked briefly in New York City as a service station attendant. But his fellow workers and neighbors could only reveal that he was a loner, not at all talkative, not one to make friends. Nothing was known about his family or where he had come from. He steadfastly refused to talk about himself, appearing to enjoy total anonymity. He did confess to the murders, however, after learning that West Virginia had done away with the death penalty the previous year. Editorial cartoonists had a field day depicting him as the personification of evil.

When pressed for the reason he had committed such atrocities, Hemingway calmly explained that the farmer had insulted him by accusing him of stealing a watch. But why kill the others? They were all tainted with the same bad blood, he contended.

Psychiatrists examined him and branded him a sociopath, but quite sane and able to stand trial. A lawyer assigned to his defense sought to get the confession thrown out but only succeeded in having the case moved to a court in the capital, Charleston. The trial was set for July.

MARGE READ about the case in the Nashville newspapers. She was intrigued by the name Grantland Hemingway. The only other time she had heard the name Grantland was of a local sports writer named Grantland Rice when she was a kid. It was also close to the name of the street she grew up on, Gartland Avenue. As for Hemingway, she could only think of Ernest Hemingway, a writer she did not care for. But she recalled a stack of newspaper articles from the war in Spain with Hemingway's by-line that her brother had collected before he left home. The thought gave her an uneasy feeling. At the moment she wasn't quite sure why.

Reading another story closer to the trial date, Marge noticed Grantland Hemingway's age listed as forty-six. She recalled her brother Ed's birthday was May 5, 1919. She could hardly have forgotten it, not after seeing that "5•5•19" he had carved in the door facing of his room so many years ago. He would have been forty-six.

Was all of this pure coincidence, she wondered? Surely it must be. This mass murderer could not possibly be her brother.

She had seen Hemingway's picture before but had never looked at him too closely. However, as she studied newspaper photo now, she saw a startling resemblance to Brad James, her father, when he was in his forties.

Was it all coincidence? She had to know the truth. She talked her husband into visiting former neighbors who had been transferred by DuPont to a plant in West Virginia. They arrived on the Fourth of July weekend and planned to make a long holiday of it.

Marge found the mass murderer's trial the main topic of conversation in Charleston. Sandy Terry, her hostess, had closely followed the case. When the news came on television, Marge watched with a growing sense of dread as the upcoming trial of Grantland Hemingway was reported. A shot of him at the jail wearing a T-shirt filled the screen. And as the camera zoomed in, she saw a tattoo on his arm that said "Freedom," and below that "7•7•37." The same style numbers her brother had used to carve his birth date on the door facing of his bedroom on Gartland Avenue. What would this date be? July 7, 1937? She remembered it clearly. It was the day her mother had cried softly as Ed James rode off in a bus, smiling, supposedly bound for a Civilian Conservation Corps camp, actually headed for Spain.

At that moment, it hit her with all the devastating force and fury of a hurricane. Her brother was undoubtedly the mass murderer.

She had come completely unglued, bordering on psychotic. Bewildered, Keith had taken her home the next day. She spent most of the week in bed before getting herself together enough to face the world again. With a sheer force of will, she had managed to maintain her sanity, but one thing she knew for certain:

She could never dare risk having a baby with the same genes as Ed James.

The whole episode put a severe strain on their relationship, but Keith stood by her to the end, even though he never understood what had happened. She was thankful her parents had not lived to witness their only son convicted as a despicable mass murderer. She feared they might have made the same connection that she had.

Now in his eighties, Ed James was still biding his time in the West Virginia State Prison at Elkins, still maintaining the anonymity of his infamy. And years after she had finally reconciled herself to living with that ghastly secret, Herbert Hunter had gleefully thrown the horror back in her face. He explained how, while stationed at the Pentagon in 1990, he had attended the christening of the *USS West Virginia*, an Ohio class Trident ballistic missile submarine. The governor had invited him to visit Charleston. As a result, Captain Hunter was there during the twenty-fifth anniversary of the Grantland Hemingway trial, which, to the governor's chagrin, triggered a new wave of newspaper and TV rehashing. When Herb saw pictures of the tattoo, he remembered having seen the identical lettering on Ed James's arm. He put the rest together much as Marge had. But he said nothing, because he was not certain of his facts. Not until the day he had confronted her with the horrible truth.

The prospect of her relationship to the mass murderer becoming public knowledge was unthinkable. The family name would be blackened forever, making her the subject of unbearable harassment from the press and television news crews.

Tonight, when she saw Bryce brandish a gun as if about to shoot someone for no obvious reason, all of the trauma and pain and hurt she had gone through because of Ed James had been suddenly and shockingly resurrected. And, she now realized, all for naught. Bryce had merely handed the gun to the man at the door.

As they walked toward the bus in the street outside

Preservation Hall, she turned to him, keeping her voice low. "What was that all about with the gun you gave the man at the door?"

Bryce's smile was apologetic. "I saw it lying out in plain view, in the open drawer of that table. I told him he'd better hide it. I was afraid somebody might get it and do something really stupid."

AS BRYCE CLIMBED aboard the bus, he looked around in an attempt to spot the Mafia hoods but saw no trace of them. He was certain they would be lurking somewhere nearby. But the most troubling element he had to contend with concerned that tormenting moment in the corridor of Preservation Hall.

Would he really have pulled the trigger if Marge had not called his name?

30

BRYCE AWOKE early on Thursday and stared into a virtual void. The room's lone window flanked an interior hallway. The heavy drapes allowed only a faint glow to penetrate around the edges. But he felt right at home in the dark as he hadn't the foggiest idea what might happen next. So far he had managed to survive in the protective custody of his small circle of newly-acquired Silver Shadows friends, but the trip was fast winding down. Even if he succeeded in keeping the bad guys at bay for two more days, which would likely be no mean task, he faced the prospect of being cast out on his own once back at Lovely Lane Church in Madison. But he had an uneasy feeling that Locasio wouldn't be willing to wait that long to make his move.

Surprised there had been no overt effort to get at him thus far, Bryce knew he had misread the intentions of the trio that had crossed the street in front of Preservation Hall last night. Was that an indication they still had not pinpointed which of the bus passengers was the real Pat Pagano, he wondered? If so, he might have a little grace period left.

That was small consolation.

Of equal concern was the possibility of getting his new friends, particularly Marge Hunter, caught in the crossfire. He had too many black marks on his record already as a result of blundering choices that proved fatal to those around him. He felt like the personification of that old line from Pogo:

"We have met the enemy, and he is us."

As he lay there in the darkness, Bryce replayed over and over in his mind the scene at Preservation Hall when he had seized the revolver and prepared to eliminate the opposition. Judging by her question later, Marge left no doubt she had seen him brandish the gun. But how much had she seen? Was she watching when he picked it up? Had that influenced her to call out his name?

Seated across the aisle from her on the ride back to the hotel, he had darted frequent glances in her direction along the way. He had begun to question whether the distress she showed really stemmed from a reaction to the crawfish they had eaten for dinner. By the time Chick deposited them back at the hotel, she appeared to be suffering no more ill effects. He wondered if her problem might have been more related to trauma? The shock of seeing him holding that gun. He had a troubling feeling there was much more involved here than there seemed to be.

He had too many questions, too few answers. He finally climbed out of bed, realizing there was little chance of disturbing Troy, and headed for the bathroom. He had just finished shaving and wandered back into the bedroom when Troy's travel alarm began to beep. Seven o'clock. Bryce switched on the TV as the alarm lapsed into silence. The light spilling from the bathroom and the sound of the television finally accomplished what the alarm had failed to achieve. Troy slowly sat up like a corpse rising from a casket. He rubbed his eyes, then pried them open wide as a local forecaster began an ominous report on Hurricane Nora's overnight progress.

"The storm is presently one hundred and fifty miles south of Port Arthur," said the serious-faced weatherman. His wavy hair piece, like Hurricane Nora, had gone a bit askew. He pointed to a map of the Gulf coast and continued. "It has veered slightly to the east over the past couple of hours, but it is still on track to make landfall around the Texas-Louisiana state line late this afternoon. Winds of near hurricane-force are already lashing coastal areas from south of Lake Charles westward to Galveston. If Nora continues on her current path, she should hit the coast around four o'clock, with winds of up to one hundred and thirty miles an hour. This would put her on the borderline of a Category Four hurricane, whose winds are capable of extensive structural damage and flooding for several miles inland.

"Our current cloudy and windy conditions in New Orleans are unrelated to Nora. They stem from a different weather system, one that came through last night and is moving rapidly off to the northeast. However, the National Hurricane Center has issued a tropical storm warning for the New Orleans area for later today, with strong wind gusts and rain possibly moving in by early evening. You are advised to stay tuned throughout the day for further progress reports on Hurricane Nora, potentially one of the season's most destructive storms."

Troy looked up from the side of the bed where he was sitting, his face as rumpled as the sheet around him. "Sounds like our boat ride tonight may be a washout."

Bryce started pulling on his shoes. "At least the morning and afternoon tours should be okay. It's just cloudy and windy now."

"Do you think Tillie might decide to cancel everything and head for home?"

" I don't know, but she's got an awful lot of herself invested in this tour."

"I guess we'll soon find out."

" Right. Want to try breakfast at the hotel restaurant?"

"Might as well."

When they were ready, they knocked on the door to the women's room. Marge stuck her head out. "I'm trying to get Sarah Anne in gear," she said. "It takes her awhile to put her face on. You fellas go ahead."

"We'll be in the restaurant downstairs," Troy said.

They rode down the elevator with Clara and Horace Holly. Apparently ignorant of the weather situation or its possible consequences, Clara babbled away as usual, entertaining them with detailed descriptions of her tour through the French Market Wednesday afternoon. The complex of long, mostly open-sided buildings dating back to 1813 was strung out along both sides of North Peters and Decatur streets. Its stalls offered everything from fresh produce to hot sauce to souvenirs and hats and jeans and the ubiquitous T-shirts.

"I found the darlingest little white dress for my youngest granddaughter," Clara said, her owlish eyes dancing. Then she proceeded to describe the garment in such lavish detail that Bryce felt he could almost reach out and touch it.

WHEN EVERYONE was seated on the bus, Tillie took the

microphone and greeted them. "We're happy to have Yvonne Deschamps back with us this morning as we tour St. Louis Cathedral, then visit the Garden District. After lunch we'll tour Mardi Gras World, where we'll see hundreds of floats and props used in the big parades. But before we get started, I'd like to address some of the comments and concerns I've gotten this morning about Hurricane Nora. According to the news reports, they don't expect the bad weather to get here until tonight. If the winds are too strong, we may have to scrub the river boat ride. Yvonne has volunteered to help us come up with an alternative. Nora is supposed to stay well west of here, but depending on how she moves after landfall, it might possibly affect our visit to Bellingrath Gardens tomorrow. We'll just have to wait and see what happens."

The sky was gray with elastic clouds stretching over the city as Chick steered his bus into the morning traffic. As they approached Jackson Square, Yvonne Deschamps gave a brief history of the cathedral. She said the current building, the third constructed on the site, dated from 1794 and was the oldest active cathedral and one of the most photographed churches in America.

When they entered the statuesque basilica with its three tall spires pointing heavenward, Bryce was tempted out of a long ingrained habit to give the sign of the cross before venturing into the sanctuary. But he restrained himself and followed the others in, exhibiting the typical look of a tourist, wide-eyed and filled with wonder.

After listening to a brief history of St. Louis Cathedral given by a white-haired nun, they strolled past the front pews and the ornate altar.

"Isn't this something?" Betty Lou's voice was hushed. "All those beautiful paintings on the walls, and high up there on the ceiling."

Fred grinned. "It's certainly bigger and fancier than Lovely Lane. I'll have to give 'em that."

"True," Bryce agreed. "But it isn't the trappings that make a church a shrine. It's the people who inhabit it."

Marge looked at him thoughtfully. "Was your wife active in the church?"

He remembered how a despondent Ellen had become reclusive after the explosion at their home. She became a chain smoker until the cancer struck. "After our sons were killed in an accident, she devoted most of her time to church work," Bryce said, not mentioning it had been with nuns, where she had become virtually cloistered.

"Were they your only children?" Fred asked.

Bryce nodded. "Ellen never really recovered from it." He had not spoken her name in years, and truthfully he had not intended to do so now. But what difference did it make any longer? He was becoming more convinced that the Mafia squad already knew, or certainly would soon, that he was really Pat Pagano.

"Something like that can really try your faith," Troy said. "I keep wondering why Virginia? Why did Parkinson's have to pick her?"

Bryce gave a slight shake of his head. "I know the feeling, but I blame what happened to the boys and to Ellen on my own shortcomings." His crisis had involved faith in himself. "I'm afraid I haven't been in a place like this in quite awhile." He glanced across at the altar.

"Whenever you feel like affiliating with another church, we'd sure love to have you at Lovely Lane," Fred said.

Bryce's face brightened. "Frankly, I can't think of any place that would be more appealing."

Looking around at Fred and Betty Lou, at Marge, Sarah Anne, and Troy, he felt these people deserved some sort of commendation. They had accepted him, a virtual stranger, taken him into their circle without question, made him feel as welcome as a lifelong friend. He wished there were some way he could repay their kindness. But as his gaze turned toward the rear of the sanctuary, he suddenly realized why the time was getting a bit late for such considerations. Standing just inside the far aisle was a familiar figure, a solidly built man in a blue suit. One of Locasio's henchmen.

CHICK HAD parked the red-and-white bus on Decatur Street in front of Jackson Square. When Tillie walked up at 10:30, he greeted her with a long face that immediately put her on guard. This was anything but typical of the normally upbeat driver.

"Miz Ellis, I got bad news," he said.

"Has the bus developed another problem?"

"No, ma'am. I've been listening to the radio. They say the hurricane took a right turn before it reached Texas. Now it's headed this way."

She flipped her glasses up and jammed them into her hair. "Toward New Orleans?"

"Yes, ma'am. It's supposed to get here sometime tonight. They're expecting rain and high winds this afternoon."

"Oh, God," she said.

Her first reaction was one of disappointment, of regret at the prospect of having to tell everyone the trip was being cut short. But it appeared the impetuous Nora left her no choice. Her own latent fear of the monstrous tropical storms made her realize that many of her charges were likely to be terribly frightened at the prospect of a deadly hurricane bearing down on them. That seemed to be almost a self-fulfilling prophecy. Those within earshot began to relay something of what they had heard to their neighbors farther back. Tillie decided she had better get everyone aboard before someone touched off a full-fledged panic.

"Find your seats, people," she said. She tugged at arms and sleeves to hurry them along. "I'll make an announcement regarding the weather as soon as we're all here."

She turned to Chick. "Can you find a newscast and rig that radio up to play it over the loudspeakers?"

"Sure," he said. "Give me a couple of minutes after we get inside."

As the group began to climb the steps, a few attempted to question Tillie about what was going on. One was a wide-eyed Polly. "I heard the hurricane's already hit just west of here," she said, fear in her voice. "Is that right?"

Tillie pushed against her backside. "Get in your seat, Polly. Don't believe everything you hear. I'll tell you in a few minutes."

Others climbed aboard with drawn faces, clearly alarmed at the uncertain outlook.

Bryce was near the back of the group waiting to board. "I was thinking the other night that I'd never had a chance to meet a hurricane up close," he said to Troy. "I wonder if this just might be my time."

Then Sarah Anne passed the word back that Nora was headed their way. "I vote we run for the hills," she said, only half-joking.

"I'm with you," Troy said. "I was in a tornado once and that was bad enough. These babies not only pack deadly winds, they can hang around and beat up on you for hours."

Horace and Clara were last in line. Hustling up the steps as nervous as a cat at a wheelchair derby, tugging at her husband to hurry aboard, Clara glanced over at Tillie, who stood beside the driver.

"Is that storm really about to hit us, Tillie?" Her voice shook with genuine fear.

"Don't worry, Clara. Just take your seat. I'll explain everything."

As soon as Horace had reached the top step, Chick closed the door and began working with the audio controls. Tillie took the microphone.

"I'm sure you've heard all kinds of rumors about the storm, but, basically, this is the story. It has turned to the east and is headed this way. Chick is looking for a radio newscast that we can put on the speaker system so you can learn firsthand what the situation is."

The driver turned to her. "I've got it."

The announcer's voice flowed urgently out of the speakers. "The latest word from the National Hurricane Center in Miami places Nora approximately one hundred and twenty-five miles south of Lake Charles, just over two hundred miles southwest of New Orleans. She is in the process of turning eastward. It will be awhile before it's clear whether she's headed straight for New Orleans or will veer to the south of us. But one thing is certain. She's in a lot bigger hurry than before. The hurricane trackers report Nora has nearly doubled her forward speed from a couple of days ago, reaching almost twenty miles per hour. At that rate, the major brunt of the storm should arrive in our area around nine p.m. Wind gusts of fifty to sixty miles per hour could hit

New Orleans by mid-afternoon, accompanied by heavy rainfall. Police report coastal areas have been ordered to evacuate and an exodus of tourists has begun. Traffic is already heavy on highways leading out of the city. It could be worse than last year when 1998's Hurricane Georges missed us but created massive traffic jams."

Chick had the bus moving by the time Tillie signaled him to switch off the radio. Facing emergencies on a tour was nothing new for her, but she had never encountered one quite like this. She worried that some of her "little old ladies" might go bonkers. She picked up the mike and spoke in what she hoped was a reassuring tone.

"We'll go back to the hotel, get our bags and check out as quickly as possible. Yvonne says she'll see if the restaurant can fix us some sandwiches and things to eat along the way. Don't worry about anything. We're in good shape. We should be able to get moving within an hour. I don't think Chick will have any trouble outrunning a twenty-mile-an-hour storm. You saw how fast he can make this old bus move coming down from Natchez. Just relax till we get back to the hotel, then pack up as quickly as you can and get back on the bus."

She hardly felt as confident as she sounded, but she hoped and prayed they could get on the road by noon, before the highways became totally clogged. Just the traffic itself would be bad enough. The high wind and rain on the way could make for a real white-knuckle ride. She wondered how competent Chick would be at driving under such adverse conditions.

EVERYONE ON the bus recalled the devastation of Hurricane Andrew a few years back, and though they might have been a bit shady on the details, most remembered reading about Betsy and Camille. MacArthur was the only one who had actually experienced a hurricane. He captured the attention of everyone in the middle of the bus with his tale of riding out a storm at a "hurricane party."

"We were in a friend's apartment. When the lights went out, we listened to music from a battery-operated tape player and played cards using kerosene lanterns. The wind howled and the rain poured and the surf crashed with a roar along the waterfront. But we just laughed and joked.

"That was in my younger days," he said. "I've got more sense now. We were lucky that it wasn't a terribly large hurricane and did not have much of a storm surge. That's what usually kills people. In a big storm, the surge can hurl a huge mass of water over a beachfront, like a tidal wave twenty or thirty feet high. Totally destroys everything in its path."

"Could something like that hit our bus?" asked a fearful Polly.

MacArthur gave her a tolerant smile. "We should be far from here by the time Nora arrives. But even if we were still around, I hardly think we would be driving anywhere near the waterfront. I should imagine the main problems around New Orleans would be from flooding."

LOCASIO HAD just hung up from talking to Marco in Nashville when the call came from Ziggy on the cell phone.

"It looks like the bus is headed back to the hotel," said Ziggy. "We didn't get close enough to know what was going on, but the old lady in charge looked pretty damned excited."

"They must have heard the news," Locasio said.

"What news?"

"The damned hurricane is on the way to New Orleans. They probably plan to leave town as soon as they can get checked out of the hotel."

"What are we gonna do?" Ziggy asked.

Locasio's voice was grim. "What Boots would have wanted us to do. I just got word from Marco. Boots is dead."

There was a painful pause, then a muttered, "Damn."

"You guys get back here as fast as you can," said Locasio. "I've already talked to The Barber. He'll be here in about half an hour. We just move up the time schedule a bit. Actually, the weather should make things easier, give us a good opportunity to carry out the plan. Is Joe ready?"

He could hear voices murmuring in the background. Then Ziggy said, "Joe says he'll get it done as fast as he can."

31

THE HOTEL LOBBY was a bedlam, people scurrying in every direction, hauling out baggage, crowding the front desk to settle their bills, getting change for the vending machines down the hallway. Just as the locals were rapidly cleaning out grocery shelves around town, the tourists would soon deplete the hotel's snack food supply.

Bryce had his bag ready moments after arriving at the room, then turned his attention to the TV. Regular programming had been suspended for continuous updates on Hurricane Nora, along with instructions from emergency preparedness officials. So far the storm was continuing to swirl directly toward New Orleans, the radar display showing pale fringes lashing out like wispy white tentacles groping for a hold on the Mississippi Delta.

"Wallace Bradley is in a mobile unit somewhere on I-10," said the rumpled news anchor. He had pulled off his jacket and sat before a pile of news clips and announcements of closings and warnings. "What can you tell us, Wally?"

"It's one big mess out here," said the harried newsman. A still photo of him filled the screen. "All of the lanes are full and we're moving like in a funeral procession. I'm almost to the Highway 90 exit. I'll get off there and see how things are going on Chef Menteur Highway."

"Thanks, Wally," the anchor said. The picture switched back to the studio. "We'll come back to you for another update shortly."

Troy finished with his bag and frowned at Bryce. "That doesn't sound too good for getting out of town, does it?"

"I'll wager the secondary roads are just as bad as the interstates," Bryce said with a shrug. To him the storm appeared more of a nuisance than a worry.

Troy grabbed his bag and headed for the door. "Not much we can do about it but get in amongst 'em. You ready?"

Bryce switched off the TV and followed him out. "Let's check the ladies. See if they need any help."

He knocked next door and Sarah Anne appeared in the doorway. Anxiety showed in her face. "Did you see the TV?"

"Looks like it'll be slow going," Bryce said.

"What if the hurricane should catch up with us?"

"Then we'll have a nice tail wind. That should speed things up."

She shook her head. "You men. It's a macho thing, isn't it? You're supposed to act like nothing bothers you."

If she only knew, Bryce thought. But as far as the hurricane was concerned, she was right. Nora didn't worry him. If anything, the lady might make his trail more difficult for his pursuers to follow. Chick's bus was a sizable target, but unless the blue Cadillac kept in close proximity, the big vehicle could get comfortably lost in the mass of traffic and the poor visibility that should be accompanying the storm. Although the full force of the hurricane was still several hours away, he knew they could easily get hit with heavy rain and stiff winds within the next hour or two. There was also a junction to contend with. Just to the northeast of New Orleans, Chick would have the option of continuing on I-10 east toward Biloxi or taking I-59 north to Hattiesburg. Unless Locasio's people remained in sight of the bus, they would have a fifty percent chance of making the wrong choice.

"For the moment, let's just worry about getting all our stuff on that bus," Marge said. She pushed her bag out into the hallway.

They carried their luggage across to the elevator, then stood and waited. Although there was only one floor above them, the lone elevator was already packed with passengers and baggage when the door opened on four. Bryce promptly pressed the "up" button to snare it on the return trip. They climbed aboard and continued on to the fifth floor.

Seeing the crowd of people who attempted to squeeze inside when the door opened at the top floor, Troy slapped Bryce on the shoulder. "Helps to have a smart man around to look after us."

They finally reached the lobby and toted their bags out to

the waiting bus. Tillie was already fussing about, counting noses and herding people aboard. She snagged Bryce and Troy as they shoved their suitcases into the baggage compartment.

"Would you fellas mind helping carry out the lunch boxes?" A look of concern shadowed her pale cheeks.

They walked back to the restaurant, where they found stacks of boxes packed into tall white plastic garbage bags. With a load in each hand, they made their way back to the bus and handed them inside to Fred, who had been pressed into service to parcel them out two to a seat.

With the delay caused by the elevator congestion, plus the fact that several of the Silver Shadows moved at a speed somewhat akin to that of the sun's shadow, Tillie did not get her wish to be on the road by noon. The dashboard clock showed closer to 12:30 when Chick finally closed the door and put the bus in gear. Fortunately, the wind was still reasonably gentle and there was as yet no sign of rain.

"I told you not to worry," Tillie said into the microphone. "We're running a little late, but the weather is still not bad at all. The big problem we face is a glut of traffic on the highway. I'd advise you to just sit back and relax, enjoy your lunch. If you haven't looked, your box contains a sandwich, chips, cookies, and a piece of fruit. We'll pass around the soft drinks as soon as we get on the interstate."

That took longer than expected, with cars and trucks bumper-to-bumper on the entrance ramp back to the street.

BRYCE HAD taken the window seat on the back row. Finding the overhead rack already stuffed, he shoved his carryon under the seat in front of him. Then he turned his attention to the window, making a careful search in every direction for a blue Cadillac. He continued to twist his head back and forth as Chick nosed the big bus onto the entrance ramp, but there was no sign of Locasio's car.

He finally leaned back and forced his muscles to relax. Maybe they had been caught off guard and failed to see the bus leave, he speculated. The thought was a heady one, but he didn't waste much time on it. He would keep looking.

Troy opened his box lunch and dug out the sandwich. He turned to Bryce. "You gonna eat now, or wait till we get a little father along?"

Bryce set the box in his lap. "I'm not too hungry, but I might as well get it out of the way. Looks like it may be a good while before we get much farther along."

IN THE RIGHT-HAND front seat, Tillie leaned forward and surveyed the glut of cars and trucks and buses that stretched out along the highway like links in a chain. A chain that reached as far as the eye could see. The rippling mass moved at glacial speed. Each time Chick managed to nudge the bus forward, he quickly crept up on the van in front and was forced to slow down, almost coming to a stop. After a stretch of time that resembled a film running in slow motion, the bus would pick up speed, then the whole process repeated itself.

Tillie had a low tolerance for forced inaction. She would have loved to step outside the bus and scream at the top of her lungs for the drivers to get their acts together and move on. They seemed totally oblivious to the hurricane bearing down on them from the rear.

Glancing back, she noted mostly sober faces among her charges. Polly, Sadie and Clara all looked like they expected Armageddon. Happily, a few seemed to take things in stride. Fred chuckled at something as he spoke to Betty Lou, and MacArthur sat with a bemused smile on his face.

Tillie scooped up a white lunch box from the floor in front of her, flipped the lid up and surveyed its contents. In times of tension she did not enjoy much of an appetite, but eating meant doing something, and doing something was infinitely better than sitting there doing nothing.

The act of eating had no effect, however, on her growing displeasure with what she saw happening, or not happening, on the glutted highway. After finishing her lunch, she leaned toward the driver, now clearly irritated. "What do you think is the big holdup, Chick? Accidents?"

"Possibly," he said. "But I'd say more likely it's construction work. That and just too darn much traffic. We passed a stalled car back there in the left lane. I'd be surprised if we don't see more along the way."

She hadn't thought of that, but he was probably right. And the longer they sat out here, creeping along with engines running, the more likely other vehicles would run out of gas or suffer from overheating. She glanced at her watch and frowned.

One-fifteen.

She unfolded her map and studied it. They were traveling among a series of exits on the north side of New Orleans along Lake Pontchartrain. She made a quick estimate that they had covered only about eight miles in the past forty-five minutes.

32

MARGE SAT a few seats behind Tillie, arms crossed in thought. Sarah Anne had talked herself out for the moment, having exhausted all the "what if's" regarding Nora's path and destructive potential. Her tortured ramblings sounded too much like the Chicken Little syndrome. Marge had been more impressed with Bryce's light-hearted approach, joking that the hurricane might provide a good tailwind. Despite the slow pace along the jammed highway, she saw no need to speculate on all the dire possibilities.

Reflecting upon her observations of Bryce, she admitted that overall he'd made a quite favorable impression. She liked what he had said this morning at the cathedral, about the worshippers being responsible for making a church a shrine, and not blaming God for his problems. She wondered if his sons had been killed in an auto accident, with him driving. In any event, as she thought about him, she realized she liked most of what she had heard. He was sensitive, plain-spoken, easy-going.

There were so many similarities between Bryce and Keith Walden. But such comparisons were unfair, she knew. Unfair to both men. They were two entirely different people, each with his own set of qualities, good and bad, though she could not put her finger on anything really bad about either of them. Maybe a few shortcomings, but nothing truly objectionable. She recalled those apparently odd mood shifts she had noted in Bryce, but saw nothing sinister in them, nothing that could not likely be cleared up with a simple explanation.

Despite her disclaimers to Sarah Anne and Troy, he did seem somewhat attracted to her. But was she really ready for this?

AROUND TWO o'clock, the wind picked up. Along the

highway, gusts lashed the trees from side to side. Traffic remained bumper-to-bumper, and though the pace had improved, Bryce guessed they were not averaging more than fifteen to twenty miles per hour. He'd had difficulty keeping up with road signs on the right side of the bus, but they had crossed the outlet from Lake Pontchartrain and he knew they should not be far from the junction with I-59.

As rain began to pepper against the windows, Troy looked around. "Must be some kind of problem up ahead. A blue light just passed us on the right."

They had seen vehicles occasionally traveling up the emergency lane in search of an exit to escape the tie-up on the interstate. And as they watched now, they felt the bus slowing, then veering to the right. Chick braked to a halt and they could tell he had opened the door and was talking with someone.

TILLIE FIRST spotted the vehicle with the blue light passing her window, then alerted Chick. "He's waving us over," she said. She stood up to get a better look.

The vehicle was black with no police markings. She couldn't tell much because of the rain and the dark overcast, but the flashing blue light appeared to be a portable one fixed to the roof. As Chick pulled over and stopped, a man wearing a hooded yellow slicker hurried back to the bus. When Chick opened the door, the man stuck his head in, climbed onto the bottom step and half-shouted.

"There's been a big pileup near the junction up ahead. Probably have the highway blocked for a pretty good while. If you want to take this next exit, I can lead you around it on the Mississippi side."

"Let's take it," said Tillie. With the weather obviously worsening by the minute, she had no desire to sit parked on the interstate.

Chick threw up his hands and glanced toward the man in the slicker. "She's the boss."

Judging by the badge clipped to the yellow fabric, the man was some sort of policeman, though only his face was visible inside the hood. He waved a hand. "Okay. Follow us."

As they moved slowly along the shoulder of the highway, Tillie got on the microphone to explain what was happening.

"We just had a stroke of luck," she said. "Some officers saw our bus and took pity on us. It seems there's been a big accident that's closed the highway up toward the junction of I-10 and I-59. They volunteered to lead us around it into Mississippi, so we won't get stuck and have to wait while the storm nips at our heels."

IN THE BACK, Bryce listened to her, then turned to Troy. "Did you get a good look at the car?"

"No. Just saw the blue light. Why?"

"I wonder what kind of cops they are, why they aren't headed up to help out with the accident?"

"Must be county rather than state troopers."

"Yeah. Maybe so."

Maybe, but why would a Louisiana deputy be leading them into Mississippi? He would feel better if he knew the car was something other than a blue Cadillac. Locasio's having anything to do with this seemed a rather remote possibility, but he decided to have a look anyway.

"I think I'll wander up toward the front, Troy," he said. "If you wouldn't mind letting me out?"

Troy scooted over in the seat and Bryce slid out. He strode quickly up the aisle, pausing to banter a few words with Fred and Betty Lou, then stopped beside the seat occupied by Marge and Sarah Anne.

"Thought I'd stretch my legs a bit and see what's going on up here," he said. "Everything okay?"

In the aisle seat, Marge smiled. "We're fine so far. Sarah Anne hasn't been too happy the way the storm seems to be catching up with us. Thank God these fellas are going to help us keep moving."

"I wondered where they were from. Did you get a look at the car?"

"It wasn't a car. It was a van. Appeared to be black."

"Maybe it's a sheriff's deputy."

He walked on up to where Tillie sat staring out at the

strengthening storm. The big windshield was made in two sections, with the wipers operating independently of each other. The long blade on the driver's side clacked noisily as it slapped rapidly back and forth, while the blade on the right moved more slowly, giving Bryce a bit of difficulty in seeing out.

"Looks like we're coming to an exit," he said. He squinted at a sign indicating U.S. Highway 190.

Tillie studied the map in her hand. "Going east it intersects with Highway 90. Ninety crosses the Pearl River, which is the state line with Mississippi, then goes along the shoreline to Mobile. There must be some road not far along there that leads back to I-10."

Bryce watched as the van with the flashing blue light moved onto the exit. He could now see the vehicle was large and black, not unlike a flower car from a funeral home. The perverseness of the thought brought a grin to his face, along with a realization some of his fellow passengers might take that as a bad omen. He had seen Highway Patrol vans in Tennessee, though none had been black. Whatever branch of law enforcement was involved, he thought, the truck might be used in conjunction with accidents along the waterways. Perhaps its role was to pull a boat trailer.

Feeling a bit better about their prospects, Bryce had started toward his seat when a strong gust broadsided the bus. He grabbed the back of Marge's seat as the big vehicle shuddered.

"Whoa, Nellie," he said, grinning.

Marge frowned. "That felt almost like somebody had run into us."

"We're a big target. The wind could hardly miss us."

She looked toward the window. "It's getting pretty nasty out there. I hope we get back on the main highway before we get blown over."

"No danger of that," he assured her. "I-10 isn't far away. Just hang in there. This bus is a heavyweight. It would take a lot more wind than we're likely to encounter to turn over something this size."

As he made his way toward the back, he wished there were a rear window so he could see the vehicles behind them. Hopefully, if the blue Caddy had been following, Locasio and his buddies had managed to get caught in the wrong lane when Chick unexpectedly eased onto the shoulder of the highway. Feeling a little more upbeat, he paused to dispense smiles and words of encouragement to some of the long-faced, frightened passengers.

One was Clara. "Come on, cheer up," he said. "We're warm and dry in here. I've seen worse storms than this in Madison."

"I suppose so," she said. But her look was skeptical. "One thing's sure, I'll certainly be glad to get back to Madison."

"Look at it this way, you can tell your grandchildren about how you were almost caught in a hurricane down in Louisiana. They'll certainly never see one in Nashville."

"Thank goodness for that," she said, almost managing a smile.

Before she could open her mouth to continue, Bryce had slipped away and disappeared toward the rear of the bus.

33

CLAIRE HOLZMAN sat at the small table in the mobile home and stared at the whirling image on the thirteen-inch TV screen. Where the devil was Ike, she fretted? They had a cell phone in the trailer and another in the truck, but she hadn't been able to get a rise out of him. Sipping at a tall glass of iced tea as she listened to the news reports on Nora's progress, she pondered what to do if he didn't show before long.

Claire had never been in a hurricane, but she had heard and read enough to know a mobile home was not the place to be should one come calling. And that ominously spinning mass on the TV was obviously chugging along a direct path to New Orleans. She was on the far side of the city from the storm's approach, but a hurricane this large could sweep right onto the coast where she sat without so much as a how-do-you-do to New Orleans.

She had almost everything packed and ready to roll. Only the paintings on the wall remained, a couple of beach scenes and a venerable old live oak reaching out with its gnarled and twisted limbs. Ike's easel still sat in the corner by the sink, holding a half-finished pelican perched on a weathered post. She didn't like to move his work until he gave his okay. He could get a little testy at times. But she could take care of that while Ike hitched the trailer to the truck.

A muffled rumble rose from the rear where a gasoline-powered generator did whatever such things did, spit out watts and volts and amperes, she supposed. Claire was aware of the noise only in a subliminal way. Since the engine ran constantly, except for occasional brief periods of maintenance, the sound formed part of the natural background.

Claire and Ike Holzman were certainly cousins if not full-fledged members of the family known as "workampers," nomads who shifted with the wind and followed the beckoning lure of seasonal jobs. Most of them set their compasses according to some rational plan, like mountains in the summer and sunny climes in winter. Not the Holzmans. They were completely free spirits, as unique as their DNA. They moved without rhyme or reason, without plan or pretense, with no clear route or destination in mind. When they decided the time had come for a change of scenery, they would simply hit the road and go wherever the strip of asphalt led them.

Not by accident, there was something of the sixties flower child in them, the utter abandonment, the break with tradition, the yearning for absolute freedom. But their link to that tumultuous era did not cause them to shun traditional creature comforts. While zealously guarding their self-reliance, they equipped their mobile home like a self-contained island. All the modern conveniences were there--stove, refrigerator, microwave, TV, stereo with CD player, laptop computer, cellular telephone. They even had a Global Positioning System satellite navigation device, although neither of them had the slightest care about where they happened to be located on the face of the globe at any particular moment in time.

As the wind began to kick up noticeably, causing the trailer to make strange screaking noises and shudder gently like a frightened animal, Claire heard the sound of a vehicle pulling up on the graveled parking area. She hurried to the door, expecting to see the big red pickup. Instead she found a white patrol car from the county sheriff's force.

A lanky young deputy with long blond hair tossed about by the wind stepped out and frowned at her.

Claire felt a catch in her throat. "Has something happened to Ike?"

"Not that I know of," said Deputy Carl Floyd. He planted his hands firmly against slim hips. "But something's gonna happen to both of you if you don't get this danged trailer out of here pretty soon. Haven't you been listening to the news?"

"I have. But there's not much I can do without Ike's truck to hitch onto this thing."

"Where is he? He can't be out making the rounds today. Everybody's closing down."

"He went into New Orleans this morning. Took a couple of paintings to one of the galleries, then planned to pick up some supplies, including some spare parts for the generator. He should have been back by now."

"Oh, boy," said Deputy Floyd, shaking his head. "I heard on the radio the traffic coming out of there is pure hell."

"You think he's stuck in it?"

"Unless he's found a way to get that pickup airborne, he is."

"What should I do if he doesn't show up soon?" Claire asked.

"Surely he'll make it before long. But if he doesn't, call me and I'll get somebody out here pronto. Write down my cell phone number." He read it off to her.

"Will you be in the area?"

"Yes, ma'am. The sheriff's got me going door-to-door warning everybody around here to leave. He's real worried. He worked over in Pass Christian back in 1969 when Camille hit. Said he tried to get a bunch of people to break up a hurricane party and get out of there, but they just laughed at him. Told him to arrest them if he wanted to. Of course, he couldn't do that. But when Camille blew in, it hurled a wave over the place high as a three-story building. Not a single one survived."

Claire bit at her lower lip. "How much time do we have?"

"An hour or so. The storm surge isn't expected until after dark. But it's gonna get pretty rough before too long. Winds may be strong enough to give this trailer fits by late afternoon."

She folded her arms against the slight chill of the wind gusts. "I sure hope Ike hasn't gotten involved in a fender bender."

"If you're running late, it would probably be best to drive over and park at the high school. They're setting up an emergency shelter there. Even have some school bus drivers on standby to go pick up families, if necessary."

The rain started just as Deputy Floyd pulled out past the large live oak that had modeled for one of Ike's favorite paintings. He turned onto the hard-packed sand of the rural road and disappeared into the cloud-shrouded afternoon. A narrow two-lanes wide, the road came off Highway 90 a few miles to the north, ran past the small plot the Holzmans had rented and continued on to the beach along the Gulf shore.

Claire ducked back inside the mobile home and returned to her table. She kept thinking about those poor people in Pass Christian. She had already seen her share of the aftermath of disaster and wasn't keen on witnessing any more. Growing up as an Air Force brat during the Cold War, she had traveled about various parts of the world where man as well as nature had taken his toll. Rebellion against the life she had led in a tightly-structured military household was one reason she had taken so readily to the unorthodox lifestyle of a headstrong young landscape artist with an unruly ponytail. Even more compelling was the release she'd felt from the strictures of a disappointing career. Claire had graduated from nursing school with visions of making important contributions to the health of her patients. But she quickly learned that nowadays the initials RN usually meant Recording Nonstop. She had only limited time for treating patients. Her chief duties appeared to be shuffling papers and entering endless data in the hospital's records. When Ike proposed, she promptly turned in her resignation, spread her wings, and flew. They were in their late thirties now, married ten years, and she had not regretted one minute.

BRYCE RESUMED his seat next to the window. As he looked out, the trees swayed like tall green dancers and the rain swept over passing vehicles in undulating bursts, propelled by strong gusts of wind. Though still heavy along Highway 90, the traffic didn't seem as bad as on the interstate.

After they had gone a few miles past the Pearl River, the bus abruptly slowed, then turned to the right.

Bryce looked at Troy. "Wonder what we're stopping for?"

Troy craned his neck to see out the right-hand windows. "We're not stopping," he said. "We've just taken another road."

As Bryce looked out, he saw they now traveled a narrow, unpaved road. He turned back to Troy, a puzzled look on his face. "This isn't going to lead us to I-10. We should have taken a left. We're headed toward the ocean."

UP FRONT, Tillie and Chick made the same assessment.

"Where in the world are they headed?" she asked. She slipped her glasses down over narrowed green eyes.

Chick stared ahead. "I don't know. But I don't like the looks of this road."

"Blow your horn and stop," she said. "Let's find out what's going on."

Chick gave a couple of blasts on his air horn, then braked to a stop. Up ahead, the flashing blue light also stopped, then the black van began moving in reverse toward the bus. The vehicle halted just in front of the clacking windshield wipers. Chick opened the door as two men jumped out of the van and ran toward the bus.

To Chick's shocked surprise, he watched as two of the New Jersey "businessmen" they had encountered in Natchez bounded onto the bus.

The younger man shook the water off his large hands and wiped them across his face, then turned to Chick. "Shut the damn door."

Though uncertain what he should do, Chick didn't like the wind blowing all that rain into his bus. He closed the door and looked up at the husky man, a scowl on his dark face.

Tillie glared at the intruder. "What's going on?"

"This," he said, pulling a semi-automatic from his jacket, "is a pistol, lady. And this is a hijacking. Where's the microphone?"

Tillie's eyes widened. Chick stared in silence, still unable to comprehend what was happening. The man looked around and found the mike, then snarled at Chick. "Turn on all the lights in here. I want to be able to see everybody."

After the overhead lights had flashed on, he lifted the microphone.

"Ladies and gentlemen," he began, "we're going to take a short ride and then conduct a little business. Just keep your seats and do what you're told and you won't get hurt. Otherwise, it could get rough. I assure you, this is no toy."

He waved the gun for all to see. Then he turned to the heavyset man who stood on the steps drying his face with a large handkerchief.

"Take out your piece and get up here, Ziggy. Keep an eye on everybody while I deal with Old Black Joe."

Chick bristled at the words.

"Blow your horn, then follow the car," the man said. He pointed the gun at Chick for emphasis.

Chick looked around as the man called Ziggy yelled, "Hey, what the hell!" He bolted down the aisle, heading straight for MacArthur. "Gimme that thing," he said. He snatched a cellular phone from MacArthur's grasp.

"Anybody else got one of those things?" the younger man demanded. He looked around and grabbed one off the seat beside Tillie. Then he glared out at the frightened and helpless passengers. "If you got one, you damn well better hold it up. We find anybody else trying to use a phone, they'll have hell to pay."

34

ON THE BACK seat, Bryce had watched with a shock more pronounced than Tillie's as Locasio's tall frame suddenly materialized at the front of the bus. At first, Bryce sat stunned, unbelieving. Clearly, he had miscalculated. The Mafia hoods had obviously ditched their Cadillac and switched to the black van. With all of the gasps and murmurs coming from the seats around him, he couldn't hear what was being said up front. But as he awaited the next move, he caught a flash of headlights beyond the window. Looking out, he saw a red pickup truck moving slowly past the bus.

Whoever was driving would unlikely be of any help even if he were to stop, Bryce realized. And in this rain, with that blue light flashing up front, he figured the odds extremely long that anyone would take the trouble to stop.

When Locasio's voice came over the speaker, Bryce concluded that his pursuers still had no idea which passenger was Pat Pagano. If they had known, they would have marched back to his seat, forced him to accompany them off the bus and then disappeared into the storm. He had no idea what the "little business" was that they planned to conduct. But if the Vicario enforcer intended to trick him into revealing his identity, Bryce thought, Locasio had better have a really clever scheme up his sleeve.

MARGE SAT close enough to see and hear everything. Watching the man wave his gun in a threatening manner was frightening, but she quickly found herself more incensed than scared. Robbery was the only motive she could imagine. Had they been stalking the Silver Shadows since Natchez, just waiting for an opportunity to strike?

As the younger man turned and gave his orders to the driver,

182

she thought back to Tuesday afternoon at the rest stop, when he had asked her to point out Bryce. She puzzled over why he had specifically asked about Bryce. Obviously Bryce did not know him or his father, if that story about the father's friend had been something more than an imaginative concoction.

"What do you think they're going to do?" Sarah Anne whispered, her eyes wide with fear.

"I wish I knew."

They felt the bus begin to move again as the rain continued to pour and the wind drove the droplets against the windows with the sound of hail.

IN THE FRONT seat across the aisle, Polly and Sadie sat with horror-filled eyes as the two men brandished their weapons and glared out at the passengers they held at bay. The idea of being pursued by a deadly hurricane had been enough to shake everyone to their foundations. And now this. The women cringed beneath the cold stares and held hands as if in an effort to shore up their faltering courage.

Seeing their reaction, Tillie bit her lip and fought back the rage that had begun to seethe inside her. She had managed to cope with Hurricane Nora, but this went beyond her imagination. Torn between fear and outrage, she held herself in check, waiting to see what would happen next.

CLAIRE HOLZMAN slammed the door to shut out the storm as soon as Ike jumped inside, water dripping from sun-browned ears, bushy beard, and a blue cap inscribed "Save the Whales." He grabbed her by the arms, blinking big dark eyes that appeared as wide as an owl's.

"Are you okay?"

She gave him a wan smile. "You're the one I've been worried sick about. Did you have your phone turned off?"

He pulled her to him for a big hug, apologized for the dampness of his T-shirt, then took out a large handkerchief and began to clean the spatter from his hornrims. "The stupid battery went dead on me. I thought I had charged it. Good thing yours still works. I considered stopping to call you, but I was afraid if

I got off the highway I'd never be able to get back on. I never saw such a mess."

"Deputy Carl Floyd came by earlier, warning us to get out of here. He says we can go to a shelter at the high school if necessary."

"I'd just as soon head out of town and keep going," Ike said, knitting his heavy brows into a pronounced V. "I've had about enough of this place."

"I sort of feel the same way."

His face suddenly stretched into a broad grin. "Hey, I almost forgot. How could I?" He patted his shirt pocket, then removed a note pad and slipped out a folded piece of paper. "Got some good news. The Wells Gallery sold two paintings and has a nibble on another. I picked up a nice check. Remind me to call them with a forwarding address."

Claire moved over to switch off the TV. "If we don't get moving, we may not have anything left they can forward to. I've got most everything packed but your easel and those paintings. What do you want to do about them?"

"Just fold the easel up and stash it away. I'll put the paintings with the others. God, it's wet out there."

"I know. Do I need to help you hitch the trailer to the truck?"

"I'll handle it. No need for both of us to drown. Oh, I meant to tell you about the bus."

"What bus?"

"Up the road a way, not far off Highway 90. I passed this big red and white tour bus. I think it had Tennessee plates. Looked like it was full of people. I don't know if they had gotten lost, or what. There was this black van in front of it with a portable blue light on top. Wasn't one of the sheriff's. He doesn't have any black vans."

"Maybe it was D-O-T."

"I don't know. They'll probably have to pull into a field somewhere to turn it around."

Claire crossed her arms and grasped her shoulders as wind gusts pummelled the trailer. "Put on your poncho and go hitch us up, Ike."

AS HE STEPPED out into the driving wind and rain, Ike

thought back to his childhood in Haight-Ashbury, where horizontal squalls would come calling on short notice, battering the white houses that camped along the steep streets like lines of pot-smoking hippies. Ike's mother had divorced his father in the mid-sixties, taking the boy to raise in the counter-culture of San Franciso's peace and love generation. He had somehow survived and made his way through art school, then headed east in search of those quaint New England scenes his mother had described in her more lucid moments. Urged on by a wealthy patron, he had succeeded beyond his wildest dreams. But success, he found, quickly led to an unwanted feeling, one of being corralled, hemmed in, restrained like a caged songbird. Breaking the chains had led to the wandering odyssey that he and Claire still pursued.

AS JOHNNY Barbarino, dressed in the yellow poncho, drove the van down the narrow road, he dodged a succession of small branches that had blown off the trees. The sandy surface was littered with leaves and clumps of Spanish moss torn loose by the wind. He slowed to a crawl when they came to a line of massive old live oaks on the left. Some of them had long limbs that reached out and down to the ground like octopus tentacles.

"This is it," he said. "I haven't been over here in a good while, but those trees are the landmark. There should be an old trail...there it is."

"What's back in there?" Joe Blow was not happy about playing around in this storm. He had never been this close to a hurricane before.

"There's an open field beyond the tree line. The property belongs to a friend of the family. We used to come out here and camp, go fishing, swim, get drunk, you name it."

"You sure there's nobody around?"

"I called to check before I left. The place is still vacant. There's some people with a mobile home down the road, but they should have got the hell out of here long before now."

"What about that red truck?"

The Barber shrugged. "May have been checking to see if everybody down this way was gone."

He drove through the opening in the trees and followed the trail on out into the field, then stopped to wait for the bus to roll up behind him. "Okay," he said, pulling the slicker up over his head. "Let's make a run for it."

WITH AN occasional glance back at the cold steel of the automatic, Chick had followed the black van with grave misgivings. They took a turn for the worse as he saw the vehicle head between the trees. If his bus got mired up in the sand, he'd never get turned around and out of this godforsaken place.

He started to object but cringed as the younger man drew back the pistol as if to aim a blow at his head.

"Follow the damned van," the man said.

Chick drove out into the middle of the field and parked behind the flashing light, which was abruptly extinguished. Looking around, he saw the visibility had become so poor the trees were little more than a blur in the distance. He opened the door on command and two men jumped in, one the yellow-slickered "officer," the other a short, wiry man with a sharp nose who gingerly carried a plastic bag.

LOCASIO PICKED up the mike again and let his gaze slowly drift about the sea of frightened faces. They were scared shitless, he gloated. Good. That should make them easy as putty to pull or push or twist as he chose. He held the mike to his mouth.

"Here's the deal, folks. My friend Joe here has a little gift for you. Show it to us, Joe."

Joe Blow reached into the plastic bag and lifted out a large block of white material with a small device attached with copper wire. He held it up for everyone to see.

"He's going to take it back and place it under a seat in the middle of the bus," Locasio said, his voice matter-of-fact. "I wouldn't advise you to mess with it. You see, it's a big hunk of plastic explosive. The Army calls it C-4. Maybe some of you gents have heard of the stuff. It packs enough force to turn this bus into scrap metal. I won't say what it would do to anyone inside. Just let your imagination run wild."

Gasps went up from the passengers.

As Joe returned to the front, Locasio held out his hand. "Give me the other gadget."

"Be careful," Joe said. He handed over a small plastic box. "It's pretty damned sensitive. I didn't have enough warning. It's sort of a make-do job."

Locasio held up the device, which had a small metal rod protruding from one end and a toggle switch on the other. He spoke into the microphone. "This is an electronic detonator. One little flip of this switch and we're all history."

He paused to let that have the desired effect, which was manifested in a chorus of moans, a few whimpers and a new wave of horrified facial expressions.

"Now I hope it won't be necessary to flip that switch, but there's something we need from you. We have reason to believe there's a guy among you whose real name is Pat Pagano. We would like Mr. Pagano to stand up and identify himself, then we'll send you on your way. If Mr. Pagano should fail to do that, my friends and I will leave the bus, then we will flip this little switch."

He held up the detonator again. The Silver Shadows began to look around at each other, staring in wonder.

35

Troy TURNED and whispered to Bryce. "That's the wildest thing I ever heard of."

"Yeah," Bryce said. And though he appeared calm on the outside, he was churning wildly on the inside. He had not anticipated anything remotely like this. But was the threat for real, or just a bluff? He had concluded earlier that they would not purposely harm anybody else just to get at him. Now it appeared they were prepared to take forty-four other lives, if Locasio was to be believed.

Bryce simply could not bring himself to accept that they would follow through on such an inhuman threat. He knew Tony Vicario would never approve of it. The old Don had insisted that no harm come to innocent civilians. According to what he had heard, the only Mafia mass murder had been the St. Valentine's Day Massacre in 1929 when members of Al Capone's gang had killed seven rival mobsters.

These were Italian-Americans, not Middle Eastern terrorists. The prospect was beyond his imagination. But could Locasio be a rogue elephant?

What if he were wrong?

IN THE MIDDLE of the bus, Hamilton MacArthur exhibited a look of dismay. He also found the whole scenario unbelievable, but the plastic bomb had been placed directly beneath his seat. Was one of the men on this bus actually named Pat Pagano? he wondered. Who was Pat Pagano? The name had a vaguely familiar ring, but he couldn't remember where he might have heard it.

He wondered if someone among them would actually stand up and admit to being the wanted man. And, more imperative, did these people really intend to blow up the bus if Pagano were not identified?

Now that his fate was suddenly and inextricably linked to that of his fellow passengers, he found his perspective somewhat altered. He was no longer the privileged outsider looking in. All around him others experienced the same fear, the same dread, the same apprehension over what fate might have in store for them. And the same feeling of helplessness.

He had always prided himself on being an effective agent of compromise in the corporate boardroom, but when he tried to think of some way he might defuse this situation, he drew a blank.

MacArthur had discovered humility.

MARGE WAS having thoughts in somewhat the same vein, though a more disturbing path of reasoning had begun to insinuate itself into her mind. She recalled those strange mood shifts she had observed in Bryce, his inquiring about Pauline when she was talking at Gloucester House with this man who now held them captive, and the incident at the rest area, when the same man approached her as to where he might find Bryce. Was there something here more than mere coincidence?

After a short span of silence, during which no one rose to identify himself as Pat Pagano, she saw the young thug reach into his pocket and pull out a medallion with a star-studded ribbon attached. He held it up next to the microphone.

"Know what this is?" he asked. "It's the Congressional Medal of Honor. On the back it reads, 'Sgt. Patrick O. Pagano, December 22, 1944, Bastone, Belgium.' You'd think a man with that kind of bravery wouldn't be afraid to admit who he is."

Marge's heart nearly stopped. Bryce had admitted that he fought in the Battle of the Bulge at Bastogne, Belgium.

As Locasio stood beside the woman on the front seat with *Ellis* on her badge, she squirmed and leaned forward. "Why do you want him? What do you intend to do with him?"

"That's none of your damned business," Locasio said. He swung his arm, catching the side of her face with the back of his large hand.

A red welt rose on her cheek as she tucked her head, raising a protective arm.

The driver shouted, "Leave the lady alone!"

"Keep that nigger quiet," Locasio ordered.

Using the butt of his gun, Ziggy Ferrante struck the black man in the head.

As the driver fell back, dazed, a man leaped to his feet a few seats back. "That's enough. I'm Pagano."

Locasio took a few steps down the aisle, reached over and shoved the man with the *Scott* badge back into his seat. "Sit down, old man. You're too tall."

From across the aisle, an attractive woman looked up at him with a frown. "And you, sir, are a coward," she said. "With that gun, you think it's great sport to push elderly people around, don't you?"

Locasio scowled as he read *Hunter* on her badge and drew back his hand.

From the rear of the bus, a voice boomed out, "Don't touch her!"

The words were so cold and threatening that Locasio was struck with shocked surprise. He flinched, dropping his hand.

The man standing beside the window in back spoke again. "I am Pat Pagano. You have no quarrel with the rest of these people. Let them go."

As he stared, Locasio slowly broke into a grin. "Mr. Reynolds, right?"

"Right."

Locasio turned to his companions. "I do believe we've found our man."

Then he looked back at the passengers, his jaw tightening, his eyes cold and menacing. "I want you people to listen very carefully to what I have to say. You're damned lucky to get out of here alive. When they ask you what happened, tell them you were hijacked by robbers. They'll also ask you to describe us. Well, you better be as vague as hell. Just remember, I have a list with everybody's name and address on it. If you get blabbermouthed, we'll come after you. You can count on it. And you won't like what we have in mind, I promise."

Looking around, he spotted an empty box on the floor that had held somebody's lunch. He leaned down, picked it up and motioned to Ferrante. "All right," he said into the microphone, baring his teeth like a dog ready to bite, "just so you won't have to tell a lie, you will drop your money and jewelry in this box as you pass by. Now get the hell out of here...all of you. And fast. Move it!"

"In this rain?" someone asked.

"Unless you'd like to die on the bus," Locasio said. "You can take cover under those trees over by the road."

IN THE BACK, Bryce watched Sarah Anne and Fred forcibly push Marge up the aisle. Then Troy turned toward him, a look of fear and anxiety in his eyes. But there was determination in his voice. "I'll stay with you," he said.

"No, you won't." Now that Bryce had taken the ultimate step, he was devoid of indecision. "You've got a wife at home to look after. No one's depending on me. Don't worry about it."

Troy hesitated, then reached over and gave Bryce a fierce hug. He moved slowly out at the end of the line. Bryce was so touched by the gesture that he had to blink his eyes to stem the rise of tears. But he broke into a grin as he saw Troy pointedly ignore the box in the big man's hand.

WALKING THROUGH the wind and rain was difficult at best. Some of the women sobbed hysterically. Troy and MacArthur, along with a few others, including Tillie and Sarah Anne, managed to herd everyone over to the cluster of trees. A few had raincoats, some umbrellas, which did little good in the fierce wind. Most huddled together behind the large tree trunks, on the side away from the storm's approach, trying to eke out as much shelter as possible. Unfortunately, the sparse leaves of the live oaks formed a canopy that was about as effective as a sieve.

Betty Lou and Fred grasped Marge's arms as she stood out in front of the others, eyes fixed on the bus.

Unsure if there were tears, for the rain pelted her face unmercifully, washing away whatever might have been there, Marge could hardly bear not knowing what was happening inside that bus. "They're going to kill him, aren't they?" Her voice was a mixture of bitterness and sadness.

"Let's wait and see what happens," Betty Lou said. She did not look hopeful.

AS SOON AS the last passenger had stumbled off the bus, Locasio walked toward the back. Bryce remained standing at his seat. The other men stayed at the front, watching through the windows at the retreating seniors. Locasio held the detonator in one hand, cradled the automatic in the other. He stopped a few feet from Bryce. He grinned and held up the bomb-triggering device.

"I'll bet you wondered whether I would really use this, didn't you?" he asked.

"It crossed my mind."

"Well, you can be damned sure I would have. Boots Minelli died this morning. It might have been helpful to send a load of church people along with him." The laugh that followed had a hollow sound.

Bryce frowned. His first impulse demanded that he snap back. *You're nothing but a cruel, heartless bastard* immediately came to mind. But the previous night at Preservation Hall had been one of his rare concessions to impulse. Everything boiled down now to a game of matching wits. He knew such a reply would hardly gain him any points.

"How did Boots find me?" he asked. The question had been tormenting him ever since that shocking confrontation in the drugstore parking lot Monday morning.

"He tracked you down through that bank in Switzerland. Got some hackers to break the bank's codes. Then he knocked off the guy who ran that mail drop in the English Channel and found your name and address. But he was too damned tight-lipped to tell me what name you were using."

Bryce had heard about the murder on the Isle of Man. He never connected it with the Mafia, though. Recalling his brief conversation with FBI Agent Burger, he asked another question that concerned him. "Boots didn't know about my move to Portland after the trial, did he?"

Locasio laughed. "Hell, yes. We got a man on the inside at the Justice Department."

That shocked him. But now Bryce knew what he had to do. He looked across at Locasio with all the sincerity he could muster. He spoke in his most convincing manner.

"Then you know I'm a wealthy man. I've got enough money in that Swiss bank to take care of both of us the rest of our lives. All you need is my signature on a piece of paper, and you're a rich man beyond your fondest dreams."

As he spoke, he reached one hand up and pulled a pen from his shirt pocket. Locasio listened with a disparaging look. Obviously he considered this plea the final act of a desperate, doomed man.

"I've got some bank transfer forms in my bag," Bryce said, pulling the cap off his pen.

He counted on the young hood pausing to consider the possibilities. Maybe think he could get Bryce's signature, then kill him. It appeared to be working. A grin began to tug at the corners of Locasio's mouth.

With a move so quick Locasio was caught completely off guard, Bryce raised the pen and pressed a white plunger. A stream of fiery pepper spray squirted squarely into the mobster's startled face. As the burning irritant struck his eyes, Locasio let out a guttural scream of pain. He threw up his hands, dropping the pistol and the detonator.

Bryce had prepared for this moment from the time the Mafiosi had entered the bus. First he had reached down to remove the spray pen from his carryon bag. Then he had turned to the window, where lettering at the base instructed:

Emergency Exit
Lift This Bar
Push To Open

Carefully and unobtrusively, he had shifted the metal bar, which secured the window at the bottom. Now he jumped onto the rear bench. He bent forward to grab the seat-back in front with his right hand. He swung the window out with his left foot, steadied himself with his left hand on the edge of the window. He swung his right leg through the opening, pushing off with both hands.

He felt a sharp pain in his back as he scraped against the

edge of the window before falling straight down. The drop was about six feet. Remembering his old airborne training, he flexed his knees as he landed, rolling onto his side when his knees buckled.

Despite the cushioning effect of the wet sand, the impact gave him a severe jolt. He might have been dazed, but the driving downpour soaked him immediately. His head quickly cleared.

As he pushed himself up, he felt a needle-like pain in his right ankle. But with the adrenaline pumping, and the knowledge that at any moment someone could lean out the window and start firing, he managed to overcome the pain in both ankle and back.

He started running as fast as he could. He tried to keep to the rear of the bus, where he would present a less visible target.

As they drove into the field, he had noticed a line of pine trees jutting out at an angle from the road. They appeared to be surrounded by some sort of bushy undergrowth. If he could just make the tree line, there should be enough cover to hide from his pursuers. What he might do when the full force of the hurricane hit was a question he would defer to the future.

If he had one.

INSIDE THE bus, Joe Blow, Ferrante and The Barber began racing toward the back as Locasio screamed like a wounded tiger. Seeing Reynolds disappear through the window, they came to a sudden halt. Momentarily immobilized by shock and uncertainty, they stared wildly at each other.

Joe, who was closest to Locasio, finally collected his wits and yelled, "Go get the bastard!"

The other two turned and started toward the door. They never made it.

As he rubbed his face and squirmed in pain, Locasio blindly kicked his foot against the detonator. He did not trip the switch, but he jarred loose the wires that Joe Blow had been unable to secure as well as he would have liked.

The result was catastrophic.

36

TIME SEEMED caught in a cosmic vacuum. Unsure how long he had been running or how far he had made it from the bus, Bryce leaned forward to wedge his body against the wind gusts. Pain had begun to inhibit his pace. The pine thicket remained at least thirty yards ahead.

Suddenly a tremendous explosion tore through the air. The roar deafened him, drowning out the noise of the storm. Heat struck his back like the rush of air from a blast furnace. The shock wave sent him sprawling. He almost choked at the acrid odor of burning flesh and charred fabric. For one fleeting moment, as he fell, the terrible smells took him back in time. Back to an equally horrific scene at his home on Long Island when he had endured the agonizing cries of his dying sons. The memory died as his face slammed into the sand. Bits of debris mingled with the mass of raindrops that showered over him.

The blast succeeded where the leap from the bus window had failed. It stunned him. He lay on the soaked ground for some indeterminate time, then rolled over and slowly sat up. Looking toward the bus, he could see only flames licking around remnants of the frame. Smoke, both billows of black and columns of white where intense heat had turned the rain into steam, swirled about in the blustery wind.

His ankle felt as though caught in a vise. His back could have felt no worse had he blistered it lying much too long in the sun. Yet despite the pain and the watery lashing he took, he sat in the drenched field and slowly looked about, marveling that he was still alive, wondering if he really deserved to be, considering what his presence had done to the innocent members of the Lovely Lane Silver Shadows.

BRYCE'S FELLOW passengers were far enough away and so thoroughly battered by the approaching hurricane that they were somewhat distracted from the physical effects of the explosion. What they felt mostly was a shaking of the ground, almost like an earthquake. But they received a full dose of its visible and psychological aftermath. Most watched in stunned silence as the big bus disintegrated before their eyes.

Not Marge.

Fred tried to restrain her when she started to bolt as soon as the debris had settled. "You can't go over there," he shouted above the roar of wind and rain and flame.

She pulled away from him. "I think I saw something move behind the bus just before it exploded."

She began running in that general direction with Fred close behind her. Troy and MacArthur quickly took up the chase. She looked about frantically, dodging pieces of sheet metal, torn bits of luggage. As a severed hand lying on the ground nearly gagged her, she heard a voice to one side.

"Over here!"

She spotted a bedraggled figure resting on the ground and knew at once it was Bryce. Darting over to him, she knelt at his side, took his outstretched hand and stared at him. His face appeared lined with pain. Otherwise he looked intact.

"Thank God you're alive," she said. The tears streamed now, though it was difficult to separate them from the drenching rain.

"I think I sprained my ankle when I jumped out the window," he said. "I don't know what I did to my back."

Fred had bent down over him and moved around to look at his back. "Your shirt's torn and bloody. Looks like the skin has been peeled back. You need a doctor."

Bryce finally mustered a weak smile. "I'm sure one will be along any minute."

MacArthur had arrived, Troy just behind him, puffing from the exertion. "Were those guys still on the bus?" Troy asked.

"I doubt they could have gotten out." Bryce looked around slowly.

MacArthur gazed at the smoldering hulk. "I don't see how anybody could have survived." Then he turned back to Bryce. "While I was huddled under those trees, I remembered where I had heard the name Pat Pagano. It was in the stories about the trial of the Vicario crime family in New York. Must have been eight or ten years ago. Pagano had worked as an investment advisor for the family corporation. He was the chief government witness against them."

Bryce gave a heavy sigh. "You have a good memory."

Troy looked incredulous. "Mafia?"

Bryce nodded.

"As I recall the story," MacArthur said, "Pagano wasn't a member of the Mafia. He had just been hired to handle investments."

Listening in silence, Marge now saw how it all made sense. Those strange looks, the odd reactions. Bryce had recognized those men for who they were back in Natchez. He had been living with that knowledge ever since, yet he never flinched. And he had admitted who he was to save her from that horrible man.

"I remembered something, too," she said. She still held his hand in both of hers. "Keith told me a little about the Battle of the Bulge. He said some real heroes came out of it. With that Medal of Honor, I'm sure you were one. You were very brave back then. You still are."

"I've also been very foolish," he said. Then he gave them a brief account of how he had innocently fallen into the Mafia trap, resulting in the death of his sons and his wife's demoralization. He was interrupted at one point by a loud whumping noise as the black van's gas tank erupted and a new display of flames danced beyond the bus's funeral pyre.

When Bryce had finished, MacArthur responded with a sympathetic frown. "You did nothing worse than any of us would have done. I daresay we would all have jumped at such an opportunity."

"But I should have gotten out as soon as I fully understood what I was into," Bryce said.

Fred stared at him. "If those men were sent to kill you, what happens now?"

"That's the sixty-four-thousand-dollar question."

Troy straightened up. "Maybe we ought to go check and see if any of them survived."

"Good idea," Fred said. "I wish we could get Bryce some

medical help, but I didn't see any sign of life on the way in here. Marge, you stay with him while we take a quick look around."

As they moved away, Bryce turned to her, his face drawn. "I'm sorry I didn't turn out to be the man you thought I was. I lied last night about that gun, too. I picked it up when I saw three of those hoods start across the street toward Preservation Hall. I had it in my mind to shoot them. I'm still not sure if I really would have, but thank God you stopped me."

As disheveled as a water-logged scarecrow, her jacket and pants and everything beneath soaked to the skin, hair plastered down around her face, Marge felt no better than she looked. But she summoned all her courage and moved close to him, placing one arm carefully across his shoulders to shelter his injured back from the storm.

"You aren't the only one who's been hiding from reality," she said. She struggled to find the right words to verbalize the torment in her heart. "I have a secret, too. One that I've been running from for years. I wasn't really ill last night. Not from what I ate for dinner, anyway. I know Troy told you something about my problems with Herbert Hunter, but neither he nor Betty Lou knows the real story."

She told him about her brother and how it had left deep scars on her life, and how Herb Hunter had tormented her with knowledge of the secret.

"I don't care what happened in your past," she said. "I know the real you is the man I've come to respect these past few days. I would hope you could somehow overlook my tainted past and–"

"You aren't responsible for what your brother turned out to be," Bryce said. "I know exactly what you've been going through. And I think we've both suffered from the same mindset. We've been playing games with ourselves. When you're a private type of person, as we are, you tend to internalize things. You feel terribly vulnerable. Instead of opening up and confiding in someone who might help you see there are other ways to cope, you lock your troubles away inside and begin to play games with your mind. It's easy to psyche yourself out, then get locked into a pattern."

Marge knew she had failed at trying to fight her debilitating dilemma alone. Perhaps he was right. Surely they needed each other. That was the message, wasn't it? She smiled through the tears. "My guardian angel must have sent you."

"I'm not too sure about that," he said. "I'm afraid my problems with the Vicario family have only come to a temporary standstill, not a final solution."

As he flinched, Marge realized her arm had brushed against the raw skin on his back.

"I'm sorry," she said. "We've got to get you out of this mess somehow."

37

IKE HOLZMAN started to make the dash from the trailer to his truck when a loud rumble boomed somewhere to the north. Thunder first came to mind, though he had seen no lightning. As close as the noise had to be, he knew it should have been preceded by a slashing, fiery streak through the sky.

Then, as the rumbling continued for a few moments, sounding as though it were compounding in waves, he realized what he had heard was an explosion.

A big one.

Nearby.

Reaching the truck, he scampered into the cab and pulled out his handkerchief again. The poncho didn't help much where glasses were concerned. Once he had them reasonably dry, he pushed his face toward the windshield and stared northward. He saw a slight reddish tint to the sky ahead. He thought he detected smoke, as well, though he couldn't be sure because of the tenacious sweep of the rain.

He pulled the truck in front of the trailer, got out and went to work. Attempting to maneuver in the midst of the storm made it nearly intolerable, but he tugged and pushed and fought and cursed until he had truck and trailer married together.

Claire came flying out in her yellow poncho like a dwarfed version of Big Bird. She jumped into the truck and looked around at Ike with the pinched face she wore during moments of alarm.

"Where did that thunderbolt come from? It shook the trailer."

"That was no thunderbolt." His voice mirrored his concern. "It was an explosion, apparently just up the road. I thought about that bus, but...I don't know what it could have been."

He eased the mobile home out past the big live oak and turned onto the road. A tree had blown over a couple of hundred feet north of them, partially blocking their path, but Ike was able to ease around it. He continued at a slow pace, dodging the litter Nora's reaching tentacles had scattered about indiscriminately. They had gone no more than half a mile and were just passing an opening in the trees when Claire shouted:

"Ike, stop!"

He jammed on the brakes but they had already moved beyond the gap. "What is it?"

"Back up. I think I saw a fire."

When he had maneuvered back to where they could get a clear view, both of them saw it, the dim outlines of a large frame mingled with scattered tongues of flame and a smoky haze that seemed to swirl in agitation from the gusts of wind.

"Oh, God," Claire said. "You don't suppose—"

Ike turned into the opening and drove out along the trail toward the remains of the bus. When he saw someone waving, he pulled up and stopped. Claire was already out before he had his brakes set.

"What happened?" she asked the bedraggled looking woman who stood beside a man sitting on the ground.

"He injured his ankle and his back when he jumped out of the bus. Can we get him out of the rain?"

"Let me check him." Claire bent down for a look. "I'm a nurse."

The man swiveled his head to look at her. "You're an angel in yellow, as far as I'm concerned."

She checked the peeled skin, then shook her head. "You'll think angel when I start patching that up. It'll be painful, but I don't see anything seriously wrong." She looked around at her husband, who had just walked up. "Let's get him inside the trailer. I'll break out the first aid kit."

"What happened to the others?" Ike asked. He bent down to help the man to his feet. "It looked like the bus was loaded when I passed it."

"Most of them are under the trees over there," the woman said. She pointed toward the line of live oaks. "I'm Marge Hunter and this is Bryce Reynolds. We're with a church group of senior citizens."

"Anybody else hurt?"

"Not from the bomb," Bryce said. "The driver got bashed in the head, and I'm sure the others are totally miserable."

Ike stared in disbelief as he balanced Bryce on his good leg. "Bomb?"

"There were four hijackers inside when it went off. Some of our people went looking–"

"Hey, who's that?" a man called out as he and his companions came charging out of the gloom toward the headlights.

"We've got some help," Marge said, almost smiling now. "She's a nurse."

After everyone was introduced, Claire pulled one of Bryce's arms around her shoulder to help support him. "Let's get inside."

They boosted Bryce up the low steps and got him into the mobile home. Marge joined them, but the three men remained outside in the rain. "You guys come on in," Ike said. "Don't worry about the water. This thing will dry out."

With the lights turned on, they looked like shipwrecked sailors pulled from the briny depths. After they got Bryce into a chair, Claire pointed to the small dry erase board by the door.

"That's Deputy Floyd's number, Ike. Call him on the cell phone and tell him to send some school buses. He said they had drivers on standby to rescue folks." She looked around at Marge. "How many people do you have?"

"Forty-five in all. Did you find anybody else, Fred?"

"Not alive."

Claire dug into one drawer for towels and another for her first aid kit as the others watched Ike make the telephone call.

"CARL, THIS is Ike Holzman. You're going to find this hard to believe, but we just found a busload of senior citizens marooned in the rain, off the road about half a mile north of our place."

"What fool bus driver went down that road?" the deputy asked.

"I don't know the details, but the bus is blown all to hell."

"Blown? By the wind?"

"A bomb, they said. Look, Carl, there's forty-five old folks out in this God-awful storm. Claire said you had some school buses on standby. We need them right away."

"Anybody badly hurt?"

"No, just scratches. A sprained ankle. Claire's taking care of it."

"A bomb." The tone of the officer's voice said it all. It was, indeed, unbelievable. "We'll be there soon as possible, Ike. May take twenty minutes or so. Tell 'em to hang in there."

Ike switched off the phone. "Twenty minutes or so."

MacArthur had dried his face and blotted his sandy hair. "Fred and Troy and I talked this over on the way back," he said, draping the towel Claire had given him around his neck. He looked across at Ike. "You people have been very kind, but we have a bit of a problem we need your help with. I think the less you know about it, the better off we'll all be. You see, Bryce here got innocently involved with some rather unsavory characters. In order to protect him, we need to be careful what is said about that explosion."

"What do you want us to do?" Ike asked.

"Tell the truth, basically, just as you did on the phone. How you found us, that we mentioned a bomb. Just don't speculate on anything else. And don't mention Bryce's name, that he was injured."

Ike's ready grin was that of a schemer. "I was raised in a climate that frowned on collaboration with the law. Personally, I don't have any of those hang-ups. But you can count on our discretion."

"If anybody wants to ask us any questions," said Claire, "they had better do it before early in the morning. As soon as this storm abates, we're on the road to God knows where."

Bryce looked around at them and wished that his mother could have been there. How many times had she told him that people were basically good and had an innate desire to help one another? Still, it involved a risk that he was not sure they should bear.

Pulling on a blue knit shirt that Ike had brought him, Bryce felt the heavy hand of fate on his shoulder. "I don't know what I've done to deserve all your help. It's really sort of overwhelming. But don't do anything that might put yourselves in jeopardy. The police will be asking lots of questions. They may bring in the FBI."

"You're in southern Mississippi," Ike said. "You will be dealing with the local sheriff and his deputies. A bombed out bus and...you said hijackers? That will get their attention. But they're short on manpower. Right now everyone is concentrating on this hurricane that's just down the road. They won't have a chance to do anything about this bus until Nora moves on. You're from Tennessee, right? I'd find another bus as soon as possible and get your folks out of here and back home."

MacArthur pulled the towel from around his neck and laid it on the sink. "I think we're reading from the same script. Fred and I plan to approach the police, or sheriff, as you say, and volunteer to answer their questions. We'll plead that the others are too distraught and should be given dry clothes and fed and bedded down. We'll ask Chick Townes to arrange another bus for us and head for Nashville at the first opportunity. Meanwhile, we want to keep Bryce out of sight."

"What about the other thirty-nine people?" Bryce asked. "They heard what that hood said. And they heard me get up and say I was the man he was looking for."

38

IKE LOOKED around as he headed for the truck. "We need to get everyone over toward the road. I don't think it would be a good idea to bring those school buses into this field. I'm holding my breath till we get this trailer out of here."

Fred suggested that Marge stay with Bryce, but she wanted to be on hand when his fate was discussed with the others. After Bryce assured them he didn't need a baby sitter, they trudged back out into the storm wearing plastic bags Claire Holzman had given them to ward off some of the downpour. Ike shifted the truck into reverse and backed down the trail to the opening near the road.

The weary, demoralized Silver Shadows huddled together like cattle beneath the trees, some looking as forlorn as motherless calves. Those who could had instinctively offered consolation to others. Clara and Horace clustered around Sadie, attempting to shield her from the worst of the storm. Claire moved among them, checking out the worst cases and offering words of comfort and hope. Help was on the way. She pressed her fingers gingerly on Chick's face and decided nothing was broken. Apparently he suffered only a large bruise and a king-size headache.

"Bryce Reynolds jumped out a window before the explosion," Fred explained when he had everyone's attention, or at least those with enough alertness to listen. "He's got some scratches and a sprained ankle, but he's okay otherwise. The sheriff is on the way with some school buses to get us back to safety and shelter. However, there's a problem we need your help with. Hamilton MacArthur wants to make a suggestion."

MacArthur resembled some weird alien from another planet with the plastic bag seeming to cover an elongated head, but he spoke with force and authority. "All four men who held us hostage apparently died when their bomb accidentally exploded. They robbed us of our money and jewelry, and that's the way they wanted to be remembered. I could only speculate on why they were looking for that man Fred Scott and Bryce Reynolds claimed to be. But I'm sure Fred and Bryce saved our lives by what they did. And therein lies the problem.

"The ringleader said Fred was too tall, which means Bryce must have been about the right size. If word were to get out, through the sheriff or the media, that Bryce Reynolds said he was the man they were after, whoever sent those men would likely accept it as the truth. They might dispatch more vicious thugs looking for Bryce. There's no telling what might happen. I think it is up to us to protect him. I suggested, and Fred agrees—"

"So do I!" Marge Hunter shouted.

"—that we should say nothing about their looking for anyone. Our only explanation for what happened should be the robbery. They threatened us with a bomb if we didn't do whatever they demanded, then they took our money and our jewelry. They probably intended to take our bus and abscond with all of our belongings. Fred and I will volunteer to speak for the group. Hopefully the authorities will let the rest of you get some well-deserved rest."

"Does everybody understand?" Fred asked. "Don't forget the threat they made to come after us. Those men won't, obviously, but they're sure to have friends back wherever they came from. Are we all agreed on this?"

There were some mumbles and nods. The only disagreement came from Tillie Ellis.

"You two can be the spokes-men," she said. "I will be the spokes-lady."

Fred quickly took her aside to impress upon her the importance of adhering to the party line. He was still talking to her when a car with flashing blue lights appeared in the road behind them, followed by two yellow school buses.

AS THE SOAKED, shivering and bedraggled Silver Shadows were herded aboard the buses, Deputy Carl Floyd cornered Ike Holzman.

"What the hell happened here?"

Ike pointed to the smoldering carcass of the late Nova Tours bus. "They said some hijackers commandeered their bus and robbed them, then forced them off. The guys must have accidentally set off their bomb." He turned to Fred, MacArthur, and Tillie. "These people over here are the leaders of the group. They can fill you in on the details."

"You folks go get in my car," Floyd said. "Lemme take a look at the mess, then we'll get out of here. Any investigation will have to wait till later. That nasty gal Nora is getting too close for comfort."

As Ike walked with him through the downpour, Floyd could feel the gusts getting stronger. He leaned into the wind, wandering through the scattered remnants of what had once been suitcases stuffed with clothing and souvenirs. Closer to the bus, bits of shattered glass, mangled seats and other torn and twisted pieces of metal lay strewn about. Floyd almost tripped on one rectangular object. When he kicked it over, he saw the destination sign that said "Goin' Places."

"I bet they sure didn't realize they were goin' to Hell," he said with a look of disbelief. "It couldn't be any more devastating down there."

As a matter of fact, it wasn't too different than the aftermath of a tornado, something he'd had the misfortune of witnessing on more than one occasion. The destruction was incredible.

"What happened to the hijackers?" he asked suddenly, already guessing the answer after seeing what looked like a leg torn from its socket.

"They were apparently on the bus when it blew," Ike said. "I believe that MacArthur fellow said it was four men."

"Damn." Floyd stretched the word into two syllables as they reached the blackened frame. "Anybody who was in there sure didn't survive."

THE WINDS HAD reached dangerously close to hurricane force as Deputy Floyd drove toward the high school. After introducing himself as the retired president of an insurance company—it turned out Floyd's mother owned one of the firm's policies–Hamilton MacArthur gave the sanitized version of what had happened, starting with the bus being lured off the interstate by a bogus policeman.

"What did they do with the bomb?" Carl Floyd asked.

"Put it under the seat where I was sitting," said MacArthur. "That was a scary thing. They threatened to blow us up if we didn't do everything they demanded."

"It may be un-Christian to put it this way," Tillie said, "but I think those horrid men got what they deserved."

"We'll probably have a devil of a time identifying them," said the deputy. He was already dreading the inevitable return to the scene of the tragedy. "Maybe the license plate on the van will help."

THE HIGH SCHOOl gymnasium resembled the casualty ward in a military field hospital. Rows of canvas cots had been set up at one end of the hardwood floor. Many of the Silver Shadows rested beneath blankets provided appropriately by a team from UMCOR, the United Methodist Church's disaster relief agency. One of the first on the scene, there to provide comfort to victims of Nora's expected devastation, the team had not counted on a bombing incident adding to the ranks.

A local Methodist minister was among the volunteer workers and arranged two emergency calls at Fred's request. One was made to Dr. Peter Trent in Madison, offering assurance to worried families that everyone was safe. The other went to the headquarters of Nova Tours. After Chick had given a brief explanation of the problem, his boss promised to dispatch the standby bus immediately. Two drivers, one a company official, would alternate on the journey, putting them on the Gulf Coast the following morning. The management representative would remain to assist law enforcement officials in their investigation.

Bryce had changed into a dry outfit of Ike Holzman's during the ride into town. Remaining with him in the trailer, Marge had donned one of Claire's housecoats. They found the high school entrance sheltered by a canopy.

"I doubt it'll still be here in the morning," Ike said.

But it allowed Claire, Marge and Bryce to rush into the

building without getting soaked again. While Claire put her nursing talents to work with the others, Marge and Bryce sat in folding chairs near the cots, drank strong black coffee and talked about their beleaguered pasts.

After hot showers in the team dressing rooms, Fred, Tillie and MacArthur donned ill-fitting but dry clothing provided by a local thrift store. They were then ushered into the music room and directed to chairs facing the school band director's desk, now occupied by Sheriff Andrew Cooper. He was a burly man with a double chin who attempted to compensate by squeezing himself into a tan uniform at least a size too small. The resulting discomfort gave him a frown that most people took for the skepticism of a professional cynic.

After brief introductions, Andy Cooper looked across the desk. "I expected the worst out of this hurricane, but what happened to you folks adds a disturbing new dimension to it."

His audience of three listened in polite silence. He wondered if they might be suffering still from the shock of their harrowing experience. Deputy Floyd had reported all he knew about the situation, which wasn't much. Cooper had talked with Ike Holzman as well. He'd never understood people who looked and dressed like weirdoes, but the beatnik artist seemed to be a decent sort. If he hadn't come along at the time he did, there was no telling what might have happened to those unfortunate old folks from the bus. As it was, they had come out of it as stunned and bewildered as a band of zombies. Mrs. Holzman, who Floyd said was a nurse, had advised Cooper against trying to question any of them except these three.

"This is Miz Jennings," the sheriff said. He waved an arm toward a dark-haired, matronly woman who sat at the table beside him. "She teaches business at the high school here. She's agreed to take down your statements and type it up tonight. You can sign it and be on your way when your new bus comes in the morning."

Fred Scott smiled at him. "That's very accommodating of you, Sheriff Cooper. We appreciate it."

"Normally I'd interview every person involved, but that doesn't seem too practical with this hurricane almost on us. The nurse, Mrs. Holzman, convinced me it would be best to limit it to you three folks. However, I need a list of everybody on that bus, just in case there's any need for a follow-up." He looked at Mrs. Ellis, who had introduced herself as the tour director.

"I can get that for you," she said. Then she narrowed her eyes. "I'd prefer that you kept it confidential, however. Not give it to the news media. The last thing I want is a bunch of reporters sticking microphones and cameras in everybody's faces. They've had a hard enough time as it is."

The sheriff scratched the stubble on his cheek. "I understand, and I agree. Of course, you realize once it goes into the file, it becomes a public record. But I think I can keep it out of the press boys' hands for a couple of days, at least. By that time you'll be back home."

"Thank you, sheriff," the tour leader said.

"Normally I would talk to each of you separately and get individual statements, but under the circumstances, a joint statement's probably the best we can do. For one thing, I need to get back out on hurricane duty. Also, there's a pretty good chance we could lose power and be left in the dark most any time now."

He had them recount the story of the ill-fated bus ride, then followed up with a few questions.

"They didn't take the ladies' handbags or the men's billfolds?"

"No," said MacArthur. The other two shook their heads. "They just held out a box and demanded we put our money and jewelry in it."

Scott leaned forward. "We were too scared to do otherwise."

The sheriff sat back and rubbed his large chin. "And you'd never seen any of these men before?"

"Not before they turned up in Natchez," said Mrs. Ellis.

"And you have no idea why they picked your bus?"

"The leader approached a few of our people," the tour leader said. "He gave some cockamamie story about a friend of his father's being from our church. I didn't believe it. One of the ladies thought they were confidence men, out to pull some sort of trick on us. Turned out she had it about right."

Andy Cooper had questioned literally thousands of people

during his career in law enforcement, and he was convinced he could spot a lie at twenty paces. He didn't want to accuse these good church people of being untruthful, but he had a strong suspicion that he wasn't getting the whole story. Something had happened they were not willing to talk about. Judging from their reaction, he diagnosed it as fear. They seemed to be awfully prudent in their answers. What kind of threat could those men have made that would hold up so well beyond the grave, he wondered?

Sheriff Cooper instructed them to give detailed descriptions of the robbers, and in this case they didn't hold back. One of his men burst through the door as he started to wind things up.

"It's gettin' bad out there, sheriff," he said. "Emergency Management just called. They say winds of a hundred and thirty-five are comin' at us fast."

And with that, the lights flickered like flames on a candle, then went out. The room abruptly became a blackened dungeon. Cooper groped for the flashlight on his belt, switched it on and led them out into the gym, where kerosene lanterns were being lit. With everyone suddenly hushed by the power failure, the howling, shrieking sounds of the wind outside seemed terrifyingly close. To most it sounded like a horde of banshees racing by in the night.

39

Hurrricane Nora blasted ashore around nine Thursday night with winds clocked at 129 miles per hour, on the verge of Category 4. She made landfall west of New Orleans and damage throughout the area was significant. Buildings were demolished, trees uprooted, roads blocked, power and telephone lines downed. Torrents of rain swelled rivers and streams to overflowing, causing extensive flooding. Initial reports put the death toll at seven. Hundreds were left homeless. Upwards of a hundred thousand homes had no electric power.

By early morning, the storm had pushed northeast beyond the Louisiana border. Its forward speed and force rapidly diminished over land, but the rains continued to pour as if an ethereal dam had burst somewhere in the sky.

Damage on the eastern side of New Orleans was not as severe as that to the west. Consequently, newspaper and TV crews concentrated their efforts in the western sector. Around daylight, a New Orleans newspaper received a report of a bus blown up somewhere in the vicinity of Bay St. Louis, Mississippi. The reporter who took the information thought the caller must have meant "blown over," since he reported no serious injuries. Because of communications problems and the difficulty of moving around, it was an hour later before a TV station received a more definitive report. A bus had blown up and four people were dead. The news director dispatched a reporter and cameraman to the area.

Sheriff Andy Cooper, Deputy Carl Floyd and another officer were wandering about the devastated area, looking for bodies, when the TV crew arrived shortly after nine. One of the dead men had been torn apart and the other three appeared badly mangled. After viewing the utter destruction of the bus, Cooper knew he would have to call in federal bomb experts, the ATF and the FBI.

The initial story was aired at ten o'clock as part of the station's continuing coverage of Hurricane Nora.

"An investigation is just getting under way on the Mississippi Gulf Coast this morning of a bizarre incident that occurred late yesterday. As Hurricane Nora's initial winds and rains pummeled the area, four unidentified gunmen hijacked a busload of senior citizens from a church in a suburb of Nashville, Tennessee. According to Sheriff Andrew Cooper, the men planted a bomb on the bus and threatened to blow it up if the passengers failed to cooperate. But after forcing the people to hand over their money and jewelry, ordering them off the bus, the robbers apparently did something that proved a fatal mistake. Their bomb went off, killing all four and destroying the bus. The forty-four passengers and their driver were rescued safely by Sheriff Cooper's men. After spending last night in an emergency shelter, they left for home this morning on a new bus sent down overnight by the tour operator. The sheriff said names of the robbers would not be released until positive identification had been made and next of kin notified."

THE NEW NOVA Tours bus pulled away from the high school just after nine o'clock. The Silver Shadows had been fed a hot breakfast, cooked with power from an emergency generator supplied by the National Guard. Everyone had dressed either in their own clothes, which had dried out overnight, or in outfits given them by the thrift store.

Bryce and Marge had roused themselves early to thank Ike and Claire Holzman. Ike provided Bryce with a walking stick, among other things. Ike had carved the cane from a birch limb picked up at some point in their wanderings. The couple had parked their trailer in a sheltered area near the building, away from the storm's path, protecting it from the worst of the winds. It survived intact, and they started out to the pickup as soon as there was enough light that they could see to maneuver their way around downed tree limbs.

"I guess we'll chart a course to the east," Ike said, scratching his head. "Don't know where in the world we might wind up, though. Best of luck to you folks."

Bryce looked a bit distressed. "I wish there was some way we could repay you for all you've done for us."

"Just take care of yourselves," Claire said.

Marge hugged both of them. "Drive carefully. It's still awfully wet out there."

Bryce patted her shoulder as the couple headed out into the rain. "Said like a good mom, Marge. I'll bet you'd have made a dandy."

"I'm afraid we'll never know," she said, taking his arm and helping him over to a table.

Tillie took a vote before everyone boarded the bus. "Do you want to stop somewhere and spend the night? Or do you want to keep on going till we get home? It'll be quite late tonight."

The vote was almost unanimous. Don't stop, except to eat, of course, or go to the restroom.

With the empty seat on the rear bench where the water cooler had sat, they had room for the extra driver, who would share piloting duties with Chick. Marge volunteered to let him take her place so she could go back to sit with Bryce and Troy.

Up to this point, they had avoided speculation on what the Vicario family might do about Pat Pagano, but as they rode northeast toward Birmingham, Marge finally broached the subject.

"Do you think they might give up looking for you after this?" she asked.

Bryce had done quite a bit of pondering on that one himself. "If they think I'm dead, they will."

"Maybe they won't be able to identify one of those bodies on the bus," Troy said. "They could think it was you."

"I wouldn't count on it. But I have an idea I intend to pursue. Something resulting from that phone call I made from the Riverwalk in New Orleans."

DURING A LUNCH stop near Meridian, Mississippi, Tillie called Dr. Trent at Lovely Lane UMC and received some unwelcome news. The story of the bus bombing had made the TV network roundups on Hurricane Nora. CNN had showed pictures of the burned-out hulk.

Tillie came over to the table where Bryce and Marge were seated with Troy, Sarah Anne, the Scotts, and MacArthur. After finding all her charges had weathered the storm in good shape that morning and were eager to travel, Tillie had been unusually upbeat. Now they noticed the smile was gone.

"The word is out," she said. "Dr. Trent has had calls from the TV stations and the newspapers. They want to know what time we'll be arriving."

Sarah Anne covered her face. "Oh, God. They'll have lights and cameras waiting for us, and I look like a disaster area."

"What did Dr. Trent tell them?" Bryce asked.

"That he didn't know. Because I hadn't told him."

"So did you?"

"No. He said not to tell him because he didn't want to lie about it."

"What time do you expect to get there?" Fred asked.

"Around eleven. That'll be after the news. I'd hate to have everybody subjected to all that. Maybe they won't come that late."

"Don't kid yourself." MacArthur's voice conveyed the assurance of a man who had traveled this road too many times before. "They'll be out in force."

"But if they don't know what time--"

"They'll know," MacArthur said. "I imagine they've already contacted the bus company to inquire about it."

Bryce looked thoughtful. "I have a suggestion. What if we unloaded the bus somewhere besides the church?"

Tillie's smile began to return. "Good idea, Bryce. Maybe we could do it out at Rivergate Mall. I'll make up a list of relatives that need to be called and informed about the change. We can get somebody at church to contact them."

The Silver Shadows also liked the idea. A few had left cars in the church parking lot but said they would bum a ride home with someone else, then retrieve their cars the following day. Bryce and Marge landed in that category. Fred promised them a ride with the Scotts' son.

"There is only one problem," MacArthur said after all had agreed. "You're going to make the news media mad, and they'll come after you with a vengeance tomorrow."

Tillie folded her arms. "I hadn't thought of that."

MacArthur promptly came up with a solution. "I don't mind talking to them. I'm accustomed to dealing with all kinds of media questions. Lord knows I did enough of that with my company. I think I can give them enough to make them happy, hopefully, keep them from coming back to pester the others."

AFTER THE SILVER Shadows "snuck back into town in the dead of night," as Fred put it, the story received top billing in the Nashville newspapers and on local TV newscasts. But direct quotes were sparse, coming only from Hamilton MacArthur, Fred Scott, and Tillie Ellis. Despite repeated requests, Dr. Peter Trent politely declined to release the bus passenger list. Sheriff Andy Cooper kept his word. He locked away the sheet Tillie had given him and furnished the inquiring news media only the identities of the trio he had interviewed for signed statements.

It was Sunday before Sheriff Cooper and the FBI released the names of the four "robbers" who had died in the bus explosion. It brought a new flurry of media coverage when they were identified as three Mafia members from New York and one from New Orleans. There was much speculation in print as well as behind the scenes regarding the real motive for the incident. Few knowledgeable observers believed the Vicario troops would have been involved in a simple robbery that far from home. But no one could come up with a plausible explanation. The FBI would say only that it was continuing the investigation.

The bomb that wreaked such havoc was composed of a large block of military C-4 plastic explosive. The authorities assumed that Joseph Capparella, a.k.a. Joe Blow, had concocted the device, which, oddly enough, had mangled him the worst.

IN THE DAYS that followed their return, Marge chauffeured Bryce to the doctor, the grocery, any other places he needed to go. The physician instructed him to stay off his injured right ankle for a week or two, which effectively kept him out of the driver's seat. Marge cooked for him part of the time, and they sampled several of the many restaurants that dotted the Rivergate area.

A few days after the story of the ill-fated bus faded from the coverage of Hurricane Nora's disastrous aftermath, Bryce sat in Marge's neat, spacious kitchen while she put the finishing touches on a carrot cake she was making for a bake sale at the church. They had chatted idly about a variety of things, but both had studiously avoided the subject that concerned them the most. Finally, Bryce decided it could wait no longer.

After watching a few moments in silence as she deftly smoothed the icing, he set his cup of decaf on the table. "I think it's time to make my call. Hopefully it will help clear things up."

She turned, studying him with narrowed eyes. "What things?"

"This Mafia business. I've got to know where I stand. I can't ask you to risk your neck by getting any more involved with me."

"You don't have to ask. I volunteer."

"No, Marge. I've ruined too many people's lives already. I won't do it to you."

"I thought we settled that the other day in the midst of that storm. You said we'd been playing games with our minds, that we needed someone to confide in. We need each other, Bryce."

He couldn't argue against his own logic, but he wasn't prepared to see her name added to the Mafia's hit list. "I won't deny it. I need you," he said. "But unless I can get free of the Vicario family–"

"If you're still worried about them, let's leave right now. We'll pack what we need to reach our destination, pick some faraway place, change our names and go."

"You'd do that?"

"Neither of us has anything holding us here."

"What about Betty Lou and Fred and Troy and all your other friends?"

"They'd wish us bon voyage."

He hobbled over, pushed an errant lock of silver hair from her forehead and kissed her. "Okay. But before we do anything drastic, let me make that phone call. You remember my telling you about attempting to reach that FBI agent, only to learn he had retired? I'm going to make some calls and see if I can get his home number."

40

A RELATIVELY SHORT commute to Manhattan, White Plains was where Matthew and Phyllis Kravitz had lived the past ten years, the place they had chosen for retirement. In the early days of their marriage, Phyllis, a college beauty queen, had worked as an American Airlines flight attendant (they were known as "stewardesses" back then). Despite all the miles she had flown, she never got the urge to travel out of her blood. Taking the exact opposite view, Matt contended his frequent journeys on FBI assignments had more than satisfied any desires in that category. He had seen all he wanted of the length and breadth of the U.S.A., not to mention the world beyond.

Since his retirement, Matt Kravitz had reinvented leisure. The fast pace and long hours of his law enforcement career had left little time for his favorite sport, golf. As an economically deprived kid, which people called "poor" in those days, he had found work as a caddy around Chicago and acquired a lifelong love of the game. Now that he had the time, the opportunity and the resources to afford golf, he had bought a new set of what he called "sticks," joined a local club and become a regular on the course.

October was a great month for golfing. Not too warm, not too cold. This had been one of those perfect days, the sun creating a jewel out of every glistening drop of dew, the wind putting just enough nip in the air to make it invigorating. Matt had scored a seventy-eight, his best round since taking up the game anew, and he was in an expansive mood. He retrieved a handful of mail from the box, entered the house and found Phyllis in the kitchen slicing bread with cookie cutters. She had cut the bread in diamond shapes, heart shapes...

He gave her a big kiss and looked down at the cluttered

cutting board. "What the devil, may I ask, have you got there?"

"Sandwiches, dummy. I'm experimenting with a new recipe. Something I plan to make for the bridge club next Friday."

Now he could see the bread was also club-shaped and spade-shaped. She was always doing weird things like that in the kitchen. "Why do you want to play that stupid card game?"

"It isn't stupid. You should play it, Mr. Deduction Specialist."

"I don't deduce anymore. I'm retired." He stifled a yawn as if he should have said "tired" instead of "re-tired." Actually, he was relishing a semblance of happy exhaustion after eighteen strenuous holes. "You should have been out on the golf course with me, getting a little exercise."

"I prefer to exercise my mind, dear. Anyway, what we need is a vacation."

"Vacation? You're daft, woman. Retirement is a permanent vacation."

She planted her hands on still-shapely hips. "Then why aren't we doing what vacationers do?"

He knew what she meant—travel. "Finish your sandwiches," he said. "I presume they're what's for lunch."

"You presume correctly." She turned back to the counter as he scurried out to the den with his mail like a thief in the night.

The first piece of mail Matt opened contained a colorful brochure showing golfers basking in the sun at Kaanapali on the island of Maui. How did they get his name, he wondered? The next one touted a similarly enticing view of golf courses on the Kona Coast on the Big Island of Hawaii. When he saw the third Hawaii postmark, his powers of deduction suddenly came out of retirement. She had set him up bjg time. Despite a penchant for frowns cultivated during his Bureau days, he broke into a wide smile.

The smile carried over into his tone as he answered the phone that rang on the table beside his chair. "Kravitz here," he said blithely, another holdover from his recent career.

"Former FBI Agent Matthew Kravitz?" asked an unfamiliar voice.

Matt frowned. He hated these businesslike intrusions into his purposeful life of leisure. "That's right. Are you Mr. Hunter?"

There was a stunned silence, then, "Where'd you get that name?"

"Off my caller ID box. It shows 'Hunter M.' in area code 615."

"Oh. I hadn't thought of that. I'm calling from a friend's house. Actually, I'm a dead man. Or so I've been told."

"You sound pretty lively to me."

"You knew me as Pat Pagano," said the caller. "Until you changed my name to William Holder."

Matt laughed, feeling the elation of a theory vindicated. "Who told you you were dead?"

"An agent named Burger. I called that number you gave me to use when I found myself in dire straits. Why the laugh?"

"I knew it wasn't you they found on that beach. Back when I learned you had disappeared from Portland, I was certain you'd gone underground, that you wouldn't be back. You're too sharp for that. Are you still in trouble?"

"Not as bad as I was a few days ago, but it could be only a temporary situation."

Matt listened in amazement as Pagano's story unfolded. He registered surprise at Boots Minelli's ingenuity in tracking down the investment advisor through the Swiss bank, but his mood turned decidedly sour on hearing the mob had learned about the move to Portland.

"Locasio said they had a source at Justice?"

"I think his actual words were: 'We got a man on the inside at the Justice Department.'"

"Damn!"

"I had hoped you might have some suggestions for me," Pagano said as he finished his tale of deception and deceit.

Matt considered the ramifications for a few moments. He talked now and then with some of the guys he had worked with. That's how he had heard about the discovery of William Holder's body. On the rare occasion when he ventured back into the city during business hours, he usually stopped by the office. However, most of his trips were with Phyllis for an evening at the theatre or some special event at Lincoln Center. Heavy doses of culture really weren't his bag, but since he couldn't play golf at night, he went along for her sake.

"I've kept up with Vicario's shenanigans," Matt said, "but I had no idea they were up to something like this. When I read that Boots had died of a heart attack in Nashville, I called my old partner. He told me about Dom Locasio and the others getting themselves killed in what looked like a bus hijacking. But it didn't make any sense. Now I understand. I think, just maybe, I can be of help."

"To get them off my case?"

"Right. The current consigliere is a guy named Nick Caggiano. I've had dealings with him on many occasions. He's bound to have been in on this. The weather is supposed to be lousy for golf tomorrow. I think I'll go in and see if I can spoil Mr. Caggiano's lunch. What name are you using now?"

"If it's okay with you, I'd as soon not say."

"I understand. I was only interested in having it to call you back after my little chat with the consigliere."

"How about I call you?"

"That'll work." Matt chuckled. The man was nobody's fool. That was why it had taken so long and such desperate measures for the Vicario mob to track him down. Matt admired his spunk. He hoped the little plan he had in mind would work.

THE RESTAURANT was a small Italian place on Mulberry Street in the heart of Little Italy, which in recent years had begun to look more like Little China, a consequence of its rapidly encroaching neighbor from the south, Chinatown. But this eatery was part of the authentic remnants wedged in between an Italian grocery and a pastry shop. The peeling yellow wallpaper was just one indication that the restaurant's better days were behind it. The food, however, was decent and the late lunchers were mostly gray-haired, some with full beards, a few with the wizened look of shrews. It was a place where Nick Caggiano could relax and enjoy a meal or, if conditions in the family warranted, pick the brains of some older and wiser heads.

Matt was thoroughly familiar with Caggiano's habits and guessed he would be here. If not, there were only two other places he would likely be found at this hour of the day. But on this occasion, Matt guessed correctly. As soon as he walked in, he spotted the Mafia mouthpiece seated alone at a corner table.

He walked over to where Caggiano had nearly finished eating. Pulling out a chair across from the consigliere, he dropped into it.

"Sorry I'm late."

"I don't remember inviting you," said Caggiano. The look of disdain made his black eyes shine like lacquered pellets. He was a slight man dressed in a heavily-padded brown jacket that exaggerated his rounded shoulders. Everything about him conveyed the message that here was a man who was not at all what he appeared to be.

Matt's smile never flickered. "I thought I had an open invitation."

Caggiano dabbed a napkin at his thin lips, blotting a reddish spot of marinara sauce. "I thought you had retired."

"You're right. This is a social call, not business. I just wanted to pay my respects on the passing of Boots Minelli. Sorry to hear about that."

"Yeah, I'll bet."

"No, really. I always felt a bit of admiration for Boots. We respected each other. He was a sharp guy. I never could get enough on him to put him away."

"Not for a lack of trying."

"True." In fact he probably could have gotten an indictment on a couple of occasions, but he had held off for bigger things. He was still looking when he retired.

"I also wanted to offer condolences on the loss of Dom Locasio and Boots' other soldiers. I understand it was quite a messy scene."

Caggiano's eyes narrowed warily. "I wasn't there."

"Lucky you." Matt rubbed his chin with his thumb and forefinger, as though pondering the imponderable. "I hear by the grapevine that they were out looking for Pat Pagano."

He paused expectantly.

"You Feds hear all kinds of strange things. You've been listening to your hidden tape machines and watching your jumpy videos too long."

Matt ignored the remark. "What made it really puzzling is

that we had given Boots credit for feeding Pagano to the sharks six months ago. That was when what was left of him washed up on the Oregon coast. We had changed his name to William Holder." He paused momentarily, a smile playing at the corners of his mouth. "But you knew that, of course. Your man over at Justice had tipped you off."

Matt had been speaking in a casual, offhand manner, a bland look on his face. But the reaction he got from Caggiano was a further narrowing of the eyes, a tightening of the jaw muscles.

"You're dreaming, Kravitz."

Matt shook his head. The time had come for a little creative embellishment. "I just came from the office. This is all the gospel, Nick. Pagano's body was pretty well mangled, so we couldn't get any prints. But the medical examiners identified him through dental records and DNA. They're positive. It was Patrick O. Pagano."

Caggiano squirmed uncomfortably in his chair. "So it was Pat Pagano. What do I care?"

"I don't know about you, but old Tony sure does. Pat really wrecked his red wagon."

Nick Caggiano sat back and folded his arms, finally mustering a semblance of a superior air. "So if Pagano got himself eaten alive six months ago, why the hell would Boots be sending his boys looking for him in Louisiana or Mississippi, or wherever the hell it was?"

"I'm glad you asked that, Nick. The guys at the office have worked like crazy on that question ever since we got word about the bus incident. After checking a bunch of old surveillance logs and consulting some Swiss bank sources, here's what they came up with. I'll admit it's all conjecture, but it fits.

"We think Boots went over to Switzerland and bought or threatened somebody until they gave him a look at Pagano's bank records. He found that Pagano had transferred funds into another account, which had an address on the Isle of Man. When we looked into that, we discovered the owner of the mail drop had been murdered, his place ransacked. We know Boots was over there at the time. So he must have found the name and address of a man in Tennessee. But what Boots apparently missed is it wasn't Pagano, but a guy who had learned Pagano's investment system and worked with him. This fellow would bring the profits back into the States, take his cut and send the rest to William Holder in Oregon. After Holder/Pagano died, the guy got a windfall. But it seems he also attracted Boots and Dom and associates. We still haven't figured out what happened down there in the middle of that hurricane, but somehow your boys managed to blow themselves to bits in the process."

Nick Caggiano glanced nervously at his watch. "I have to get back to work. Is that all you came here to tell me?"

"That's about it. But you also have my condolences, Nick. I'd hate to be the one to tell old Tony that he lost a capo and four soldiers on a wild goose chase. To make it worse, you're getting some terrible press for hijacking a busload of church folks—senior citizens at that. Naughty, naughty."

Caggiano rose abruptly. It was not at all what he wanted to hear. Kravitz was right. Being the bearer of such terrible tidings would certainly not endear himself with Tony Vicario. Especially since he was the one who had originated the idea of tracking down Pagano through the connection to the Swiss bank.

Caggiano felt he had aged a few years since sitting down to lunch. "Thanks for the sympathy," he said in a mocking tone, though the voice was more dispirited than defiant. He steamed out of the restaurant, knowing a grinning Matthew Kravitz stood there in his wake.

THE FOLLOWING Sunday morning, Marge Hunter and Fred Scott stood at his side as Bryce Reynolds was welcomed into the membership at Lovely Lane United Methodist Church by Dr. Peter Trent. As a Catholic, Pat Pagano could have been accepted on the transfer of his membership, but since Reynolds had not belonged to any church, it was necessary for him to join on a profession of faith. He particularly liked the vow that asked:

"Do you accept the freedom and power God gives you to resist evil, injustice, and oppression in whatever forms they present themselves?"

He had seen them in their worst forms imaginable. He had resisted them and, thank God, succeeded.

On a Saturday afternoon four weeks from the day they had arrived back home in Madison from Mississippi, Marjorie Hunter and Bryce Reynolds were married at the church altar. Many of those who had been on that fateful bus trip attended the ceremony, including Hamilton MacArthur, who was accompanied by his stylishly attired wife, Andrea. Following the reception, Bryce and Marge Reynolds left on a honeymoon trip to Acapulco, with a stopover in New Orleans. It was a small gesture to assure the world, and himself, that at long last, he was truly a free man.

www.ingramcontent.com/pod-product-compliance
Lightning Source LLC
Chambersburg PA
CBHW050315110726
47899CB00007B/2250